"You have what I've always wanted."

Louisa looked as surprised as if Emmet had announced he carried rain in his back pocket. "Really? I can't imagine."

"Family. Siblings." His voice had thickened, but he couldn't help it. "I always felt lonely growing up alone." Abandoned.

She looked away, her gaze seeking the far edge of the field. "You know what I want?"

"No. What?" Whatever it was, he wished he could give it to her.

She paused for a beat. Two. Shuddered as if a chill had raced across her shoulders. She tried to speak, but her voice caught.

It obviously meant a lot to her. And his heart softened with such a protective urge that it was all he could do not to pull her into his arms and hold her close, keep her safe.

"For it to rain." Her voice rang with determination. "I pray for it every single day."

He knew without a doubt that wasn't what she'd started to say. Disappointment stained his insides. What was she afraid to admit she needed?

LINDA FORD

shares her life with her rancher husband, a grown son, a live-in client she provides care for and a yappy parrot. She and her husband raised a family of fourteen children, ten adopted, providing her with plenty of opportunity to experience God's love and faithfulness. They've had their share of adventures, as well. Taking twelve kids in a motor home on a three-thousand-mile road trip would be high on the list. They live in Alberta, Canada, close enough to the Rockies to admire them every day. She enjoys writing stories that reveal God's wondrous love through the lives of her characters.

Linda enjoys hearing from readers. Contact her at linda@lindaford.org or check out her website, www.lindaford.org, where you can also catch her blog, which often carries glimpses of both her writing activities and family life.

The Cowboy Father

LINDA FORD

Recycling programs
for this product may
not exist in your area.

 LOVE INSPIRED BOOKS

ISBN-13: 978-0-373-82903-3

THE COWBOY FATHER
Copyright © 2012 by Linda Ford

FIREWORKS
Copyright © 2009 by Harlequin Books S.A.

www.LoveInspiredBooks.com

Printed in U.S.A.

Dear Reader,

In 2012, Love Inspired Books is proudly celebrating fifteen years of heartwarming inspirational romance! Love Inspired launched in September 1997 and successfully brought inspiration to series romance. From heartwarming contemporary romance to heart-stopping romantic suspense to adventurous historical romance, Love Inspired Books offers a variety of inspirational stories for every preference. And we deliver uplifting, wholesome and emotional romances that every generation can enjoy.

We're marking our fifteenth anniversary with a special theme month in Love Inspired Historical: *Family Ties.* Whether ready-made families or families in the making, these touching stories celebrate the ties that bind and prove why family matters. Because sometimes it takes a family to open one's heart to the possibility of love. With wonderful stories by favorite authors Linda Ford and Ruth Axtell Morren, an exciting new miniseries from Regina Scott and a tender tale by debut author Lily George, this month full of family-themed reads will warm your heart.

I hope you enjoy each and every story—and then come back next month for more of the most powerful, engaging stories of romance, adventure and faith set in times past. From rugged handsome cowboys of the West to proper English gentlemen in Regency England, let Love Inspired Historical sweep you away to a place where love is timeless.

Sincerely,

Tina James
Senior Editor

Dedicated to the memory of my father, who was widowed with six children during the Depression and fought to provide for them so they weren't taken away. He succeeded despite the harsh realities of that era. Through it all, his faith survived and grew, and when he later remarried he was able to pass that strength, faith and hope on to myself and my siblings born to that second marriage. I thank God for the godly example he lived.

* * *

If God so clothe the grass, which is today in the field, and tomorrow is cast into the oven; how much more will he clothe you, O ye of little faith.
—*Matthew* 6:30

Chapter One

Golden Prairie, Alberta
April 1933

Louisa Morgan paused before the battered door of the Hamilton house. She'd prayed for an opportunity to earn money to help pay the medical bills—bills accumulated on her behalf. Influenza had struck many over the winter, but Louisa had been particularly ill with infection raging throughout her body. The doctor, meaning to be encouraging, said it was amazing she was alive and she should be glad. She was. Truly. But the illness had cost her something very precious…the ability to have children.

She vowed daily she would not let her disappointment turn into bitterness. She would enjoy what God still had in store for her. There was much to be grateful for…the ability to walk about and breathe in the spring air, the chance to continue her studies. She might have been content to keep on with her self-studies at home and not consider looking for a job, except she'd seen Mother slip cardboard into her shoes to cover the worn soles. She'd been about to confront Mother and insist she buy a new pair, but she noticed the pile of bills on the desk and knew Mother wouldn't buy anything until they were paid.

From that day, Louisa had prayed for a way to earn some money. Unfortunately a depression held the country in its grip. Able-bodied men were out of work. Many of them rode the rails or worked in government-run relief camps. Why would anyone hire a woman with no experience and a history of ill health when there were strong, family men eager to do any available job?

Then the teacher at the local school had asked her to tutor a bedridden little girl.

This job was truly an unexpected blessing and opportunity.

Still she did not knock.

A blessing it might be—and she had no doubt it was—but she had not expected to be thrust into a position that mocked her dreams. Dreams of a child of her own, a family and home of her own. Things she could never have now.

If she stood here long enough, she'd change her mind about the opportunity and answered prayer, decide it was only cruel mockery and walk away. *Lord, I believe You are in control and have opened a door for me in answer to prayer.* Pushing determination into her limbs, she knocked. Her heart battered against her ribs in determined anticipation.

The door opened. Louisa stilled her face to reveal none of the surprise she felt at the sight of the man in the doorway. He was stocky yet gave the impression of strength and authority. He had a thick mop of dark blond hair. His eyes looked as if they smiled, even though his expression revealed only wariness.

She'd expected an older man. A widower, she'd been told, and for some reason she'd imagined someone like old Mr. Knowles, who had married late and lost his wife to some unnamed illness a couple of years back. Mr. Knowles was bent, his hair almost gone except for a comb-over that caught in the wind, should he remove his hat. Mr. Knowles's face resembled a pale orange.

The man before her looked like someone used to being outdoors. The clothes he wore bore no resemblance to the broadcloth suit jacket and shiny trousers Mr. Knowles wore. No town clothes on this man, but a yoke-fronted shirt and soft denim jeans. Louisa knew he'd left his ranching life to bring his little girl home to recover from her broken leg.

The little girl was why Louisa was here. "Miss Ross, the teacher, said you need a tutor for your daughter." Adele Ross had said Mr. Hamilton insisted he approve the tutor she recommended. "I'm here to see if I'm—" Suitable. The word stuck in her throat. She wasn't suitable. She knew that. She had no formal education, unless one counted the few months Judd Kirk had tutored her last summer, before he married Louisa's sister, Madge, and moved to a nearby farm.

No formal education. No experience. A history of poor health. And barren. The word thundered through her head.

However, she was not here as a marriage candidate. She simply needed the job. She had no intention of letting her emotions become involved in any way. That would only lead to deeper sorrow.

"My name is Louisa Morgan, and I think I can provide your child with adequate tutoring."

"Miss Morgan." His voice was deep and gravelly. "I'm pleased to make your acquaintance. I'm Emmet Hamilton, as I'm sure you know. Please come in and we'll discuss the position." He stepped aside and indicated she should enter the house.

She tucked courage under her heart, strength into her legs and crossed the threshold. It took a moment for her eyes to adjust to the dim interior. Something brushed her ankle and she pressed her fingers to her mouth, stifling a squeal of alarm. It was only a cat, and she sighed.

"Auntie May is very fond of her cats. If you have an aversion or dislike of them, best you say so right away."

"I'm quite fond of them." She bent and stroked the big gray cat that meowed at her feet. Suddenly cats sprang from every corner until six crowded around, demanding attention. Louisa chortled at their antics. "Well, look at you guys. Aren't you pretty little things?"

"They're a nuisance."

She straightened and met his eyes, wondering if he objected to his aunt's pets, but she could read nothing in his expression. Seems the man had learned to hide his opinions rather well. Or perhaps he found it inappropriate she should spare the animals attention. Despite the continued demands of the cats, she determinedly ignored them, hoping it would prove her seriousness.

"Have a chair." He pointed toward a wingback chair in maroon upholstery.

She sat and glanced about. The room was crowded with furniture—three armchairs, a sagging brown sofa, at least eight little tables, their tops cluttered with knickknacks. And not only the sort of pretty decorations one would expect. Among ornaments of birds of various colors and in various poses there were also china and wooden cats, bits and pieces of hardware, a doorknob, a lantern, books, dog-eared catalogues and magazines… Would she do the same as she grew older? Fill the lonely places that called for children with pets and possessions?

"Goodness me, boy." May Hamilton burst into a doorway on one side of the room. "Bring the miss into the kitchen where it's warmer."

So the cold in Louisa's bones wasn't just nerves.

She half rose then subsided, waiting to see what Mr. Hamilton intended to do.

He nodded. "Come along then." His eyes said far more though. They said he found his aunt both amusing and endearing.

Louisa relaxed marginally and followed Auntie May into a warm room as crowded with furniture and odds and ends as the front room. The whole place had the appearance of many projects on the go or abandoned at some point.

Auntie May studied Louisa. "Hello, my dear."

"Hello, Miss Hamilton."

She snorted. "Since when does anyone call me Miss Hamilton unless they are about to present a bill? I'm Auntie May. Always have been. Always will be. Now park yourself and talk to my nephew while I pour us tea."

Louisa "parked" on one of the mismatched chairs crowding around the table, as if Auntie May normally fed a large family instead of being on her own most of the time. Louisa had heard how she'd taken in her brother's son after his parents' untimely death and finished raising him. But he had left before Louisa and her family moved into the community. He'd returned a week ago with his injured daughter. Some suggested he came back so Auntie May could care for the child, but Louisa said where else would one go but back home if they needed help?

Auntie May nudged her way through a swarm of cats to set cups of tea in front of Louisa and Emmet. "I know Emmet will have hundreds of questions to ask you before he accepts you as tutor to little Ellie, but Emmet, let me say this. I've watched Louisa these past few years. I've seen her overcome challenges and emerge stronger and sweeter and kinder for them. I'm here to say you couldn't do much better than her."

Louisa's face burned with embarrassment at the praise. But at least Auntie May hadn't gone into detail about the challenges Louisa faced. Thankfully, only her family and Doc knew of her greatest challenge. One she must face with dignity and faith every day of her life.

"Thanks, Auntie May. I'll certainly take your opinion into consideration."

"Of course you will. Now come on, all of you." She spoke to the cats running after her as she stepped into the porch. "I've got some food ready." The meowing made conversation impossible until the door closed behind them.

Emmet laughed. "My aunt and her cats."

Louisa, twenty years from now—the local cat lady. "She'd be lonely without her pets." Auntie May was slightly eccentric but a good soul. There wasn't a person she wouldn't help, and the entire community knew it. The thought cheered Louisa marginally.

"Shall we get down to business?"

Louisa nodded, her tension returning tenfold.

"There are things I need to know about you."

"I understand." She'd tried to guess what questions he'd ask and how she'd answer them.

"First, what sort of training and education do you have that qualifies you to teach my daughter?"

She'd rightly guessed that would be uppermost in his mind. "I'm sure Miss Ross explained my education."

"I'd like to hear it from your lips."

"I do not have university education. Nor have I attended Normal school." If finances and health allowed it, she would love to go to Normal school and train to be a teacher.

"I see. And yet Miss Ross feels you are well educated. Tell me, formal training aside, what qualifies you for this job?" His voice was low, his look insistent.

Apart from the fact that it's the only one I've been offered and I need the money? "I did well in school and have continued my education since. Mostly I am self-taught, but last year my mother hired a tutor with a teaching degree and he helped me. I have a strong background in English, Greek, the arts and history."

"I see."

She wondered if he did. She must prove she could do this job. "I am also uniquely experienced for a situation such as your daughter's. I spent three winters unable to attend school. I kept up my studies while at home.

I learned how to work on my own and how to amuse myself while confined to bed."

He studied her, then sighed. "Unfortunately, Ellie is used to being outdoors, riding her pony, climbing trees, running across the fields. School has always been a necessary evil in her opinion. I don't think she is going to find contentment in quiet activities."

"Does she have a choice?"

"Not at the moment. What else can you tell me about yourself? How old are you?"

"I'm twenty. Almost twenty-one."

"I would have taken you for much younger."

She squared her shoulders and tried to look wise. Realizing how silly her reaction, she had to steel herself not to chuckle.

"I assume you are only passing time until you marry."

"You, sir, assume incorrectly." He could not possibly know how his words hurt. For that she was thankful. "Marriage is not part of my plans." No man would want her, nor would she marry if one did momentarily profess love. It wouldn't be fair to deprive a man of children. Besides, wouldn't he grow to resent her? Better to remain single than take such a risk.

He gave her narrow-eyed concentration.

She refused to blink before his study, instead choosing to try to decide what color his eyes were. Green? Blue? Just when she'd decided on one, they shifted to the other. Ah. She'd learned something that might be useful in the future, should she get the job. His eyes changed color with his emotions. He had gone from green-eyed doubt to blue-eyed relief. For some inexplicable reason, it pleased her to have learned this tiny bit of information.

"Are you saying you have no beau?"

"I am indeed." She fully intended to protect herself from further pain by avoiding anything but friendship with any man.

"Daddy. Where are you?" A young, demanding voice called from a room past the kitchen.

The smile on the man's face made Louisa blink. The man looked as if the sun had come out and the sky turned blue at the sound of a little girl's voice. He was obviously very fond of his daughter. "I'll be right there."

Her eyes stung. Her father had loved his daughters in such a fashion. It had been almost four years since his passing, but she missed him as though it was yesterday.

"Would you like to meet Ellie?"

"Yes, please." Did this mean she had the job? Or would if she could relate to his daughter? *Please, God. Give me wisdom.*

"Come along."

She followed him into the adjoining room. A china cupboard and sideboard, groaning under a collection of mismatched dishes, took up most of one wall, but in the middle of the room stood a bed, raised to elbow level on blocks. A blonde child lay on the bed, her chocolate-brown eyes watching Louisa with unblinking interest.

"Who are you?"

"I'm Louisa Morgan." She glanced toward Emmet, but he stood back, observing her. Apparently he meant to see how she would handle the situation on her own. "And you are Ellie Hamilton."

"So?"

"Ellie?" Her father's voice carried gentle warning. "Be polite."

The little girl gave Louisa an unrepentant stare, then smiled at her father. "Okay, Daddy."

"Good girl." He stepped forward. "Her cast goes from here—" he pushed the blanket to show a cast up to her chest "—and down to here." This time he lifted the bottom of the covers. Only her toes peeked out. "So you can see she can't move around much."

"I'm sorry, Ellie. It can't be much fun." Louisa reviewed what she knew of the child. Seven years old. Motherless. Had fallen out of a tree and broken her leg.

"It's not any fun. I hate it." Crossing her arms over her chest, she put on a full-blown pout.

"It's necessary so your leg will heal." Emmet's voice was tight. It must hurt to see his child like this. "Even as it's necessary for you to continue with your schoolwork. Which is why Miss Morgan is here."

"No. I don't want to. Don't make me." The child screamed and cried at the same time. "Please, Daddy, don't make me."

Emmet stepped to Ellie's side, cradled her face between his palms. "Hush, sweetie. Don't upset yourself like this." He crooned wordless comfort.

Ellie wrapped her arms about Emmet's neck and pulled his face down to rest on her cheek.

Louisa turned away, her throat clogged with emotion at seeing his gentle pain over his daughter. Feeling his helplessness. Understanding how Ellie felt. How often had Louisa had to watch life move on while she observed from the sidelines? *Lord, all I want is a job, but perhaps You have something more for me here.* She would follow God's leading, but she would keep her heart under lock and key.

Emmet extricated himself from Ellie's grasp. "You'll be okay. I need to talk to Miss Morgan for a minute, then I'll be back."

"Then will you play with me?" A quiver in her voice tore at Louisa's resolve. The poor child. If she got the job of teaching her, she would do everything she could to make the days pass quickly with fun activities.

"Miss Morgan?" Emmet indicated she should follow him. He led her through to the front room. "I don't want Ellie to hear us."

She sat while he went from one side of the room to the other, his strides long and hurried.

"I'm sorry. I can't imagine how you feel."

"No, you can't." He ground to a halt and jerked his thumb toward the room where his daughter lay. "It's my fault—"

"How can you blame yourself for an accident?" She ached to explain that sometimes things just happened despite our best efforts. For no good reason. A person simply had to accept it and move on. The only other choice was to be angry and bitter. Not a pleasant alternative, to her way of thinking.

"I should— Never mind. It has nothing to do with the job." He sat down and faced her. "I need to get Ellie into a routine of sorts as quickly as possible." He sighed deeply, as if he regretted the decision he must make.

"Miss Ross spoke highly of you. Let's see how you do with Ellie. If you're still interested in the job…"

At first all she cared about was getting paying work, but seeing the child, witnessing their affection, sensing the frustration in both of them…well, now she *wanted* the job. "When do you wish me to start?"

He laughed, his face suddenly years younger. "Is tomorrow too soon?"

"I'll have to get lesson plans and advice from Miss Ross but tomorrow is fine."

"I hope you can make her happy."

"I'll do my best." Though she knew a person, whatever age, was only as happy as they chose to be. But she could imagine getting Ellie to laugh, seeing Emmet smile at his daughter's cheerfulness.

It wasn't until she stood on the street, smiling with anticipation, that she realized she was imagining all the things she could never have—teaching a child in the safety of home, sharing the pleasure with a man.

She'd strayed wildly from her intention of guarding her emotions. This was only a job, she scolded herself. A child who needed to learn. Nothing more.

Now all she had to do was face Mother and inform her of her decision. She already knew how she'd react. Warnings she would make herself sick. Advice that she must take care of herself. But Louisa was tired of being coddled, of being careful. It certainly hadn't prevented her from getting sick in the past. From now on, she intended to enjoy every bit of what she could squeeze from life. Certainly she knew her limitations. But no amount of hard work would make her barrenness more…or less…than it already was.

An ache the size of Alberta lay tightly tied and buried in a secret corner of her heart—where she would make sure it stayed.

Chapter Two

Emmet closed the door softly behind Miss Morgan's departure and stared at the wooden slab. She was much too young and pretty to be…what? Young and single? Not planning marriage? Most certainly a temporary condition. No doubt she waited only for the right man to show up. Not that it mattered one way or the other to him. He no longer sought after dreams such as marriage, home, success…. All that mattered now was taking care of Ellie. And he had failed badly in that area. Something he intended would not happen again. Nothing must divert him from caring for her.

"I hope you're going to let Louisa help Ellie."

His aunt's voice thankfully jerked him back from the dark trail his thoughts headed down. He turned to meet her intent look.

"She's a good person."

"She starts tomorrow."

"Good for you. I was afraid you'd see her pretty face and immediately count her out."

"Now, why would you think that?" He purposely

kept his voice soft. Sometimes Auntie May responded better to a gentle warning.

But not always.

"I know you, boy. You've been hurt too many times. And now you've locked your feelings in a deep vault someplace."

How wrong she was. Not that he hadn't tried exactly that. But he'd failed miserably. He'd never felt anything as deeply, as frighteningly real as when he'd found Ellie hurt. "My feelings are not buried. I care about Ellie. So much it hurts."

A cat jumped to a table next to Auntie May and leaned over in an attempt to get her attention. Several things clattered to the floor.

Auntie May scooped up the cat and retrieved the fallen objects. "I don't mean Ellie. Of course you love her. She's your flesh and blood. But don't you think she needs a mother? Just as you need a wife—a partner?"

"I've already tried that, remember? And it ended with Jane dying." Like everyone he cared for. His parents. Even his pet dog. "Ellie is enough for me."

"She can't be, you know. A man needs a wife."

He snorted. "This from a woman who never married." He considered her. "Are you saying you regret that?"

She chortled. "I have you and Ellie. And my pets." She scrubbed the heads of four cats sitting at her feet. Then she gave him a look full of both challenge and regret. "I loved once."

"You did? What happened?"

She shrugged and buried her face in the fur of the gray cat in her arms. Seemed the animal was the favored of the bunch, or perhaps the most demanding, as it always ended up being held. "Didn't work out."

"Why?" In the dozen or so years he'd lived here, she'd never once hinted she had loved someone. Nor expressed regrets at being single. Did the man die? Seems death stole a lot of people.

"I've been happy. Nothing to complain about, but take it from me. Cats aren't the same as humans."

"No kidding."

"They're more loyal for the most part, however."

Emmet considered the statement. Had Auntie May's love interest been disloyal? The idea only reinforced his decision. "Auntie, I'm sorry your love didn't work out. But you say you've been happy. That's more than many can claim, and likely all any of us can expect. I'm content with my life. I have Ellie and you." He bent to pat two furry heads. "And the cats."

"I always wanted more for you. I wanted you to have the things I didn't."

"You're sweet, but I had a wife. She died. But she gave me a daughter. Do I deserve anything more?"

"I don't know what any of us deserves, but God, in His mercy, blesses us anyway. My concern is you've shut your heart to more. Likely wouldn't take it, even if God sent it your way."

Emmet didn't want to argue with her. Didn't have an argument to offer. He had all he wanted. Anything else would only invite more pain. Auntie May was right. He had barred his heart.

A crash rattled from the kitchen. No, it was Ellie's room. Had she fallen? Hurt herself while he stood two rooms away making silly conversation? He would never forgive himself if—

He crossed the room in long strides and hurried to her bedside, Auntie May at his heels.

Ellie's covers were rumpled, but other than that she looked in one piece.

"What was that racket?" he demanded.

Auntie May continued past the bed. "I'd say this would explain the noise." She held up the shattered base of a lamp. "Now, I wonder how that ended up on the floor."

"I bumped it," Ellie said, "trying to get something to play with." She put on a pretty pout. "Daddy, you said you'd come back and play with me."

"I was on my way." He shouldn't have lingered talking to his aunt about things that didn't matter.

"I'll clean this up." Auntie May brought a broom and dustpan from the kitchen. "You go ahead and amuse your daughter."

"Thanks." He caught Ellie's eyes and tilted his head toward his aunt, silently signaling her.

Ellie smiled sweetly. "I'm sorry for breaking your lamp, Auntie May."

"Goodness, child. Don't you fret about it. Accidents happen."

His daughter made him proud. "What would you like to do?"

"Ride my pony."

He chuckled. "I guess you would, but how do you think he'd feel with a big white stiff body on his back? Wouldn't he be frightened?"

Ellie giggled. "He'd kneel down and dump me off."

"I expect he would."

"Is that lady going to be my teacher?"

"Miss Morgan? She's coming with lessons tomorrow."

"Do I have to do schoolwork? Please don't make me."

He hated doing so, but surely it was the best thing for her. "It will help you pass the time and you'll be able to keep up with your friends at school."

"But Daddy, all my friends are where we used to live. I have no friends here." Her bottom lip quivered. "Why did we have to move?"

"I'm sorry, Button. But I couldn't take care of you and run the ranch."

"Betsy could look after me."

Anger surged up his throat at how Betsy had looked after his daughter. He'd arrived home early to find Ellie on the ground, screaming in pain with a broken leg and Betsy absent. She'd gone to a nearby homesteader's place—a single man—and left Ellie on her own. From all accounts, not an unusual occurrence. Seemed he was the last to discover it. Shouldn't he have been the first? "I didn't much care for the way Betsy watched you."

"Miss Morgan is very pretty, isn't she?"

Far too pretty to be single. But that mattered not to him in the least. "She's passable, I suppose."

Auntie May, mussing about in the kitchen, snorted loudly. Emmet chose to ignore it.

"You might like her better than me."

"Oh, Ellie." He pulled a stool close to her side and cradled her in his arms as best as the body cast allowed.

"I will never like anyone better than you. Not so long as I live."

"You promise?"

"I promise." He held her close a moment longer, then she squirmed free.

"Tell me a story."

"I'm not much good at storytelling."

"Tell me about Grandma and Grandpa."

He sucked in air. All she knew was they had died when he was nine. He never talked about them. It was another life. This was his life now. "How about if I tell you about the night you were born?"

"Okay." She sounded less than enthusiastic. Perhaps because she'd heard the story before.

So he tried to up the drama and suspense of that long-ago night when the doctor had come in the middle of an October snowstorm and the electricity had gone off. His little daughter had been delivered by flickering lamplight. And he'd fallen smash, dash in love with his tiny girl. "I loved you from your first breath, and I will love you until my last breath." He squeezed her gently.

Ellie giggled. "Daddy, you're silly."

"Silly about you."

"Then you won't make me do schoolwork?"

Emmet laughed, pleased at her wily ways. "You'll still have to do schoolwork." He scooped up the gray cat and put it on the bed beside Ellie. "You play with the cat while I do some chores." He didn't intend to sit around and let Auntie May do everything. He'd noticed a number of neglected things he planned to take care of while he was here.

Later, after he fixed a broken step and cleaned out

weeds blown around the back shed, he returned to play with Ellie.

"I wish you would stay with me all day."

"I wish I could too, Button. But I can't." Having Louisa Morgan spend a few hours each day with Ellie would make it better for both him and his daughter.

Next morning, Emmet waited at the front door for Louisa to arrive. He'd had a restless night, wondering if he did right by Ellie, forcing her to take lessons while confined to bed. But Louisa said she'd spent time in a similar situation. Had she been ill? It was hard to believe. She looked in perfect health.

A battered-looking car, a Model A, wheezed to the front gate. Louisa stepped daintily from the vehicle. She moved as if she anticipated what life had to offer. Her cheeks glowed. Her skin was like pure silk, and curly dark hair framed her oval face. A dark pink dress with a flowery pattern accented her chinalike complexion and swirled about her legs as she turned. If she had any physical flaws, he did not detect them, and if she suffered any chronic illness, it didn't reveal itself in the way she moved.

She leaned into the backseat and pulled out a satchel so heavy it required she use both hands to set it on the ground. Then she dragged an awkward board out, set it beside the satchel and bent to extract some lengths of wood.

All this to teach Ellie a little reading, writing and 'rithmetic? He stepped outside. "Can I give you a hand with those things?"

She sent him a smile full of gratitude that sneaked

through his defenses and delivered a king-size wallop to a spot behind his heart.

He sank a mental fist into the area and pushed it into oblivion. "Seems you're serious about this tutoring business."

She laughed. Music seemed to fill the air. He glanced around to see if a door was open, if someone was playing the piano. All doors were closed. He shifted his gaze to the trees. Birds sang an accompaniment to the sound. He concluded the music came from Louisa's laugh. "I like to do a good job."

"I'll take the bag. It looks heavy." He grunted as he hoisted it from the ground. "Did you bring bricks?"

Another musical chuckle. "Just books. Some Adele—Miss Ross—loaned from the school and some I brought from home." She tucked the longer pieces of wood under one arm and tried to tackle the bigger piece, but it was almost as big as she.

"I'll take that. What is it?"

She turned it to show the other side. "A blackboard. My brother-in-law, Judd, made this tripod. See, the legs extend so I can write on the board then raise it so Ellie can see it from her position in bed. Isn't that clever?"

"Oh, very."

She chuckled. It seemed everything amused her, pleased her.

Obviously, he thought with a shade of bitterness, she had not encountered major difficulties in her life.

They struggled toward the house and dropped the items on the floor.

"Is that all?"

"Yes. Thanks for helping."

They stood in the doorway to catch their breath. "We sure need rain." Clever conversation, Emmet mocked himself. But what did it matter? He was only being polite.

"Rain, an end to grasshoppers, better commodity prices. So many things. I know my sister thinks the government should fix the country's problems, but I prefer to trust God. He'll change things when He sees fit. In the meantime, I will trust Him for my daily needs."

Her faith sounded nice. But would she trust if everything she valued was snatched away? Would she say God was treating her fairly? Would her faith falter? But he didn't want to talk about trials and how they affected one's faith. His own hung on by a tiny thread. "I neglected to ask about your family. Do you come from a large one? Tell me about them."

"I have two younger sisters. Madge is a year younger. She married Judd last fall. Sally is two years younger. She lives at home as do I, with our mother." She paused a beat then went on. "My father died four years ago. I still miss him." Her voice thickened.

Emmet stilled an urge to squeeze her shoulder. "My parents died eighteen years ago and I still miss them."

"Oh." Her lips formed a little circle, and her eyes widened. "I thought it would get easier with time."

"It gets easier. Just never goes away."

"I remember him at the silliest times. A certain hymn will bring tears to my eyes. Or the smell of molasses cookies, which he loved. Or—" She shrugged. "I suppose it's the same for you."

It was a question, even though she didn't voice it as

one. But he remembered very little about his parents. "I leave it in the past."

Her eyes widened even more. "You mean you purposely try to forget about them?" She didn't wait for an answer but provided her own. "Although I miss my father, I wouldn't want to forget him or all the wonderful memories I have. Nor the lessons he taught."

"I suppose time has dulled my memories." He didn't want to dwell on it any longer. "You must have moved to this area after I left."

"We bought the farm two miles from town eight years ago."

"Ah. I left nine years ago."

"Daddy!" Ellie's voice wailed through the house.

Emmet chuckled. "She's been waiting patiently all morning. Seems her patience has run out." He again picked up the bag and board and trooped through to Ellie's room. Several cats, seeing the unfamiliar items, hissed. Two backed into a corner and continued to hiss and arch their backs. Four skidded from the room.

Ellie laughed. "Scaredy-cats." But her laughter died and her eyes grew wary at all the equipment Emmet and Louisa dragged in.

"Where do you want this?" Emmet indicated the blackboard.

Louisa looked around. Stood beside the bed. At the end and then on the side farthest from the door. "This would be ideal—" Except for the bookshelf, the table and the wooden chair in the room, all of which were loaded with Auntie May's belongings.

"I'll move this stuff out of the way." He shoved it

into the far corner, crowding the china cabinet. "Auntie May doesn't believe in throwing things out."

He wondered at the way the sunshine left Louisa's face and her eyes grew stormy.

"I suppose she finds comfort in being surrounded by familiar objects." She kept her back to him as she cleared the top of the table and lifted the bag onto it, but he thought he detected a tightness in her voice he hadn't noticed before. He put it down to tension at getting the room organized for teaching.

He set up the tripod, adjusted the blackboard on it then stepped back. "Looks like everything is set. I'll leave you to it." He edged toward the door, reluctant to leave them.

"Daddy, where are you going?" Ellie reached out, as if to stop him.

"I'll be close by. If you need me, you only have to call." The door was inches away, but he didn't step through.

"We'll be fine," Louisa murmured, then pulled a reader from the bag and directed her attention to Ellie. "Miss Ross sent the whole set of grade-two readers so you can show me which ones you can read."

Ellie sent Emmet a look rife with pleading and accusation. He hoped she would understand he was only doing what was best for her.

But she understood the knowledge would provide poor comfort.

Chapter Three

Louisa watched Emmet's departure, feeling the same frightening desperation she heard in Ellie's voice. *Don't leave us. I don't know what I'm doing.* Adele had laid out the lessons and told her what to expect. "The first thing to remember is the child may be resistant to the whole idea of having to do schoolwork while in bed. Find a way to pique her interest and curiosity."

Sounded so easy when Adele said it. But she could do this. Louisa drew a brave breath and began. "First, I'd like you to tell me what things you like. That way we can make your lessons as interesting as possible."

Ellie gave her a stubborn stare. "Can you bring my pony so I can ride?"

Louisa laughed softly. "I think that is outside my power. What games do you like?"

"Hide-and-seek. Racing. Climbing trees. We can't do that either, I suppose." Ellie boldly challenged Louisa with her words and her expression.

"You're quite right. So let's think of something you *can* do and enjoy."

The child made a most unladylike sound. "There isn't anything to enjoy while I'm stuck in bed."

"Do you like reading?"

"Hate it."

"Do you like stories?" Louisa held up two storybooks she'd enjoyed when she learned to read. The books were well-worn. "These were my two favorites at your age. They've been read over and over by myself and my sisters."

A flicker of interest. Good. "You've got sisters?"

"Two. Madge and Sally."

The interest died. "I've got my daddy." She grew fierce. "He'd be lonely without me."

"I'm sure he would. He's fortunate to have you."

Ellie nodded.

"Just as you're fortunate to have him. Now, shall I read a story to start with?" Ease into the lessons, Adele had advised.

"I guess." Her lack of enthusiasm was slightly dampening, but Louisa chose to ignore it, opened the book and began to read. She loved the rhythm of the words, the comfort of the familiar story, but she closed the book at the end of chapter one. "We'll read more later, but now it's your turn to read to me." She handed Ellie the primer Adele thought she would be reading from by now. "Can you read me the first page?"

Ellie fixed Louisa with a stubborn frown and made no move to open the book.

Louisa flipped the pages to the first story. "Start here."

Ellie didn't even shift her eyes to the page.

"Ellie, please read this."

Ellie lowered her eyes, skimmed the page and closed the book. "I can't."

"Why can't you? Is it too hard?"

"I can't remember."

Louisa sighed. "What do you remember?"

"Falling out of the tree and landing wrong. You should have heard my leg. It snapped. Like this." She clicked her tongue to imitate the sound. "I tried not to cry, but my daddy was gone."

"Gone? Where?" Was this what he meant when he said it was his fault?

"Out working. We own a ranch, you know. He was checking the cows."

"I see."

"So now I have to lie in bed in this horrible cast—" She banged on it, the sound a hollow thud. "I can't do schoolwork."

"Of course you can work. There's nothing wrong with your brain."

Ellie turned away and stared at the door, as if willing Emmet to appear. And he did—sauntered past as if he had other things on his mind, but Louisa knew he was checking to make sure Ellie was okay. He paused. "Things going well?"

"Daddy." Ellie's voice quivered in the saddest possible way.

"Things are just fine." Louisa grabbed a bit of chalk. "Let's do some arithmetic now. What is the answer to this?" She wrote "1 + 1=" on the blackboard.

Emmet hesitated, watched a moment longer then moved on, and the outside door whacked shut.

"Ellie?"

The child stared clear through Louisa. "I don't know."

"You aren't even looking." She tapped the blackboard.

Ellie glanced at the numbers. "Can't remember."

Louisa crossed her arms and faced the child squarely. "I don't think that's the truth. I know you know the answer to one plus one."

They did a stubborn silent duel.

"Two." Ellie was not happy about admitting it.

"Good. Now two plus two."

"Where's my daddy? I want my daddy."

"Do you need to go to the bathroom?"

"No. I want my daddy."

Louisa took two steps until she stood right next to the bed. "Your daddy is working, and you must too."

"I'm sick."

"No, you've got a broken leg."

The big gray cat Louisa had met the day before jumped on the bed and stared into Ellie's eyes.

Louisa laughed. "The cat is telling you to do your schoolwork."

Ellie shoved the cat to the floor. He landed with a thud and stalked away. "I want my daddy!" Ellie yelled loudly.

Emmet crashed into the house and strode into the room. "Did you call me?"

Ellie nodded, her eyes brimming with innocent tears. "I have to go to the bathroom and Miss Morgan won't let me."

Emmet shot Louisa a stinging look.

Louisa wisely refrained from rolling her eyes at the

child's dramatics. Instead, she quietly headed for the door. "I'll step out while you tend to her needs."

She came face-to-face with Auntie May. "How long have you been here?"

"Just got in. Emmet and I were fixing the shingles." Her eyes narrowed. "She been giving you grief?" She tipped her head toward the bedroom.

Louisa opened her mouth to answer, then realized it would be inappropriate to speak of her concerns. "We're getting a routine established." Heaven help her if this was the regular pattern she'd be forced to follow.

"The little one is a tad spoiled, though I suppose it's to be expected. There's just the two of them."

"And you."

Auntie May snorted. "The child barely knows me. Besides, I'm just an old spinster." She bent to pet the cats crowding around her ankles.

Louisa wanted to see her expression. She longed to see acceptance and peace in Auntie May's eyes. Needed to know being a spinster wasn't an unhappy fate.

Louisa straightened her spine. She would become a happy spinster doing things to help others and bringing joy to herself as well. She'd start by showing Ellie it was fun to learn. She'd help the child deal with the boredom of her body cast. It would take more wisdom than her limited experience offered, but she could ask Adele for help, and she could pray. After all, hadn't God said in James chapter one, verse five, "If any of you lack wisdom, let him ask of God, that giveth to all men liberally and upbraideth not; and it shall be given him." It was one of the verses Father had Louisa and her sisters memorize.

Emmet emerged from the room. "Miss Morgan, please call me if Ellie needs to go the bathroom again." His voice and expression clearly said what his words didn't. He judged her unkind and unreasonable to not allow his child such basics.

"Of course." She knew full well there was no point in saying she had asked and Ellie had denied such a need. This battle was between Ellie and herself. With renewed determination, she returned to the child's bedside.

At noon, when she was done for the day, she'd made absolutely no progress with the planned lessons. Ellie insisted she didn't know or couldn't remember anything and refused to do any work.

Louisa emerged from the room, knowing her hair was mussed and her face likely flushed from frustration and fighting back tears. Why had she thought she could do this job? A bubble of self-pity whispered she was totally useless, but Louisa ignored it. Fought back. She wasn't useless. Not in every aspect. She could help this child if Ellie allowed it.

Emmet walked her out, waiting until they were out of earshot to speak his mind. "I sense you and Ellie are not getting along."

"Miss Ross said I might encounter resistance. After all, Ellie has lost her freedom. On top of that, everything is new. Familiar things are gone." Let him think the latter observation came from Adele as well, even though Louisa spoke her own thoughts. "Her only defense is—" she wanted to say defiance, but doubted Emmet would appreciate such a description "—is to exert what little independence she has left. I believe she will soon tire of it and find there are more enjoyable ways to pass the time."

He looked doubtful. Louisa feared he would tell her not to return. But after several seconds' consideration, he sighed heavily. "You're right about one thing. She's lost everything. She can hardly be blamed for feeling out of sorts."

"She hasn't lost everything, though." Her words were quiet, coming from a place full of certainty that Emmet was more than enough for this child. "She has you."

"She'll always have me."

She nodded, though words pushed at her lips, wanting to warn that he couldn't promise such.

"As long as I live." He clenched his fists. "And I fully intend to raise her in such a way that even if something happened to me—God forbid—she would never feel like I was gone. I'd be in her thoughts and in her actions every day."

Peace filled Louisa. "Exactly what my father did."

Their gazes connected, forged a single thought about fathers and daughters…how each needed the other. How sweet the relationship.

Louisa tipped her head away first. "I'll see you tomorrow." It was half a question, but he nodded.

"Until tomorrow then."

She climbed behind the wheel of their old, unreliable automobile and turned toward home. She admired Emmet's devotion to his child. It reminded her of the love her father had lavished on her and her sisters. Louisa smiled as fond memories of her father filled her thoughts. Ellie was a fortunate child to know such love.

Not until she reached the turnoff did she remember that the fortunate child was also a defiant, uncooperative child. Tension grabbed the muscles of her shoulders and loosened tears. She let the car coast as she struggled to gain control.

Blinking back the moisture in her eyes, she looked at her home. Father had dreamed of operating a farm, growing crops and raising cows. But after he died and the Depression hit, the family had been forced to make sacrifices. They'd let most of the land go to the bank in exchange for the house, the outbuildings and a few acres. The Morgan family didn't have much—their home, a barn, a cow, a calf and a reluctant garden— but it was so much more than many had. Over and over Louisa had observed families—beaten and broke—load their meager possessions to the sides and roof of their vehicle and drive away. Many couldn't afford the gas for driving and left with bundles on their backs. She knew just how blessed she, her mother and her sisters were. *Thank you, God, for allowing us to keep our home and stay together.* Her illnesses brought further tightening of purse strings that were already pulled about as taut as they could go.

"I prayed for a job so I could help pay the bills. Lord, You provided one when there were none available. I am not going to accept defeat or complain that it's hard." She sent the car toward home at a faster pace.

Mother watched her approach from the window and came to the door as she stepped from the car. "You look exhausted. Come in and rest." She twisted her apron in worried hands. "I'm afraid you will make yourself sick again."

Louisa hugged her mother. "I'm fine. I have no intention of making myself sick. You can count on that." Never again, if she had anything to say or do about it. She wouldn't jeopardize her health. It was far too precious.

"How did your first day go?"

She longed to share her frustration with her mother, but she knew it would only worry her. "About as expected. We're learning to adjust to each other."

Sally stood in the kitchen doorway, her eyes watchful. Sally didn't say much, but she saw a lot. Louisa could duck her head and avoid her sister's keen gaze, or she could face her and let her try to guess what lay behind her words. She knew the latter was the easiest way to deal with Sally, so she smiled at her. "How was your day?"

"I've been busy. Clara and I went to the orphanage and put in a garden for them."

"Good for you." Ten to twelve children lived at the home on the hill. A barren spot without trees or flowers, but at least the children were housed and fed. They attended school and church and appeared happy enough.

Mother had lunch ready and they sat down to enjoy it. Afterward Mother went for a nap.

Sally waited until the bedroom door closed, then gave Louisa a demanding look. "Tell all. How did it really go?"

Louisa blew out a huge sigh. "Ellie refuses to learn." She described the morning to her sister, including the part when Ellie made it sound as if Louisa wouldn't let her go to the bathroom.

Sally drew back, looked shocked. "She sounds dreadful. Are you going back?"

"I'm not about to give up."

"You're stronger than I am. I wouldn't be able to face such a situation."

Louisa chuckled. "I'm not strong. You know that as well as I do." Her thoughts darkened, but she refused to be controlled by her disappointment.

"You're strong in a quiet way. Perhaps because you've had to fight to get over pneumonia and influenza."

The darkness drew closer. The pain beckoned. But Louisa saw it for what it was—self-pity. And refused to open the door and invite it in. "I'm going to take that as a compliment." She thought of Ellie. The child needed to learn how to make the best of her situation.

She'd return tomorrow and try again. She'd show Emmet she wasn't unkind to his precious little girl.

"The kids at the orphanage are sweet. I'm going back after school is out with cookies for them. Why don't you come with me?"

Louisa's heart flopped in protest. See kids? The idea mocked her barrenness. "I don't think—"

"I know what you're going to say. You don't want to be reminded you can't have children of your own. But these kids will likely help you. They know how to enjoy life despite their loss and disappointment."

Sally's words stung. "Are you saying I don't?"

Sally looked shocked. "I didn't mean it like that. I only thought seeing them would cheer you up. You know...after dealing with a child who is feeling sorry for herself."

"You might be right. I'll go with you. I'll even help you bake cookies." Maybe she'd learn a thing or two about working with children who had suffered unfortunate events in their life that would help her deal with Ellie.

Somehow she had to prove to herself she could handle the job God had placed in her lap. But she wondered if He had more faith in her abilities than she did.

Over lunch Emmet listened to a litany of complaints from Ellie. Louisa was too harsh. She didn't explain things well.

"I don't think she likes me."

Emmet chuckled. "What's not to like? You're a sweet, smart, funny little girl." He hoped Louisa was right, and this resistance was only an adjustment period. Strange that Louisa and Ellie hadn't struck it off right away. From his first look at Louisa, he'd thought her beautiful—not just in appearance but in a deeper way. Her beauty seemed to come from within.

He fisted the idea away. It didn't matter what he thought of her. Only that she was kind to his daughter. He would tolerate nothing less.

He carried the lunch plates and glasses to the kitchen and grabbed a cup of coffee. A stack of dirty dishes waited to be washed. "I'll sit with Ellie for a bit then clean up this mess."

Auntie May shooed him away. "I do believe I can manage to wash a few dishes. Or at least let the cats lick them clean."

"Leave them. I'll do them later." He did not want Ellie eating off cat-cleaned dishes.

Auntie May's teasing chuckle made him realize he'd been tricked. "You're joshing and I missed it."

"You sure did. There was a time I'd have never gotten that past you." She sobered. "I think you've grown far too serious."

"Sometimes life isn't a joking matter." He headed for Ellie's room.

"People should never forget to find and appreciate the good things God gives us."

He paused to consider her. "I sometimes find it hard to believe in such."

"And there lies your problem. Emmet, my dear boy, I'm not saying bad things don't happen. I'm only saying you don't need to let them steal away the good things too."

He studied the words a moment but could find no personal truth in them. Except for one thing. "I have something I appreciate...Ellie." He ducked into her room, a wide smile on his face as he planned to enjoy the afternoon with her. But her arms were flung above her head and she snored softly.

Suddenly the next few hours looked lonely and bleak. He returned to the kitchen.

Auntie May glanced over her shoulder where—he was relieved to see—she had a wash pan full of hot soapy water.

"She's asleep." He downed the lukewarm coffee Auntie May seemed to favor and yearned for a cup of strong, hot brew.

"Why don't you have a look around town and see how the place has changed since you left? I'll watch out for Ellie."

"She'll be bored."

"Seems to me I can manage a little girl for an hour or two. Now shoo."

So he "shooed," right out the back door and down the lane that had once been his playground. He didn't expect he would see any of the kids he'd grown up with. The girls would be married. And the boys who weren't also married would be looking for work, perhaps riding the trains back and forth across the land.

He cut down a side avenue and ventured toward the main street. The buildings were familiar, even if they needed paint and repair. He stopped and stared. Mr. Smith's fence had fallen down. Mr. Smith used to put a lot of stock in that fence. Emmet circled the corner of the lot and looked at the house. The door sagged. The windows were bare.

He saw a young man striding down the street and called out. "What happened to the Smith family?"

The man crossed to Emmet's side. "They used to live here, didn't they? They were gone before my time. But my wife said they lost everything in the crash and went to live with Mrs. Smith's mother. No one has lived here since. Lots of empty houses around. Mostly abandoned by the occupants who could no longer make a living. Many have been taken by the bank because the mortgage payments were in default."

The two had fallen into step and continued toward the heart of town. Emmet studied the businesses. "Sharp's General Store. I remember them. There was a girl many grades below me...can't remember her name."

"Joanie?"

"That's the one. I don't suppose she's still around? She'd be what? About nineteen or twenty."

"She's still around. I'm guessing you used to live here."

Emmet explained how Auntie May was his guardian growing up. "I moved away nine years ago. Got married and have a little girl."

"Welcome back home."

Home. It had been once, but now? Truth be told, he didn't know where home was anymore. Rather than try to answer the comment, he asked the man about himself. "Gather you're a newcomer."

"Recent. I've been here about a year. Judd Kirk. I married a pretty young gal from this area, and we bought a farm near town. It's also near her home. Perhaps you know it—the Cotton place."

"Sure, I know it. There were a couple kids in school with me. They're gone, you say?" They'd arrived at the general store and trod indoors.

"Yup. Left the place lock, stock and barrel, which was handy for me." Judd glanced around. "Why, here are my two sisters-in-law. Come and meet them." Already Judd strode toward the young women.

Emmet stared. Louisa. He didn't want to see her outside the hours she tutored Ellie. Anything more felt as if he'd crossed a mental barrier he erected around his life. But of course, in a town the size of Golden Prairie, they would naturally run into each other, unless he stayed within the boundaries of Auntie May's house and yard. He'd done that for four days and found it stifling. Still, perhaps he could excuse himself on the pretext of urgent business. But too late. Judd led the young women toward Emmet. "My sisters-in-law, Louisa and Sally Morgan."

"Louisa and I have already met. She's tutoring my daughter." Did he see the same flicker of regret over this meeting as he'd felt? The idea stung. Why should she want to avoid him? He shifted his gaze to the other girl, Sally, and greeted her.

Judd laughed. "It's a small world. Or should I say it's a small town."

Louisa gave Judd a quick smile.

"Sally and I are preparing to make cookies to take to the orphanage. We needed raisins."

"A tea party?" No mistaking the curious tone of Judd's voice.

"Why don't you pick up Madge and join us?" Sally offered.

This was obviously a family event. Emmet edged away.

Judd stopped him. "Why don't you come along too?"

"I can't."

"Bring your daughter. She'll enjoy it."

Sally groaned. "Judd, the reason Louisa is tutoring his daughter is because Ellie is bedridden in a body cast. She can't join us."

Judd grabbed Emmet's shoulder. "Right. That would be who I made the tripod for. Oh, man, I am so sorry. That's tough on a little girl."

"Thanks."

"Good thing you have Louisa to tutor her. Couldn't ask for anyone better."

"Judd." Louisa tried to stop her brother-in-law, but he ignored her.

"She knows what it's like to have to stay in bed. I admire how she's handled her illnesses so well. I think I'd want to moan and groan and feel sorry for myself. But not Louisa—"

Judd leaned close to Emmet and chuckled. "Don't be fooled by her looks. She's a fighter."

Emmet watched the pair of sisters gather up their small parcel and head for the door.

Sally whispered something to Louisa and hung back. Louisa grabbed her arm and pushed her forward. Louisa paused before they exited and gave Judd a demanding look. "You'll let Madge know right away so she can get ready?"

Judd laughed. "I'll get on it immediately." The look he gave Emmet burgeoned with amusement, and he lowered his voice to a whisper. "I better say goodbye or face the wrath of three sisters, because if one is offended they're all offended. Sure you can't come along? You know—to give me a little moral support?"

"Judd, are you coming?" Louisa's voice was sweet and inviting, but Emmet saw the way Judd jerked to attention and guessed that beneath the gentleness lay solid, unyielding bedrock.

"Sorry, I can't leave my daughter." He liked the man and wished they could spend more time together. He missed company beyond Auntie May and Ellie. "Why don't you drop by when you get a chance?"

Judd gave him a considering look. "I just might do that. Right now I better go find my wife and tell her of her sisters' plans." He hurried after Sally and Louisa.

The store felt empty when the trio left. Emmet gave himself a mental kick. He was used to being alone, out in the open, riding the range, working with cows. Company—and companionship—was sporadic and fleeting. So why should it bother him to be left behind? He must be getting befuddled.

He crossed to the candy selection, chose a red-and-white peppermint stick, paid for it and left the store. Ellie would be awake soon, and the candy would brighten her afternoon.

But later, as he sat beside his daughter, watching her suck the peppermint stick, the rest of the day stretched before him, as endless as the vast horizon. The only break in sight was Louisa's return in the morning.

For Ellie's sake only. The hours must be even longer for her.

Chapter Four

Louisa stopped at the last corner before the Hamilton home. She wasn't eager to start the session with Ellie.

Rather than dwell on her doubts and fears, she thought of the few hours she and her sisters had spent at the orphanage. Louisa had dreaded the event but was determined not to let her sisters know. However, from the first rowdy greeting to the last goodbye, she'd enjoyed every minute. The children were happy to see them. Several acted as if they especially liked Louisa, which was heartwarming. One of the older girls brought her some drawings she'd done and listened eagerly as Louisa showed her how to add shading and correct perspective to her rather appealing work. Another child, a girl close to Ellie's age, brought a book and begged Louisa to read it to her.

"What grade are you in, Leila?" she'd asked.

"Grade one. I'm six."

Louisa asked her to read aloud from her reader. The child read eagerly and clearly. Ellie was in second grade and should read even better.

Perhaps today, Louisa would discover Ellie's reading level. She turned the corner and headed toward the house. At the front gate, she parked, gathered up determination and courage and shoved them into place, then stepped forth to face the battle. *God, guide me, bless me with Your wisdom.* She took the awkward parcel from the backseat.

Emmet opened the door as she approached. He sent a questioning look at the bundle in her arms but didn't ask about it.

At the way he seemed to assess her, Louisa's cheeks burned. Judd should not have told him about Louisa's illnesses. Three bouts of pneumonia. Influenza that hit her so hard. She'd asked Madge to remind him no one outside the family must hear of Louisa's barrenness. She didn't want to be the recipient of pitying looks.

"Good morning." She kept her voice cool. Professional. She wasn't a teacher, but she would act like one. Emmet was a parent of a student. Nothing more. "How is Ellie this morning?"

"Okay. And you?"

She faltered the slightest. Why did he ask? Did he think she might get ill at the least little thing? She tilted her chin. She had no intention of getting ill. "I'm fine, thank you. Eager to start my day." Eager might be a slight exaggeration. But she would show no fear, no regret, no desperation. God was at her side. *The Lord is my shepherd. He leadeth me beside still waters.* Would the waters be still or troubled today?

Emmet kept pace at her side as she crossed the front room. "I'm glad you understand that Ellie is finding it difficult to adjust to her situation. It's a relief to know you'll be patient with her."

Did she detect a warning in his voice? She stopped and faced him. "Mr. Hamilton—"

"Please, call me Emmet."

Did teachers call parents by their first name? Would doing so cross a line she didn't wish to cross? She needed to keep things impersonal between them. Not one step further than her feelings had already transgressed.

"As you please. I am being paid to teach your child." The school board had hired her with specific expectations…keep the child up to speed with her classmates. Only, her position depended as much on Emmet's approval as the school board's expectations. Emmet had the right to say yes or no to her being Ellie's tutor. "I'll do my best to help her keep up with her class work."

"I care less about Ellie's schoolwork than about her happiness."

What more could anyone ask of a parent? But life wasn't always that simple. "I hope I can achieve the one without sacrificing the other." But it would take Ellie's cooperation. Something she suspected that would not come without a battle.

"That's all I ask."

Louisa stepped into Ellie's room and read instant defiance in the child's eyes. She was trapped between what Emmet believed was possible and what Ellie clearly would not allow—Louisa teaching her.

She considered putting aside the role of teacher and simply amusing the child, but her agreement with the board was quite specific and she couldn't, in good conscience, pretend she fulfilled the terms without doing so. If she couldn't teach Ellie she must quit. And that was something she would not do. Not with those medical bills stacked up on Mother's desk.

Adele had given her more advice. "Make it clear that there is a certain amount of work to be done each day. Be matter-of-fact about it. Then do it."

"But what if she doesn't cooperate?"

"That's where discipline comes in. You might try providing rewards, incentives, if you like."

Louisa crossed to the little table where she arranged her lesson plans that she and Adele had drawn up together, the books she intended to use and the odd-shaped parcel.

"What's that?"

"It's for you. You can have it when you complete today's lesson." She picked up the chalk and wrote on the blackboard: "Reading, Arithmetic and History." "Three subjects. We won't spend long on each, but they all have an assignment that must be completed."

Ellie eyed the package, her curiosity obvious.

Good. Louisa had already tried reading and arithmetic without success, so she went for history. "Grade twos are studying the history of Alberta. Today we are going to talk about the establishment of the North-West Mounted Police." She loved the drama of the march west and had a picture book illustrating it. She began with explaining the need for a police force to settle the troubles in the West. She showed a picture of the colorful troop ready to set out—noble and hopeful, unaware of the challenges they would face.

But Ellie stared at the present as Louisa continued reading. If Ellie cared to look at the pictures, they were there before her. Adele had assured Louisa that Ellie would soon be drawn into the lessons.

Louisa came to the end of what she planned to read for the day.

"Now I want you to choose a project. You can either draw a picture about the march west or write a story. You can pretend to be one of the young police officers or—"

"What is that?" Her gaze hadn't shifted from the parcel.

"If you want to open it, you have to do your lessons." She placed a bed tray before Ellie, tilted so the child could write, and put a sheet of paper on it. "Do you wish to draw a picture or write a story?"

"Neither." The girl certainly knew how to put on a pout. "Daddy won't like that you're teasing me. He lets me have anything I want."

"That makes for mighty poor character." Adele had prepared a list of questions should Ellie balk at working on her own initiative. "Here are questions about the North-West Mounted Police. You can do them." There were five very simple questions.

"I don't want to."

At least she wasn't insisting she didn't know or couldn't remember. Louisa wondered if this was progress. "If you want to see what's in the parcel, you must first do your work."

"No." Ellie swept the tray to the floor with a clattering racket. "Why are you being so mean to me? I don't have a mother, you know."

"Well, I don't have a father."

"You're a grown-up. You don't need a father."

"Even grown-ups need a father now and then." She picked up the tray and rescued the paper and pencil, replaced them on the bed and tapped the page. "Please answer these questions."

"I don't want to, and I generally do as I please."

Louisa sighed. "There's a name for children like that."

Ellie scowled. "What?"

Should she tell her? "Spoiled."

Ellie screeched and tried to push the tray off the bed again. But Louisa held it firmly in place. "Let's get this done so we can move on. We still have reading and arithmetic to do this morning."

Ellie screamed louder.

Emmet strode into the room. "What's going on here?"

Ellie sobbed and reached for Emmet. "She's being mean to me."

Emmet wrapped his arms about the child's trembling shoulders. "Hush now. You're okay. Daddy's here." His voice was warm and gentle, but the look he gave Louisa accused her of senseless cruelty.

Louisa sighed. She couldn't fight them both. But she wasn't about to admit defeat. She stiffened her spine and thought about how to deal with this.

Ellie snuggled into her father's shoulder and lifted her eyes to Louisa. There was no mistaking the glint of triumph.

Emmet extracted himself from his daughter's arms and faced Louisa, but she spoke before he could.

"We need to talk. I'll wait for you in the front room." Her stride was far steadier than her insides. She crossed the kitchen. Auntie May sat at the table with four cats on her lap and one draped over her shoulders.

"You're never beat until you quit," she murmured.

Louisa flashed a trembling smile. Exactly the words she needed to hear. She wasn't about to quit. Nor admit defeat.

Emmet backed out of Ellie's room, assuring his daughter he would be back in a few minutes, then he gave Louisa a curt nod and strode into the front room.

Louisa followed, and although she felt like being meek and apologetic, she kept her head high and her step firm.

"Miss Morgan, I fear you are most unsuited for this job." His eyes flashed with anger.

An answering flash burned her eyes. "I consider Miss Ross to be a fine teacher, with all the skill that experience and study can give."

"We aren't talking about Miss Ross."

"Indeed, we are. She recommended me for this job. She supervises the lessons. She also gives advice as to how to deal with a child who doesn't welcome having to keep up with her studies. I suggest if you have a problem with my methods, you consult her."

He looked askance. "I have no quarrel with Miss Ross. I'm sure she's a fine teacher."

"One of the best. We are fortunate to have her."

"That might well be the case, but she isn't the one in Ellie's room making her cry."

Louisa refrained from pointing out the tears were for Emmet's benefit to elicit his sympathy. And they worked very well. "Before you decide to dismiss me, you should consider I am the only one available to do this job, unless you intend to scoop up one of those hobos down by the tracks."

Emmet looked as if she'd suggested dipping his child in mud.

"I thought not. Then why don't we consult Miss Ross and get her help in sorting this out?"

"Sounds like a fine idea. After school today?"

"She's already expecting me." They had arranged to meet almost every day to discuss lessons. "I don't believe there is any point in me trying to continue this morning."

Louisa returned to the bedroom and gathered her things—including the wrapped gift—then paused to say goodbye to Ellie, not caring at all at the pleased look on the child's face. This wasn't over yet.

She could only hope Emmet would realize that if he let Ellie win this battle, she would be the loser, not the victor.

Later that afternoon, Louisa waited outside the classroom for Emmet. She'd arrived a few minutes before, but it didn't seem fair to go in without him. He might wonder if she was seeking to get Adele on her side. It had been tempting to do so, but in the intervening hours since she'd marched out of the Hamilton house, her resolve had grown. She would not fail.

Emmet approached, his strides firm, his jaw squared even more than she'd noticed before. He was a man determined to do what was best for his daughter.

Louisa mentally drew herself to rigid attention, as if readying for duel. How silly. A giggle tickled the back of her throat, but she wisely restrained it. They weren't adversaries. They both wanted the same thing—what was best for Ellie. Only problem was they obviously considered that to be two different things.

Her amusement died as quickly as it had come, and the prayer she had whispered all afternoon filled her thoughts. *Lord, show us a way of compromise that will enable me to teach Ellie.*

"I'm ready." Emmet paused at her side and indicated she should lead the way.

She proceeded down the hall to the room where Adele waited for her. They passed a closed door. "Before the Depression and drought drove so many people from the land, this room held the older grades. Now even the desks in one room aren't full, and there are no students above grade five." Why did she explain this to Emmet? He had attended classes here when he was younger, when both rooms held children. "I feel badly that many children will be deprived of an education because of their family circumstances." She had never before felt the need to fill silences with idle chatter.

"You hold learning in high regard, don't you?"

She cast a sideways glance at him. Was he mocking her? No, he looked serious. "I believe there is much value in learning."

"Reading, writing and arithmetic are handy skills."

"So are art, music, languages, history and so much more. The more we know about our world, the better equipped we are to live successfully in it. But learning also teaches us to think past the obvious, past our own experiences."

He chuckled softly, puckering the edges of her resistance to him. "I always thought experience was the best teacher."

"It is sometimes a cruel teacher."

They considered each other. She saw in his eyes a dark familiarity with the sort of pain she meant, and she understood something as clearly as if he had written it in bold letters across his forehead. He'd lost much and now protected Ellie, perhaps even indulged her, because she was all he had left, and he feared losing her.

Instinctively she touched his arm, signaling she understood. "There is no substitute for experience, but I believe a solid education can equip us to deal with life. Of course, our best help in life is to trust God. He promises to guide us through."

Emmet could have been frozen stiff, for all the indication he gave that he heard her or was aware of her touch. Yet she didn't withdraw her hand. She felt his troubled soul through her palm and wanted to soothe it. "You do believe in God's love and care, don't you?"

He shuddered. "I think I do. I like to think God brought me back to Golden Prairie for a reason, but I think He could have found a better way to do it than through Ellie's accident." By the time he finished, his voice grew harsh, uncertain. He shook his head. "I struggle to trust God when things are hard."

She crossed her arms about her waist, pressing tight, her palm still warm from where it had touched him. "I suppose that's what it means in Second Corinthians five, verse seven, when it says, 'We walk by faith, not by sight.' When we can't see why things are the way they are, we choose to trust God anyway."

"It's that easy, is it?"

She smiled widely. "No, it's that hard—but I prefer to trust God rather than my own assessment of the situation." It had been a struggle to come to the place of trusting God in her barrenness, but she had to believe He had something else in store for her—something that would bring her satisfaction.

Adele must have heard them outside her door as she swung it open. "Mr. Hamilton, Louisa. I didn't expect the two of you. Do come in." She glanced from one to the other. "Is there a problem?"

Emmet spoke before Louisa could answer, but it didn't matter. They'd come with a common purpose. "We agreed to seek your advice in Ellie's lessons."

"Very well." Adele waved them toward the front row of desks as she sat behind the big teacher's desk.

Louisa had no problem slipping into hers, but Emmet had to wedge into a desk designed for young children, not broad-chested men. Louisa ducked her head to hide her amusement and shifted her gaze toward Adele.

Adele Ross had become a friend when she learned of the collection of books Louisa had and begged to borrow a few. The woman pulled her hair into a severe knot at the back of her head, as if to prove her serious state of mind, as suited a teacher of young children. But Louisa knew she had the kindest heart and a long store of patience to accompany her cheery attitude. They had never discussed their respective ages, but Adele was probably nearing thirty. Closer to Emmet's age than Louisa's. She hadn't thought of that before and tried to assess if either of them showed a flicker of interest in the other. When she detected none, she relaxed. Though why she should be relieved made no sense. Emmet and

Adele would make a good couple. Except it would mean Adele would have to give up her teaching position. Although some school boards now allowed married teachers, this one did not.

Adele looked at Louisa. "Perhaps you'd better explain."

Glad to be brought back from the useless side trail her thoughts had started down, Louisa nodded. "I have been unable to get Ellie interested in the lessons and Emmet—Mr. Hamilton—feels I am not suited for the job."

Adele blinked in surprise, then did her best to hide it. She turned to Emmet. "Is that correct, Mr. Hamilton?"

"Ellie is unhappy with Miss Morgan's lesson presentation. I thought you could suggest someone else. Someone who could get Ellie's cooperation without upsetting her."

Adele nodded slowly and considered his request several seconds before she replied. "I can think of no one I would consider more suitable than Louisa."

Louisa smiled her thanks and gave Emmet a pleased look. She'd told him much the same, but it was gratifying to have Adele verify it.

Adele leaned forward, her hands clasped together, and addressed Emmet. "Why do you think Ellie is upset about the lessons?"

Emmet shot Louisa a look that reminded her of his daughter—full of defiance. "She says Louisa is mean to her."

"I see. Precisely what does Louisa do that would fall into that category?"

Emmet opened and closed his mouth, then blinked twice. "I don't know exactly. But several times I have come into the room in response to Ellie's cries." He glared at Louisa. "You must be doing something."

Before Louisa could defend herself, Adele spoke. "I have been a teacher for a number of years and I know how serious a charge such as this is. But I need something more solid than the cries of your daughter."

Louisa tried to protest, but Adele lifted a hand to signal silence. Was Adele taking Emmet's side? Just because he was the parent? Adele smiled, taking the sting from her actions. "You'll get a chance to speak, but I must get to the bottom of this."

Louisa sat back and fumed. There was no bottom. No top. No sides. Because she'd never been mean. Not once.

"Now, Mr. Hamilton, please explain. Did you see Louisa strike your child?" She waited for Emmet's answer. "No. Did Ellie accuse her of doing so?" Another pause in which Emmet could only shake his head. "No. Call her cruel names? No. Does she expect Ellie to do more work than she is capable of in her circumstances?"

Emmet shrugged.

Adele pressed him. "How much work has she done?"

"I've seen none."

"You've seen nothing that could be constituted as cruelty. And you've seen no work. Is that correct?"

Emmet refused to answer. "I've seen Ellie cry. Heard her accusations."

"I'm not discrediting that. But let's hear Louisa's explanation, shall we?"

Emmet sighed. His look said he'd like to see her get out of this.

"We have planned the lessons together. Nothing a grade-two student shouldn't be able to do. In fact, many of my grade-one students could do the work." Adele turned her gray-eyed gaze to Louisa. "How far have you come with the lessons?"

Louisa hung her head, a sense of complete failure swamping her. "I've accomplished nothing."

"And why is that?"

She shared her concerns with Adele, but hated to admit she had only failure to report. "I have been unable to gain Ellie's cooperation."

"Can you explain what you mean by that?"

Louisa brought her head up and spoke directly to Emmet, ignoring his defensive expression that indicated if there was a problem, it was not Ellie's fault. It couldn't be. "I am not a teacher, but I have a very good guide. I've followed her suggestions. She said to win the child. She said to give her time to accept the idea. I tried. Then she said Ellie must understand she has to continue her lessons. Again, I tried, but no matter what I do, Ellie says she doesn't know, doesn't remember or flatly refuses to do any of the work. When I read she does her best to ignore me. I even brought a present as an incentive, as Adele suggested. That brought on an outburst because I refused to give her the present until she did her work." She waved her hands in frustration. "I value learning. I know what it's like to fall behind. I want to help Ellie, but she won't let me." She hated to admit failure, but she couldn't continue to insist on being Ellie's tutor when Ellie resisted her. "Perhaps you're right. Ellie is falling behind because I can't reach her."

Adele held her palms toward them. "Let's not be hasty. Frankly, not only is Louisa the best person for this job, but she's the only person remotely qualified. We'd have to advertise across the province to find someone else, and let's be reasonable. How many applicants would we get for a two-month job that's only four hours a day?"

"Probably lots of unemployed teachers looking for work," Emmet muttered.

"I expect that's so. But I would think you'd want references. All that takes time." Adele let her comments hang in the air. "Emmet, what do you want for Ellie?"

"That's easy. I want her to be happy."

"Right. Is she happy with things the way they are?"

"I suppose not. She's restless, wishing she didn't have to be confined to bed in a body cast."

"So perhaps school lessons might prove a welcome distraction?"

"I had hoped so."

"Good." She turned to Louisa. "What do you want here?"

"To do the job I was hired to do. To help Ellie keep up."

"Why?"

Adele's question opened a whole vista of truth to Louisa. It was more than the money. She'd always felt a spectator on life. Never very useful. This was her chance to prove to her mother and sisters…and herself…that she could do something, make a difference. "I believe I can do this. I can help Ellie. I want to because I know how difficult it is to fall behind your classmates, to struggle to catch up and keep up. And because I firmly believe learning can and should be fun."

Adele's eyes gleamed with pleasure at Louisa's confession. "Mr. Hamilton, do you have any objections to Louisa's goals for your daughter?"

Louisa and Emmet studied each other. Wary adversaries? Or something more? Something that went beyond teaching, beyond Ellie's needs. She sensed in him a deep hurt that echoed her own. Of course he had pain—he'd lost his wife, and before that his parents, and now his child was injured. Perhaps by helping Ellie, she could help him. Ease some of his concerns. She'd told God she would serve Him in whatever job He provided. This was a job. Nothing more.

But she could not deny she hadn't expected a job to dig deep into her heart and open up longings she knew she must deny. Somewhere in the past two days, despite Ellie's cantankerous ways, Louisa had crossed a line. She'd begun to care about the Hamiltons. She wanted to help Ellie because she cared. She wanted to help Ellie because it mattered to her that Emmet, although he loved his daughter deeply, was allowing her to rule his life.

Adele broke into her thoughts, still addressing Emmet. "Do these goals contradict yours in any way?"

"I suppose not." His gaze held Louisa's, searching for what, she did not know. But she let him probe deep past the surface of their words and association until she felt as if his thoughts had reached deep into hers, found an anchor pin and secured a hook to it.

"Perhaps there is another way to address the problem. A compromise?"

Louisa forced her gaze toward Adele. Would it include her keeping the job? She darted a glance at Emmet. Did he look even vaguely interested?

He caught her looking and shrugged. "What do we have to lose?"

She turned back to Adele. "What do you suggest?"

"I think you two should become partners in this venture."

"Partners?" Louisa and Emmet echoed the word in unison. How could they possibly work together? Even being here and discussing Ellie's need had opened a window in Louisa's heart, revealed a hunger she must deny. She looked it squarely in the face. Yes, she longed to earn the love of a man such as Emmet—strong, committed, loving—but her barrenness made it impossible. Even if he knew...even if he said it didn't matter. It would be unfair to burden a man with the same limitations she must accept.

Her best plan would be to avoid him as much as possible. Whatever Adele meant by partnership, Louisa hoped it meant a simple shake of hands in shared concern.

Adele took their silence for agreement. "I think Ellie is feeling you two are in opposition. Either it threatens her, or she's taking advantage of it. Perhaps even both. I think by presenting a unified front, she will realize she has no alternative but to do the assigned work. She'll soon learn that lesson time can be fun and help her pass the long days. I have laid out the lesson plans and will continue to do so. I suggest the two of you work out how to deliver them. You're welcome to use any of the material I have." She waved a hand to indicate the books and objects in the shelves around the room.

Work together. Plan together. Louisa choked back a protest. How was she to stay professional when every time she turned around, she encountered feelings that were decidedly not professional? And now to consider spending more time in his presence…how was she ever going to keep her feelings locked away?

... ...

Chapter Five

Emmet pried himself from the too-small desk and followed Louisa out of the classroom. With a murmured
goodbye and thank-you to Miss Ross, he closed the door
and sucked air into lungs too stunned this past half hour
to function properly.

Partners? Work together? A unified front? Shoot. He
didn't want to be united with Louisa on anything. Just
sitting next to her in the classroom, feeling her fragile
resistance—he was wrong on that score too. She was
about as fragile as the first spring crocus that fought its
way up through the snow and waved its head cheerfully
through the winds and storms of the season. What had
possessed him to agree?

One thing only. And it was all that mattered. It was
best for Ellie.

Louisa too, appeared to need time to pull herself together after Miss Ross's surprise suggestion.

He'd been awed by Louisa's passion that Ellie keep
up with her classmates. And more than a little moved
by it. If he were honest, he'd felt just a tiny bit guilty

that he was concerned solely with her happiness. For a fleeting moment, it seemed almost irresponsible.

But he had his head back where it belonged after the brief period of confusion. Squarely on his shoulders. He would not let anything Louisa said or did confound him again. "Looks like we're stuck working together." He excused the roughness of his words and his voice on the need to keep boundaries firmly in place. He wanted only one thing from Louisa—help teaching Ellie, because he now realized how important it was for her to keep up with her studies. "So let's figure out a way to make this work." He headed for the outside door, Louisa at his side.

"How do you suggest we do that?"

"I suppose we need to plan our approach, as Miss Ross suggested." But when and where? "I don't like leaving Auntie May to watch Ellie too long." Ellie clearly didn't appreciate it either, but he refrained from saying so, still feeling as if he was somehow lax in wanting to keep her happy. "It's too big a chore. Besides, Auntie May has enough to do."

"What with feeding her cats and all." Her dry tone informed him that Louisa teased, and he chuckled. His tension dissipated in his amusement.

"I fear she will fall over one of them and injure herself." He'd meant to be teasing too, but realized it was a deep-seated worry. He didn't care to lose any more of his family due to an accident.

"I don't think you need to fear for her safety. She seems to know how to avoid them when she's walking. You know, I've always admired how sure-footed she was."

"Comes from dancing around cats. Keeps her nimble." He did a little side jump to illustrate, bringing a merry laugh to Louisa's lips. He tucked a smile into the corner of his mind, pleased to have amused her.

Shoot. How did he get so far off track? If this was a sample of how it would be to work with her, it did not bode well for keeping it businesslike. And yet, somehow, he couldn't honestly object. But back to the task at hand. "If we wait until after Ellie goes to sleep…" Then what? Auntie May liked to curl up with her cats and a book in the evening. He didn't want to take advantage of his aunt by asking that she be alert to Ellie's call.

"I could come back into town later. I'm sure it won't take long to deal with this."

In fact, they might be able to stand on the step and sort it out in a matter of minutes before she left. Yet somehow he didn't suggest it. "If you don't mind. That way I could be available without expecting Auntie May to cover for me."

"I don't mind. Like I say, I'm sure it will only be a short while. Then I can visit a friend."

"Good." They stood before her battered car. "I'll see you later then." He planted his hat on his head, nodded goodbye and strolled away. Not until he heard her car start and breathed in the gas fumes and dust of her departure did he wonder if spending more time with Louisa was a wise idea. But it was too late to change his mind, and because it was for Ellie he had no intention of doing so.

Emmet explained to Auntie May that Louisa would be coming because they were going to work on Ellie's lessons together.

"Excellent idea, my boy. You'll soon discover what a fine woman she is. You know, you could do worse than think about asking her—"

He cut her off right there, knowing she was about to suggest he ask Louisa out. "I have no interest in such things. Not now. Not ever."

She looked at him, her face awash with concern. "Emmet, you are a young man. You can't carry your hurt like a shield all your life."

He intended to do exactly that, though it was caution he carried, not hurt. He was long past hurt. "My life is busy enough with the ranch and a child to raise."

"Troubles shared are troubles halved."

"We'll use the front room so as not to disturb Ellie, if that's okay with you."

She studied him, letting him know she understood he ignored her suggestion of sharing troubles. "I prefer the rocking chair in the kitchen, as you are well aware. Does Ellie know about your new plan?"

Ellie slept in the next room, exhausted by another crying spell. She missed her pony. Her friends. Even Betsy. "I haven't said anything." Seems the least little thing set her into a bout of tears. Hopefully she wasn't going to end up like her mother. Jane had resorted to tears to get her own way so often that Emmet had learned to ignore them. Or had tried to, but they never failed to make him feel guilty.

"It's something Louisa and I will plan together."

A gentle knock sounded at the door.

"I expect that is her now."

"'Spect so. You better let her in. And don't worry about me. The cats and I will be quite happy in the kitchen." She sat in a rocking chair so well used that the rockers had a ridge where she changed direction. "Run along now." She shooed him away.

He crossed the room and opened the door. The sun had settled toward the horizon and slanted rays into his eyes, so he didn't see her face clearly. For some unfathomable reason, that bothered him. He wanted to see her expression, know what she really thought about this arrangement. Perhaps if he did, he could understand how he felt. Because this did not feel like business. It felt like a social call. He had struggled the past hour to try to drive that thought away, but it refused to leave.

"Come in. Have a seat." He waved toward a little table he'd cleared off and against which he had shoved two chairs, assuming she would want to show him material.

"Thanks." She sat and waited for him to sit opposite her, then she opened a notebook. "These are the lesson plans Adele helped me prepare." She pointed to the outlined notes. "As you can see, we aren't aiming to do more than basics. Her assignments have also been adjusted so she can do them without too much effort. We realize it's difficult for her to do much while flat on her back."

He glanced over the material. "These seem fairly straightforward."

"You're still thinking I'm the problem here." She sucked in air. "You might be right. I get the feeling she resents my presence. Perhaps by having you in the room and presenting part of the lesson, she can see I only want to help her."

"I agreed to do so. I'm just uncertain of my role. What do you want me to do?"

"I guess it depends on what you want."

"What I want has nothing to do with lessons. I want her to not be injured in the first place. I want—" *I want her mother to still be alive. I want my parents to be alive.*

"I'm sorry. It can't be easy raising a child on your own."

"It has its challenges for sure, but I wouldn't trade it for anything. My only regret is not having more children." He leaned forward. "I envy you your sisters. I longed for brothers or sisters when I was growing up. And when I married, I vowed I would not have an only child. But life did not follow my plan."

Louisa kept her head downturned. "Nor did mine," she murmured.

The pain in her voice seared his heart. He knew such pain. "What happened?"

She lifted her head. Her expression silently wept. His breath caught in the back of his throat at such raw pain. She drew a shuddering breath and then smiled, driving away the darkness, replacing it with sunshine as bright as what he'd faced when he opened the door. "We all have troubles, but I've learned that when we need God most, He is the closest. Knowing how much He cares for me is a gift beyond measure."

He wanted to know the size and shape and extent of her troubles. Wanted to take them from her. Just as he longed to take every trouble falling into Ellie's life and carry it himself.

She turned her attention back to the papers before

them. "I've prepared the history lesson so I can teach that. The arithmetic is straightforward. You could teach it if you like. Reading…well let's work together on that."

He pushed his thoughts back to the task at hand—the only thing that mattered—getting Ellie to do her schoolwork. Soon they had settled the lessons. The evening ahead stretched long and empty. He ached for someone to talk to. Sure, he had Auntie May and Ellie, but that wasn't what he meant.

"Would you like to go for a little walk before you leave? Watch the sunset?"

She tucked the lesson material into her satchel without answering.

Obviously she expected their relationship to be based solely on the task at hand. As did he. He shouldn't have asked. But how could he withdraw the offer now without sounding rude?

Before he could think of a way, she turned her face upward and smiled, sending rays of golden light into his heart.

"I think that would be nice."

The woman had a beautiful smile. He couldn't imagine why she didn't have a dozen young men at her beck and call. Except most young men were struggling to keep body and boots together.

Emmet pretended he wasn't relieved it was too late to change his mind. He told Auntie May his plans, ignoring her triumphant grin. They left the house, paused as Louisa put her satchel in the car, then turned their steps away from the heart of town. "I used to play scrub ball in that lot." He pointed to the empty bit of land. "Can't imagine I was once so carefree. Seems like a lifetime ago."

"Tell me about your ranch."

He gratefully accepted her attempt to pull the conversation to safer channels. "It's small. Tucked away in the foothills to the west. The land is beautiful. You can see the mountains simply by lifting your head and looking."

She sighed. "I'd love to see them up close. I've had glimpses when we went to Calgary. That's all."

"They're a sight to behold, that's for sure."

"I suppose you're anxious to get back there."

He considered the question. "Seems I should be, but I'm not."

She stopped to study him.

He grinned but knew it was crooked and uncertain. "I guess I can't think of the place without associating it with bad things."

She nodded, her eyes brimming with sympathy. "Your wife died out there."

He couldn't maintain even a shaky smile.

"I'm sorry." She touched his arm, then withdrew her hand. But just as when she'd pressed her palm to his arm in the hallway of the school, a feeling of comfort raced through his heart. How did she do that? Give a healing balm simply with a touch? "She didn't die at the ranch, for which I am grateful. We were in town buying supplies, and a team was frightened by a strange dog barking at their heels. They bolted. Before anyone could stop them, they ran over Jane."

She shuddered. "How dreadful. Where was Ellie?"

"I had her in my arms. I pressed her face to my

shoulder so she couldn't see." He'd protected her then. He'd protect her now.

"How old was Ellie?"

"Four."

"And you've managed on your own since?"

"I had an older woman as a housekeeper for almost two years, but her daughter needed her so she left. Then I got Betsy, a neighbor. She came after school and stayed until I was back for supper. But I discovered she spent as much time elsewhere as she did with Ellie. That's how Ellie came to be alone when she broke her leg."

"Poor Ellie. She must have been very frightened."

"Indeed." He didn't want to think about it. Or talk about it. If something happened to Ellie... He shifted back to a safer topic. "The town has gone downhill since I left. So many places vacant."

"I know. It's sad." She sighed, and he felt guilty at having brought up nothing but depressing topics.

"What do people do for fun around here? Sorry, I didn't mean that to sound critical. I'm just wondering."

She chuckled softly. A man could grow to appreciate amusing her.

"I enjoy weeding the garden."

That was her idea of fun?

She giggled. "Guess that's not what you meant."

He glanced at her then. He'd admired her beauty before, assessed it as more than skin-deep, but at the way happiness and joy bubbled from her sparkling eyes, he almost tripped. A man could forget all his carefully constructed fences, find them blown over and useless in the face of such deep-rooted beauty. "I can't believe it's your idea of fun." His voice deepened, revealing just how much he'd been touched. Hopefully she would assume it was only because he teased her.

"No, really, I consider it a blessing to be able to do physical work. There was a time I couldn't. A person learns to appreciate ordinary things when they've been deprived of them."

"I know you were ill enough to be confined to bed. What was wrong?"

"Pneumonia. Three winters in a row. Seems my lungs never got completely better before the next winter would start it all over." The joy in her eyes abated, as if the memory of those days hurt.

He cupped her shoulder, wanting to share her sorrow as she had shared his. He wanted to restore the bubbling happiness. "You're better now though?" She seemed fragile in appearance, but he had discovered she was actually about as fragile as steel. He didn't want to think her health was precarious.

She laughed. "I'm better. Ready to tackle life and enjoy it to the fullest. No more sitting on the sidelines idly watching. Which is why even weeding the garden is pleasant."

"But seriously, what do you do for pure enjoyment?" He wanted to know, though why he should care... He wasn't about to examine his reasons, and declared his question to be an attempt at pleasant conversation.

"I bake—"

"Like the cookies you took to the orphanage?"

"Yes. We took oatmeal raisin and also molasses cookies because they are our favorites. They were

Father's favorites." Her expression filled with sadness. He wanted to bring back the sunshine.

"How did the visit to the orphanage go?"

"Good." She told him about the children. "They appreciate the least little kindness. Poor little waifs."

"Okay, you weed the garden and bake cookies. What else?"

"I read. I draw. I sang in the church choir for Easter. I generally keep busy. But maybe you mean what is there for a single man to do in the community." They walked along a dusty trail that paralleled the railway tracks. She slowed and considered him. "Are you looking for a way to meet young ladies?"

Heaven forbid. He never wanted to marry again. But he wanted to see her reaction if he suggested otherwise. "Are there lots of young ladies around?"

She ducked her head, but not before he thought he caught a flash of disapproval—or was it disappointment? Was she even faintly interested in him as a man?

"Of course, I've already met three charming young ladies."

Her head jerked up, and she considered him with wide-eyed surprise. "You have?"

It pleased him to no end to see her interest. "Miss Ross seems like a good person."

"Yes, of course she is."

"Then there are those two young ladies I met in the store."

Her eyebrows shot up in silent question.

"You know. Miss Sally Morgan and her very charming sister, Louisa." He laughed at the confusion in her face and admired the way her cheeks bloomed pink.

"Oh, you're teasing me."

He was more than half-serious, but why was he enjoying teasing her? Their relationship was to be nothing more than business, even though they were partners now. He liked the idea more and more.

She continued down the trail, every step raising a puff of dirt. "Look." Her voice filled with wonder.

He'd forgotten they were supposed to be admiring the sunset and followed her gaze to the west.

They stood side by side and watched colors shift from pink to orange to deep red. Gold tinted the scattered, empty clouds.

She sighed. "Times like this I wish I could really paint, instead of just puttering." She continued to stare at the sky.

He angled sideways so he could watch her expression as much as he watched the sky. A chain of emotions crossed her face. Awe, a restlessness he supposed came from a desire to be able to paint, a look of determination—he wanted to ask what it meant—and then peace swept over her face so completely that he ached inside. Why couldn't he feel the same peace?

"I have only to look about to see the hand of God in the sky, the trees and the flowers. 'The heavens declare the glory of God; and the firmament showeth his handiwork.'"

"The nineteenth Psalm. I memorized it in Sunday school. I learned a hundred verses and won a Bible." He still had it, tucked away in his things. It had been a long time since he'd opened it. To his shame.

"My father had us memorize verses. He also taught

us to read our Bible every night. I promised him I would make a habit of it, so I try not to miss a night."

"Seems your father was a good man."

"Yes, he was." She shifted to look at him more closely. "I'm sorry you lost your father so early. Like I told Ellie the other day, we all need a father."

"He was a brave man. Wasn't a thing that could stop him if he decided to do something." Except he had been stopped. "Of course, we all discover sooner or later that there are things we can't change, can't move, can't correct."

"Too true." She stared again at the sky, her expression clouded. Then she smiled, and that incredible look of peace returned. "But nothing is too hard for God. Where He leads, He makes a way. All I have to do is trust and obey." Softly she sang the hymn.

He couldn't stop watching her, his heart pounding against his rib cage in hungry insistence. He'd forgotten how sweet it was to trust. "It's hard to trust when things go so wrong."

"The hymn 'Trust and Obey' was written for D. L. Moody to use in his preaching. He once said, 'The Word of God alone makes us sure. Obedience to God makes us happy.' If we want to be happy, sure and safe, seems we have to turn things over to God and let Him take care of them. He has promised to meet our every need."

Did he detect a catch in her words? "Don't you struggle to believe that?"

"Every day. But I constantly choose to trust and obey to the best of my ability. Of course, I fail badly and often, but that's my human frailness."

He laughed. "I'm beginning to think you are anything but frail."

She tilted her head and considered him. "Why do you say that?"

"Because I've seen you in action. Once you take up a cause, I think you will fight for it until the end."

She grinned. "I do believe you're right. Sally says it's because I had to fight to get well."

"It's made you—*tough* isn't the right word." He tapped his finger against his chin. "Steel disguised as china."

Her mouth dropped open. Her eyes grew dark. And she stared.

"Don't look so surprised."

"But I am. And I'm trying to decide if I'm flattered or not."

"It's not an idle compliment. It's simply an observation."

They turned back toward town.

"I will try and live up to your evaluation of me." She lifted her chin and squared her shoulders.

"It wasn't meant as a challenge, you know. You aren't going to do something foolish, are you?" He'd seen how stubborn foolishness could lead to disaster. He'd seen the runaway wagon coming. Called Jane. Warned her to get out of the road. But Jane waved away his warning. She had her mind set on getting something from their own wagon and would not move until she was done. Jane was like that. "I don't want my words to influence you to take silly chances."

She grinned. "Emmet, I value my life and my health too much to do anything to jeopardize it. However, there are other challenges I can face that don't carry any risk."

He caught her by the shoulder. "Are you talking about Ellie? Because if you think this is a battle you must win—"

She shook her head and patted his shoulder. "Emmet, I am far more interested in winning her favor and helping her than I am in proving I am more stubborn." She grinned. "Though I probably am. But I like to think I am wise enough to pick my battles." She sucked in air as if readying herself to face a challenge. "No, the battle I am prepared to win is one with myself."

She marched onward.

He stared after her.

She called over her shoulder. "Aren't you coming?"

He rushed to catch up. "You can be very unsettling at times. Just when I think we understand each other, you shift gears."

Her chuckle rang out. "Don't worry about it, Emmet. It doesn't concern you. We have a job to do—get Ellie to learn her lessons."

Emmet faced straight ahead and wished they hadn't gone so far from town. She might as well have slapped him in the face and stomped on his toe, her message was so clear. Her only interest in Emmet was teaching his daughter.

Well, wasn't that all he wanted too?

Of course it was. He'd let the warm air and the nice sunset sidetrack his thoughts only momentarily. He ought to thank her for her timely reminder. Instead he pointed toward a robin singing on the branch of a thin poplar tree.

She paused to listen. "You ever notice how birds sing no matter what their circumstances? If it's windy, they hang on and sing. If it's hot, they chirp more merrily. If it rains—and don't we wish it would?—they ignore it and sing anyway. I think God created them as a lesson for us."

"Sing anyway?"

"Yes. Don't you think that's a good plan?" She smiled at him, oblivious to the fact he had pulled his emotions back behind bars, where they belonged.

"I guess it's a good idea. But for me, I have an even better one—take care of Ellie no matter what."

She studied him. "I think you can do both at the same time. And what better thing to teach Ellie? Sing anyway."

They reached town where, in front of three houses, the residents sat on their porches. They called a greeting, and Emmet and Louisa returned with their own.

Then they made their way back home and stood by Louisa's car. "Thanks for coming," Emmet said. It had been an interesting evening.

"Thanks for the walk. It was nice." She climbed into the car and, ignoring the banging and coughing, waved goodbye. "See you in the morning."

He watched until the cloud of dust blocked her from view. "Tomorrow," he whispered. "When we make learning fun for Ellie."

Ellie. She was his only concern.

Then why, as he prepared for bed, were the things Louisa said filling his thoughts? Along with the way her face had glowed with serenity. But of course, it was easy for her to be content with life. She'd overcome her illnesses and was now as healthy as anyone. No wonder she could sing so readily.

Life was not so simple for him.

But he dug through his belongings and found his award Bible. He had neglected it far too long. Had let his faith grow dim. It was time to look for the peace Louisa revealed.

Chapter Six

Louisa banged her hand against the steering wheel. She shouldn't have agreed to go out walking with Emmet. But it seemed he was as lonely as she. Then she had asked personal questions. Given personal information. "Professional," she muttered. "A job." But every minute spent anywhere near him made her acutely aware of emptiness in her heart that ached for—

"Enough." She could have none of the things she ached for. "Sing anyway." Silly thing to say. No wonder he looked as if she'd gone crazy. But she'd only wanted him to understand the peace and contentment that was found in trusting God despite difficult things. He could experience it too if he chose. And even more important—she determinedly pulled her thoughts back to the only thing that mattered…helping Ellie. Emmet could teach her to be happy in her present circumstances. A lesson that would be invaluable as she grew older.

Mother waited for her. Beyond her, Sally roamed about the kitchen.

"Sorry I'm so late."

"I don't like you going out in the evening. You must take care of yourself." Mother's face twisted with concern.

Louisa hugged her mother. "I didn't do anything that would cause me a problem." Though she'd come perilously close to letting her heart consider Emmet as more than the parent of a child she was tutoring.

Sally waited until Mother went to her room. "Were you planning lessons all this time?"

"We went for a walk."

Sally squealed. "I'm so glad to hear that."

"No reason you should be."

"I like to think my big sister is finally allowing herself to look at a man in that way." She batted her eyelashes and looked dreamy.

"I am not. I cannot. I will not."

"Oh, Louisa, there's absolutely no reason you can't."

"Sally, it would not be fair."

"Not all men want—"

"Emmet has already said he regrets not having more children. Says he hated being an only child growing up." She didn't say anything more. She admired him for his devoted love to Ellie, reminding her as it did of her father. But her only association with him would be as Ellie's tutor. She must guard her heart. Otherwise…

But as she lay on her bed, recounting the little walk and the things he said, she recalled he asked what there was to do. Poor man. He must feel housebound. Someone should invite him out. Seems he could leave Ellie with Auntie May in the evenings after she'd gone to sleep.

Perhaps the Morgan girls could do something. She'd

noticed that Judd and Emmet were already acquainted. She'd talk to Madge and see what—

Stop. It was not her responsibility to plan a social life for him. Her job was to be his child's tutor. She'd do well to brand that on a slab of wood and nail it across her wayward thoughts.

The next morning Louisa had her resolve firmly in place as she stepped into the Hamilton home. She tucked the satchel under her arm and held it tight to her body. The sound of Emmet's voice came from Ellie's room, and Louisa headed across the floor.

Auntie May sat at the table mixing up a dreadful-looking concoction. Louisa tried not to look disturbed by the glutinous brown mixture.

Auntie May laughed. "It's for old Stormy. She can't eat regular food anymore, poor thing. But she is so sweet and gentle, I don't mind fixing her something special. Yes, you are a regular sweetheart, you are." She crooned to the ragged black cat on her lap then grinned at Louisa. "Just an old woman with old friends. They're waiting for you." She tipped her head toward the doorway, and Louisa understood she meant Emmet and Ellie, not the friends of Louisa's future—old cats.

Louisa closed her eyes to shut out the sight of Auntie May, and vowed she would find some other way to fill the lonely hours of her life. She would not become reclusive and odd.

"You're just what that pair in there needs."

Louisa jerked her eyes open and stared at the older woman. "Me? What on earth do you mean?" She wasn't what any man needed, and it seemed she couldn't even tutor a child.

"They're stuck in a narrow place without realizing it. They need rescuing more than they know."

"I'm prepared to do my best to help Ellie with her lessons." She didn't know if that was what Auntie May meant or not. Moreover, she didn't care to find out, so she hurried into Ellie's room.

Emmet stood at her entrance. He smiled. Her heart lifted in response, and her answering smile was so wide it stretched the skin of her cheeks. His eyes flashed pure blue. She knew that meant he was pleased. Pleased to see her? More likely, pleased to think of getting Ellie on track with her lessons. This was only a job for both of them. She knew that.

She shifted her gaze toward Ellie and caught a flash of defiance. The child was as unwelcoming as Emmet was welcoming. It promised to be another challenging day. Steel disguised as china, Emmet had said. She'd assured him she chose her battles carefully and vowed this would not be a battle zone.

"Good morning," she said. "Did you notice how loudly the birds are singing this morning?"

"Sing anyway?" Emmet's quiet voice reminded her of their conversation last night and reignited all the feelings she had firmly squelched. She battled them back into submission.

"Shall we begin?"

Emmet nodded, and as they had discussed, he spoke to Ellie. "El, I don't want you to fall behind in your schoolwork, so I'm going to assist Miss Morgan with your studies."

"How you gonna do that?"

"I'm going to help her teach."

"You're not a teacher. You're my dad." With each word, resistance grew clearer.

"Moms and dads help with homework, don't they?" She nodded reluctantly.

"That's what I'm going to do. Help you."

"What about her?" Ellie clearly thought Louisa wasn't needed.

For a moment, Louisa thought the same thing. Emmet could do this on his own. But she'd been hired to do a job, and she would do it if at all possible.

Emmet chuckled. "I don't think I'd be a very good teacher on my own." The way he looked at Louisa—his eyes blue and smiling, his gaze shining with approval—threatened to destroy the locks on her heart.

She sucked in a steadying breath. "Your father and I are going to work together."

The look Ellie gave Louisa was far from welcoming, but it disappeared instantly as she favored her father with a wide smile. "I guess that means you're going to stay here."

"For now."

Louisa caught the tiny note of caution. Did he sense that Ellie had manipulated him into this? Not that she could have guessed it would turn out this way.

Ellie sent a look at Louisa that warned she would be happy when Louisa was gone and she had her father to herself.

Louisa returned the look, silently informing the child she could not drive Louisa away against her will. She was discovering more steel in her core than she had ever been aware of.

She and Emmet had decided to start by repeating the failed history lesson, so while she opened the picture book of the history of the North-West Mounted Police, Emmet edged his chair closer to the bed so he could study along with Ellie.

Louisa opened the book and began her story.

Ellie interrupted. "You did that yesterday."

"Do you remember it then?" She would be surprised if Ellie heard more than a word or two.

"Of course I do."

"Then here is your assignment." She repeated the instructions as Emmet adjusted the bed tray.

His attention on his task, he likely did not see the look of raw defiance on Ellie's face. Louisa understood the child's quandary. She didn't want to cooperate with Louisa but also didn't want her father to guess at the little game she'd been playing. As soon as Emmet finished, Ellie smiled sweetly. "Will you help me, Daddy?"

"Of course."

Louisa considered it a victory—at least Ellie was doing schoolwork, even if she was getting Emmet to write the answers for her. Ellie's knowledge of the subject surprised her. The child had taken in far more than she would have guessed possible.

"Do you want to draw a picture too?" Emmet asked.

"I can't draw."

"I expect you can draw as well as I can. Look." He scratched away on the paper.

Ellie giggled. "What is that?"

"Horses. I can't believe you had to ask." He turned

the picture toward Louisa. "It's pretty obvious, wouldn't you say?"

Louisa pressed her lips together to stop a burst of laughter and tried to give the drawing serious consideration. But it was impossible. She'd never seen such awkward-looking animals. "They have such short legs…and long square bodies."

Ellie rolled her eyes. "They look like boxes on sticks."

Louisa couldn't contain her amusement any longer and laughed aloud.

"I did my best." Emmet tried to sound offended, but he laughed too.

Ellie stared from her father to Louisa, fought a battle with her resistance but a giggle escaped. She giggled until tears rolled down her face.

Emmet stared at her and pretended concern. "Don't cry, Button. It's only a picture."

Ellie giggled harder.

Auntie May appeared in the doorway. "Now that's a sound I can live with."

Louisa sucked in air that went deep into her lungs, refreshing, renewing. "That felt great. Like the Bible says, 'A merry heart doeth good like a medicine.'"

Emmet sobered, though his eyes continued to brim with laughter. He grabbed a hankie and wiped Ellie's eyes. "Are you going to be okay? Should I call the doctor?" He donned a serious expression. "'Miss Polly had a dolly that was sick, sick, sick, so she called for the doctor to come quick, quick, quick.'" He sang the words in a gruff voice.

Ellie giggled. "Daddy, you're silly."

Louisa's knees felt like strings of unbaked bread dough. She gripped the blackboard easel, hoping it was strong enough to bear her weight. The sounds of a child giggling and a father singing as the warmth of the sun puddled across the quilt on the bed were heartbreaking to her. The only thing in the scene she could look forward to in the future was the quilt. Perhaps she would make quilts to distribute to the less fortunate. But the ache inside her screamed against making them for others. She wanted to make them for her own family. Her own children.

She struggled for control. *Please God, hold me up.* And she meant more than her weak knees. She meant the future, the present, this moment of watching father and child.

When she could speak without revealing her tyrant emotions, she suggested Emmet should do the arithmetic lesson.

Looking uncertain, he wrote half a dozen simple problems on the board. Louisa stood to one side, although she longed to sink to the chair at Ellie's bedside.

Emmet read the first problem. "One plus one? This is way too easy. Ellie knew this before she started school."

"Two." Ellie's answer was brisk.

Emmet grinned. "One plus two?"

On and on they went, Ellie suddenly remembering things that only yesterday she couldn't.

"Do I get recess?" Ellie asked when Emmet declared arithmetic over.

"I think you deserve it."

She eyed the parcel on the table. "Can I open it?"

Louisa shook her head. "Not until we're done."

Ellie screwed up her face, ready to protest.

Emmet opened his mouth. But Louisa didn't give him a chance to voice his objection.

"I remember you said you like playing hide-and-seek. Do you want to play the game during your recess?"

Ellie snorted. "I can't hide."

"You could if you were no bigger than a button."

Ellie looked intrigued, as did Emmet, although Louisa did her best to avoid looking directly at him. Still it was hard to ignore his presence in the room. The place was so crowded, he couldn't return to the chair without brushing her shoulder in passing. Her heart clamored to her ribs and hung on as if drowning. Which perfectly described how she felt—drowning in her own foolish emotions.

She forced her mind back to explaining the game. "You pretend you are the size of a button. You can hide anywhere in this room, and we have to find you. You can give clues by saying warmer or colder. I'll go first to show you." She glanced around the room, being careful not to pause in any one spot and give away her hiding place. "Okay, I'm ready. Come find me."

"Are you in that jug?"

"Cold as ice."

Soon both Emmet and Ellie were guessing.

"Warm. Warmer." They drew close to her hiding place, which was on the tray over the bed.

Emmet glanced about, looked down at his shirt. "In my pocket?" His gaze grabbed her and held her in an invisible grasp.

She could not stop a jolt of something powerful and

demanding from rushing through her like hot wind off the prairie, bringing both pleasure and pain. Close to his heart. Oh, if only it could be. But she must concentrate on what she could have. Not what was impossible. Find contentment. Trust God. "Colder," she managed, though her voice felt distant.

"On the tray." Ellie tapped it.

"You found me. So now you can hide."

They played the game for a few more minutes. Time Louisa used to pull herself back to reality. When she felt she could face Emmet and speak without her heart exploding with empty, impossible dreams, she suggested they try reading.

"I don't want to." Ellie switched from happy to angry so fast, Louisa almost lost her balance.

Emmet looked as surprised. "This is your last lesson, then you can see what Louisa has in her peculiarly shaped parcel."

"I don't care."

Louisa and Emmet stared at the child. They both knew she wanted very much to open the present.

Louisa handed the reader to Emmet. "Maybe for you?"

He opened to page one. "Would you read to me?"

Ellie shook her head.

"Tell you what. I'll read a line then you read a line." He read aloud, then paused for Ellie to continue.

She gave him a defiant stare.

Louisa found the earlier reader and handed it to Emmet. The same thing happened. Could Ellie not read, or was she being stubborn?

But all three of them were getting frustrated, and there seemed no point in trying to continue.

Louisa retrieved the storybook she'd begun two days ago. "I think that's enough reading. Instead, I'll read you some more of my story." It was one of the Winnie the Pooh books. "I loved these stories. My father would read them with different voices for all the characters. Do you know how the stories came to be?"

Two blond heads shook in unison.

"Winnie was a real bear. During the Great War, a soldier from Winnipeg bought the bear cub from a hunter for twenty dollars. He took the bear with him to Britain, but when his troop was posted to France, he turned the bear over to the London Zoo. Christopher Robin was a real little boy. His father wrote these stories for him, making Christopher's stuffed animals characters in them."

Emmet and Ellie seemed mesmerized by the story.

Satisfaction slipped through Louisa like a sweet drink, and she read a chapter to the pair, wondering which one enjoyed it most. Emmet laughed as much as Ellie as Louisa made each character come alive.

She closed the book.

"Aw." A duet of protest.

She grinned. "I never get tired of the stories." She'd always thought how much fun it would be to read them to her own children, but reading them to Emmet and Ellie would have to be pleasure enough. She pushed away every trace of regret and reached for the parcel. "I think you earned this today." She set the parcel on the tray.

Ellie gave Louisa a fleeting smile and Louisa let satisfaction sift through her.

With Emmet hanging over Ellie, as curious as his daughter, Ellie ripped the brown paper away to reveal a box. "What is it?"

"Open this." She showed her how to pull open the front to reveal—

"Ooh." Ellie stared.

Louisa grinned, pleased at the reaction. "It's a dollhouse."

"In complete detail," Emmet said. "Where did you get this?"

"I made it one winter when I couldn't do much else." She handed a fat envelope to Ellie, who opened it to reveal a family of paper dolls with every imaginable outfit, from ball gowns to nightgowns to winter hats and muffs.

"What do you say, Ellie?" Emmet prompted.

"Thank you." She flashed the first genuine smile Louisa had received, and it settled somewhere deep in her heart with the doggedness of a summer drought.

Louisa told herself she was happy simply to give the child a bit of pleasure during the weeks she must remain in bed. But she could not deny the ache that echoed in her thoughts. This was as close as she'd ever get to the dream she'd cherished as long as she could remember. It was that dream—of a husband and children of her own—that made her keep her old readers, made her spend countless hours creating a dollhouse. "You're welcome. I hope you get lots of enjoyment out of it."

Ellie was already outfitting dolls and placing them

in various rooms of the house. Emmet bent close, his head touching Ellie's as they arranged things.

"It's time for me to leave." Seeing them like this, the perfect father-daughter pair, triggered a thousand errant emotions in Louisa's heart. Longing for things she could never have. Sorrow over dead dreams. And, she insisted, happiness that she had a hand in creating this sweet moment. "I'll see you both again tomorrow." She gathered up her belongings and tried to slip away before her emotions completely escaped her control.

But Emmet followed her out of the room, catching her elbow in his cupped hand as if she needed his gentle assistance. She told herself she was capable of navigating the kitchen and front room without help, but she couldn't convince herself to pull away. Because her traitorous heart rejoiced in the touch.

He escorted her to her car, but rather than open the door as she expected, he turned her to face him. He brushed his fingers along her cheek and smiled. "It was incredibly generous of you to give that dollhouse and dolls to Ellie. I would think you'd want to keep it to give to your own children."

The words sliced through her, leaving her insides torn and bleeding. She had made it for that precise purpose. But it was not to be.

She grabbed the door handle and wrenched it open. "I must go." She blinked back the moisture in her eyes. She would not cry. What was the use? What could she do but throw herself upon God's love and let Him carry her?

She turned and headed out of town, but she paused before the turnoff to cry out her pain to God and seek His strength. By the time she reached the house, she was smiling. No one must ever know the way her insides wept.

Chapter Seven

Emmet stared after Louisa long after she disappeared from sight. What had sent her scurrying away so suddenly? He'd been about to ask her to come back in the evening so they could discuss tomorrow's plans. Now he didn't know what to expect.

The generosity of her gift to Ellie filled him with awe and appreciation. She must have spent hours creating the dollhouse. Was she now regretting giving it away? Did that explain why she had suddenly turned tail and left in a rush? Didn't seem she could be in a hurry for some other appointment. He retraced the conversation. *Save it for your own children.* Had those words sent her fleeing? Was she afraid to have children? Was her health too uncertain? Though he saw no evidence of poor constitution.

Perhaps she would explain later.

Whistling under his breath, he hurried back to check on Ellie. Apart from the reading lesson, it had been a good day. Thanks to Louisa. She would make a wonderful mother.

He told himself repeatedly he wasn't interested in

her, especially in that way, but he found it harder to believe.

Ellie grinned at him. "This is fun." She had to be persuaded to set the dolls aside for lunch.

An hour later, the dishes were done and Ellie played happily with the dolls and dollhouse. Emmet sighed. He wasn't used to idly passing time around the house. He needed open air. Hard physical work.

Auntie May glanced up from mending a shirt. "Why don't you go do something useful? You're bothering me with your pacing and sighing."

"I wasn't—" Only he was. "I need some hard work."

"Then go find some. Me and Ellie will be okay by ourselves." She raised her voice. "Won't we, Ellie?"

"You'll come back for supper, won't you?" Ellie asked.

"Of course." He meant to be back in case Louisa came by to discuss lessons. And to put Ellie to bed as well.

"I met Judd Kirk. He owns the Cotton place now. I'll go out there and see if I can do something useful."

He found Judd fixing fences and lent a hand.

"It's a steady job," Judd complained. "The wind blows tumbleweeds and Russian thistle that piles up along the fences then fills with dirt. Next thing I know, the fences are buried or blown down."

As they worked, Judd talked. Emmet learned how his wife, Madge, had saved the family home from bank foreclosure. He told an amusing story about posing as a teacher and tutoring Louisa so he could spy on a man who had taken Judd's mother's money and lost it in some scheme.

"You must have enjoyed your little game." His jaw hurt at the thought of Judd and Louisa poring over books and sharing secrets.

"Not at all. I wanted to be honest. I wanted to be Judd, an outdoorsman. I wanted to openly show my growing love for Madge."

"So what happened?"

Judd leaned back to stretch his muscles. "First, Madge discovered my true identity. Then she discovered who I was watching and forced me to confront my reasons. In the end, I admitted I was trying to make things right in my own wisdom. Madge taught me to trust God for both justice and the future."

Emmet leaned back too. Extracting the wire fence from the burden of weeds and dirt was hard work. He thought of Louisa singing "Trust and Obey." "Seems the Morgan girls have a passion about trust."

"I suppose they do. But so far as I can see, they're right. God can run things much better than I can." He returned to rescuing his fence.

Emmet threw his efforts into the work as well. He trusted. Of course he did. But not like Louisa. Her trust was like a sweet nectar permeating her thoughts, her actions and her attitudes. But unlike him, she hadn't watched everything she valued get snatched away. Well, not quite everything, thank the good Lord. He had Ellie. And his determination to protect her. He'd failed in the past. And Ellie was paying. Poor little Button. But he'd be more diligent in the future.

Several hours later, he returned home sweaty but happy. Nothing like hard work to make a man appreciate life.

Ellie still played happily with the dolls and dollhouse and smiled at him as he stepped into the room to check on her. "Do you need to go to the bathroom?"

"Auntie May helped me."

That was a first. Emmet felt a mixture of relief that she had let someone else assist her, and a twinge of guilt because he hadn't been available. It wasn't as though he needed to do everything for her, only make sure it was done. Yet he couldn't dismiss a tiny thread of regret.

He and Auntie May ate their supper at Ellie's bedside to give her company. He let her play for a while after they finished. "It's time to get you ready for bed." He put the dolls and house away. "I'm afraid you will have to leave it until after your lessons are done tomorrow."

Ellie protested, but already her eyes were drooping. By the time he'd sponged her and helped her brush her teeth, she could barely stay awake. One of Auntie May's cats jumped up and curled up next to Ellie. Before he cleaned up the basin of water, both were asleep.

Auntie May sat in her rocker, her Bible on her lap... well, almost on her lap. Two cats lay between her knees and the book.

Emmet stared at the clock and then out the window. Would Louisa come tonight? But he saw no automobile approaching and sighed.

Auntie May tsked. "Go on outside and wait. I need some peace and quiet."

Good idea. He flung open the door, and his heart grabbed at his throat. Louisa stood before him, her hand raised as if to knock. "Where did you come from? I almost ran over you." His heart still bounced erratically. He stared past her. "Did your car break down?"

"I walked."

"Walked? Why? Isn't that a bit far?"

"Are you my mother?" Her voice was as soft as butterfly wings, but he didn't miss the note of warning. And it triggered unreasonable emotions. Anger. Longing. A thousand fleeting things.

"Do I look like anyone's mother?"

She giggled, and his anger evaporated. "Not like any I've seen, I must confess." She tipped her head toward the empty street. "I walked to save gas."

He wanted to say forget about saving gas. If something happened to her... But she was right. He wasn't her mother, but he'd make sure she got home safely.

"I went to see Adele and get some more work for Ellie." Louisa indicated her satchel.

"Come in." They sat as before, but Louisa didn't pull out any lesson plans.

"I asked if it's possible Ellie doesn't know how to read. She said the teacher should have informed you or dealt with it, if that were so. She gave me suggestions on how to present the work in a different way."

"I assumed—" He tried to think if Ellie had ever read anything aloud to him. "Would she be able to do her written work if she can't read?"

"I noticed she got you to write down her answers."

"But at school? How could it be possible?" How could he have missed it? Wasn't it his responsibility as her parent to know, rather than trusting someone else to take care of it?

Her eyes filled with distress. "I know. But none of

that matters. If she can't read, it's up to us to help her catch up."

Her assurance smoothed his insides. "What's the plan?"

She opened her satchel then and pulled out papers. "I have a few ideas on how to turn reading into a game. I'll work on that tonight." She handed him arithmetic sheets. "In the meantime, she can go as fast as she wants in other areas. Shall we follow the same system we used this morning?"

"Sounds fine to me."

"Good." They reviewed the planned work, then she shoved everything except the arithmetic sheets into the satchel and pushed the chair back. "I must get home and do some preparation for tomorrow."

"I'll walk you home."

"It's not necessary."

"I won't let you walk home alone." He poked his head into the kitchen to tell Auntie May.

"Run along and have fun." She winked.

Emmet opened his mouth to protest, explain he was only acting responsibly, then changed his mind. What was the point in arguing when a large portion of his brain cherished the same idea? Despite all his arguments to the contrary, he meant to enjoy her company.

They sauntered down the street, waving to a neighbor in a front yard and another on his porch. The voices of children at play carried on the air, as did the grit of dust in the dry wind. Yet he didn't mind. The evening was soft with warmth, contentment and a pretty woman at his side. "I went out and helped Judd this afternoon."

She missed a step. "You did? Why?"

"I got tired of hanging about the house. Ellie was so happy with the dollhouse, she didn't care if I was there or not."

Her cheery laugh broke forth. "I didn't mean to replace you."

"It was a very generous gift."

"I have no need of it." Again that sad note in her voice. Again he wondered at its cause. Tried not to think his explanation was correct. Louisa didn't seem the kind to shy from physical challenges, but last time the words had sent her fleeing out the door. No door to use this time, but he didn't want her retreating mentally. So he quickly sought another topic.

"Judd has some mighty big dreams for his farm."

Another burst of laughter. "When the drought ends, he's going to be a rich cattleman."

"I think that hope keeps him busy mending fences."

"He's a hard worker." She obviously adored her brother-in-law. "With big dreams."

They walked in companionable silence for a few yards. "A person needs dreams."

"Especially when circumstances offer nothing but defeat and disappointment."

"The drought will end. So will the Depression." He assumed that's what she meant. "In the meantime, sing anyway. Right?"

She studied him, her look full of teasing regret. "You aren't going to let me forget that, are you?"

"I hope you aren't trying to."

"Why?"

"Because if everyone gets down in the dumps, we

are a doomed country. We need people who can still find joy and hope, despite everything."

"You think that's me? I believe that's the nicest thing anyone has ever said of me."

"Why are you so surprised? Isn't that exactly what you said you intend to do—sing anyway?"

"I said it. I meant it at the time, but sometimes I forget and let discouragement gain the upper hand."

A shudder raked her shoulders. They had stopped walking to face each other, and he cupped her upper arm. "Louisa, don't ever stop singing."

She looked deep into his eyes, exploring, examining. He almost unlocked doors to her search, but he could not. There were some things that could not be shared, the pain too deep. These were burdens he must carry alone. For a fleeting second he remembered his mother and father, tried to recall their last day. Though if he'd known it was their last day…

A person knew some things too late.

A look of utmost peace and contentment filled her face. The look he'd come to expect and hope for. "Sing anyway," she whispered.

"That's right." He tucked her hand around his elbow and they continued down the road. "So what big dreams do you have?"

"Sorry?"

"Didn't we just decide a person needs big dreams? I wondered what yours are."

If her hand hadn't rested on his forearm, he might not have known she stiffened. "No big dreams, I guess. Seems every dream ends in a closed door."

He looked down on her dark curls. Wished he could see her face. "Tell me about your shattered dreams."

She made a little sound of protest. "They aren't important. I hoped I could go to university. That's not possible with money being in such short supply. In the meantime I am trying to take one day at a time, follow the Lord's leading and not run ahead with plans of my own."

He wanted to pull her to a stop, tip her face upward and demand she explain the tightness in her voice. But she strode onward, insistently.

"Now tell me about your big dreams."

Oh, he had walked into that one blindly. "I no longer dream. Tried that and look how it worked out."

She looked at him then. Now, though, he didn't want her to, because he feared she would see what he couldn't disguise—his disappointment, his failure, his determination to protect what little he had left. "But you have Ellie. You have your ranch. You have your faith. Surely you still have dreams."

He gave what he hoped was a teasing smile. "Nope. About all I can do is sing anyway. Or at least try."

She looked about to argue, then sighed. "Sometimes it's the best we can do."

It didn't seem right that she should accept defeat so easily. Made him want to grab the future and pull it down like a big, fat, red balloon and offer it to her. It made him want to throw aside all his own disappointments and promise to dance and sing with her into the unknown.

But he couldn't. The future was not his to offer. And

he had little faith he could walk boldly into the unknown.

She laughed.

He blinked. "What's so funny?"

"Me. 'Why are thou cast down, O my soul? Hope thou in God; for I shall yet praise him for the help of his countenance.' I have no need to feel sorry for myself with God's promise to guide me."

He wished he could find the same confidence in life.

"I turn off here." She stopped and pointed toward the house up the lane. "Do you want to come in and meet my mother and say hello to Sally?"

"I'd like to." He wanted to see her family, see her home, see the things that had shaped her into such a strong woman.

As they neared the house, she pointed to the garden. "Where I go to have fun." She grinned at him, and they shared a laugh.

"I want to warn you that my mother is overprotective of me, so don't be alarmed if she acts like I committed some horrible crime by walking to town."

"I expect she's only trying to protect you. I know how it is." He would never let Ellie do anything remotely dangerous in the future.

"Sometimes it is stifling."

They reached the door and Louisa opened it to call, "Hello. I'm home." A little black-and-white dog ran forward, wiggling as though he would turn inside out.

Louisa laughed and patted the dog. "This is my dear friend, Mouse. I've had him since we moved here."

An older woman stepped into the room. She had a

mop of curly hair like Louisa's, only it had faded to gray. She fixed Louisa with a concerned look.

"Mother, this is Emmet Hamilton. It's his little girl I'm tutoring."

The woman smiled sweetly. "Delighted to meet you, Mr. Hamilton. Please, come in and have tea."

Emmet gladly accepted her invitation. He wanted to meet her family and see where she lived.

Louisa had fought a conflicting set of emotions all the way home from town. She didn't want to spend more time with Emmet, be constantly reminded of things she couldn't have. She'd freely released that dollhouse to Ellie, a sort of sacrifice. In the back of her mind, she had whispered, *Okay, Lord, I know I will never be able to give this to a child of my own. So I choose to give it to a child who has no mother.* It seemed fitting. But it had been a wrench. She'd spent months on that project when she was fifteen. Long past playing with dolls herself. She had made it for only one reason, and to have Emmet remind her over and over that she might have kept it for her own child was like hot coals to her heart.

But when he announced he would see her home… As if there was no question. As if he considered it his duty. And then acted as if it was more than duty. Well, suffice it to say she tended to ignore the reasons why she didn't want to spend time with him.

Seeing the speculative look in Mother's eyes warned Louisa she should have listened to reason rather than give herself excuses. Mother saw a marriageable man— handsome, strong, with a child, providing a ready-made family for Louisa. What she didn't see was Emmet's clearly stated desire to have more children.

Louisa would be forced to explain it again after Emmet left. For now, Mother greeted him warmly. "Won't you come in and have tea with us? Sally just made some cookies. They're fresh from the oven."

"I'd be happy to. Smells like molasses cookies. Yum." He glanced at Louisa, held her gaze a beat, not long enough to attract Sally or Mother's attention, but long enough to signal that he remembered Louisa had said they were Father's favorites. Knowing he remembered made it even more difficult to keep her heart from tripping happily down the trail of possibilities.

There were no possibilities, she reminded herself.

Mother waved Sally forward. "This is my youngest daughter, Sally."

Emmet nodded. "We've already met."

Mother blinked. "Really?"

"Yes, at the store."

"Oh, I'd forgotten."

Sally rolled her eyes behind Mother's back. Louisa wanted to groan but feared it would only bring demanding questions from Emmet, so she indicated he should sit across from her as Mother presided over tea.

As soon as everyone was settled, and not a moment longer than courtesy required, Mother addressed Emmet. "So tell me about yourself. I know you lived with your aunt, but where were you before that? What have you done since you left here?"

Louisa did groan aloud now. "Mother, how much do you need to know?"

Mother gave a gentle smile, but Louisa knew she

hadn't relented one speck. "I probably should have made inquiries before. After all, you are in his company every day. It's my duty."

Sally chuckled, but wisely didn't encourage Mother.

"Mother, I am with his child." No need to give Mother any more hope that there might be more interest to nurture by admitting she and Emmet had agreed to work together teaching Ellie. "And Auntie May is in the next room."

Mother slid her gaze past Louisa and Sally and landed it squarely back on Emmet. "I'm sure you don't mind talking about yourself."

Emmet chuckled, sent Louisa a teasing look. "I don't mind in the least. After I left here and after working at various ranches, I found a bit of land to the west. I met and married Jane. Sad to say she died three years ago. I've been on my own since then, but when Ellie broke her leg and had to be in a body cast, I knew I couldn't stay on the ranch. So here I am."

Louisa noticed he hadn't mentioned his parents. Seems he never did. Why was that? It wasn't as if he'd forgotten them. Hadn't he told her he still missed them?

"Yes," Mother said, her voice sweet with satisfaction. "Here you are." The look she gave Louisa said as plainly as words "Here he is indeed. Just what you need."

Louisa grabbed a cookie and took a bite big enough to choke on, but she stubbornly chewed it and downed it with a gulp of tea.

Emmet grinned at her, as if knowing what wasn't being said. "Mrs. Morgan, tell me what it was like to have three little girls running around." His grin remained, but his eyes grew shadowed. "I always wanted a passel of young ones scampering about."

Louisa couldn't meet his look, couldn't let Sally or Mother see how much the idea hurt, and kept her attention on picking the tiny cookie crumbs from her plate.

Mother sighed. "It was a lot of fun. My husband adored the girls and spent a lot of time with them. And they played together well. Girls, remember the tea parties you used to have?"

Louisa lifted her head as sweet memories swept through her. She grinned at Sally. "We had a whole crowd of stuffed animals and dolls."

Sally nodded. "I remember you used to make dolls out of almost anything. Remember the one you made from corn husks?"

"I read the Indians did that, so I had to try."

"And you made one out of a potato that had eyes looking like a face."

Louisa laughed. "You couldn't stop staring at it. I think you wondered if it would open its mouth and talk."

Sally laughed. "We had a lot of fun."

Emmet's expression was hungry, full of longing. "It sounds like it."

Louisa wanted to erase that look from his face. "You had lots of playmates. What did you do besides play scrub ball in the vacant lot?"

The look he gave her said he understood she meant to make him see beyond being an only child. But she couldn't say if he appreciated it or not. At least, not until his eyes flashed blue and he smiled. "Depended on who I was playing with. The Crates family had half a dozen boys. Two were older than me, one my age and two younger, but they seemed to always do things in a group. And the things they did made people sit up and notice. They tore down an old abandoned shack and turned it into a fort down by the tracks."

Louisa and Sally glanced at each other in surprise. "I wonder if that's the same shack the hobos still use," Louisa said.

"It might be." He laughed. "We used enough nails to hold it together for a long time."

After that, they talked about people in the community— who still lived there, who had moved out, who had moved in—until Emmet pushed his chair back. "I must be on my way."

Mother sent Louisa a glance that said as loud as a ringing bell "Walk the man to the door and show a little interest."

Louisa knew it was best to follow her mother's silent instructions, so she accompanied Emmet to the door.

"I enjoyed the visit. Thanks for inviting me."

Let's not make a habit of this. Mother will start making wedding plans. And whether or not you know it, it isn't something either of us want. "Anytime. I'll see you tomorrow."

He reached out to touch his hat, realized he didn't wear it and settled for a sketchy salute instead. "Until tomorrow." He walked away.

She caught the sound of his whistle as he headed down the lane.

Sing anyway.

She needed the reminder, especially as she turned to face her mother's inquiring look.

"You didn't tell me he was so handsome. And a Christian."

"Mother, what difference does it make?" She sought strength in Sally's sympathy but Sally offered none, either by her look or in words. Of course. She was sure any man would be willing to overlook Louisa's barrenness if he loved her.

"I suppose it doesn't matter if he's handsome—though it helps—but being a Christian is the number-one requirement."

She knew her mother had purposely misunderstood Louisa's protest. "I believe in my case, there's an even more important consideration, which you well know. You both heard him. He longs for a big family. Now I really must do some work for the lesson I want to present tomorrow." She wrapped dignity about her like a shroud and climbed the stairs to her room, little Mouse trotting at her heels.

In her room, she scooped up the dog and sank to the edge of the bed. Her heart ached with unshed tears and futile dreams of living on a ranch, listening to a child's laughter and play, sharing the moment with a man with flashing blue eyes.

It would never be for her. But she didn't have time to mope. She gathered together paper and pencils and began to fashion illustrations for the lesson. But drawing pictures she hoped would help Ellie learn to read only made her insides hurt more, and she dashed a tear from her eye before it could drop to the paper and ruin her work.

Sometimes it was extremely difficult to find a song to sing.

Chapter Eight

Emmet had never got this much pleasure from lessons when he went to school. Back then he hadn't enjoyed watching the teacher's eyes flash with humor as she reminded him of how he whistled as he left the Morgan home. "Sing Anyway is my motto. Maybe yours is Whistle Anyway."

Nor had he noticed a teacher's eyes darken with emotion as she talked about the hardships of the Mounties' march west. Not only did he notice, but his heart had been tugged to join in the same sadness. He knew relief when they moved on to the next subject, which was arithmetic. At least Ellie did well in that subject.

Louisa had driven her car this morning. He felt a twinge of regret. If she'd walked, he'd be duty bound to see her home. She returned to her car when they took a short break before they tackled reading. When she came back, she carried a brown folder. "For our reading class," she explained. She must have seen his worry, though he'd tried to deny it all morning. "Don't look so concerned. We're going to play a game. Ellie will learn to read because it will be fun."

Louisa set the blackboard where Ellie could see it.

Emmet sat at Ellie's side, ready to assist and encourage in any way he could. His insides twisted and coiled. He should know if Ellie couldn't read and needed extra help. What kind of father wouldn't know?

Louisa placed a picture on the easel—a drawing of a ball with the word below. "Ellie, I'm going to show you a game. First, we have to name all the objects. What's this?"

"A ball." Ellie sounded cautious.

"Too easy, I know, but that's okay. So the word says, 'ball.' Look at it and remember."

Ellie nodded.

Louisa put up more pictures with words below—half a dozen in all. Cat. Dog. Doll. Sun. Run.

All this work for a child who wasn't her own. Louisa would make a wonderful mother. He'd often wished Jane had given Ellie more attention, but Jane was happy if Ellie played alone without interfering with Jane's chores.

He jerked his thoughts away from making a comparison between the two. It wasn't fair.

Louisa took a big pair of scissors from her bag and cut each picture in half. The top half had the picture, the bottom half the word. She shuffled them like cards, passed six to Ellie and kept six for herself. "Now let's play. As soon as either of us gets a match between the picture and the word, we put them down. For every match, you get to take a card from the other player. You go first. Do you have any matching pairs?"

Emmet glanced at the cards Ellie held and saw two

pairs. He let Ellie study them. When she matched "cat" with the picture, he wanted to cheer.

Louisa let Ellie take a card from her hand.

Emmet waited as Ellie looked at the pictures. He could almost feel her intense concentration. When she matched "run" and the picture, he clapped and she beamed with victory.

She got four out of the six matches.

Louisa beamed. "Do you want to play again?"

"Yes."

They played until Auntie May stuck her head in and said, "Lunch in fifteen minutes."

Ellie didn't want to stop.

Louisa placed the cards facedown on the bed. "You can play a game on your own. Pick up two cards."

Ellie did.

"Do they match?"

She studied them a moment, then shook her head.

"Then put one back and try another. When you find a match, put it aside and keep playing until you get them all."

Ellie's attention was on her game as Louisa prepared to leave. "I'll make some more cards for tomorrow if you like."

Ellie glanced up and nodded.

Emmet walked her out. "You could stay for lunch."

"Mother expects me home."

He didn't want her to leave. In fact, he wanted to hug her tight and thank her for all the work she'd done for Ellie. "She can read, can't she?"

"She's uncertain, but she learned those six words easily enough."

"You did so much work on this. How did you think of the games?"

Louisa's smile was sweet enough to stop the birds from singing. "Adele suggested I make it a game. I couldn't think what might work, so I prayed. And this idea came."

Emmet couldn't get his thoughts around how much she put into teaching his child. It amazed and awed him. "I truly appreciate how you're helping."

Their gazes caught and held in a powerful sense of oneness and belonging, of wanting and needing. The look went on and on, her dark eyes searching for truth and so much more. More than he could give. He closed his thoughts to her. Regretted it the moment she blinked and shutters closed her off. Then he half convinced himself there was nothing he could do differently.

"I'll see you tomorrow then." She made for the car.

"What about preparing the lessons tonight?" Just the idea she might not come back made him forget all his good intentions.

She didn't turn right away. Long enough for his mouth to go dry and a thousand arguments to change her mind crowding his own.

Then she slowly faced him, her face a mask, her eyes veiled. "Are you sure you want to do this? You must have other things you'd like to do."

He had nothing that interested him more. That thought seemed at odds with earlier promises he had made for himself, but he dismissed the idea. "We need to make sure we are doing what Ellie needs."

The mask grew more wooden. "Then I'll come back after supper."

He wanted to tell her to leave the car at home. Give him an excuse to escort her back. But how could he? He had to confine his interest to what was best for Ellie. Never again dare he put anything before her needs.

Rather than make a trip back to town when school was out, Louisa stopped to speak to Adele during the noon break and get work for the next day.

Adele asked about the reading lesson, and Louisa told her what happened. "Good for you. You've got the instincts of a natural teacher. Have you ever considered going to Normal school?"

Louisa looked around the schoolyard where Adele was supervising. Children played and swung. Girls huddled together near the garagana hedge. Boys ran after a ball.

She loved helping Ellie, working with Emmet to help his little girl with her studies, but she didn't know how she could see a whole classroom of children every day, face the fact she would not have her own. "I can't afford it." It was a convenient, and true, excuse.

"I borrowed the money to attend."

Louisa nodded, as if giving the idea some thought. But even if she found Normal school appealing, she didn't know anyone who would lend her money. What about Uncle Peter? No. She'd never consider asking. Peter was her father's brother. He had never married. At Father's funeral he had said several times, "If there is anything I can do... If you need anything... I can help with expenses." Mother had been offended.

"Your father took care of us very well," she told the girls privately. "We aren't charity cases for your uncle."

Mother would never allow any of them to ask him for anything.

Louisa left Adele a few minutes later and drove home. She dreaded facing her mother. She'd likely demand a full description of the morning. If only she could tiptoe inside and find sanctuary in her room. But as she stopped before the door, she heard Mouse barking a frenzied greeting. Everyone in the house would know Louisa had returned.

The door opened and Sally waved at her. "The coast is clear. Mother has gone to visit Mrs. Roberts. She'll be gone all day. I think Mrs. Roberts is about to have her baby."

They shook their heads. "Poor Clara," Louisa murmured. Sally's friend was the eldest of six, now about to be seven, and carried a full load of responsibility— but secretly Louisa envied the girl all those little ones to care for.

Sally laughed. "Clara considers it a blessing. She can hardly wait for this baby. She said it had been too long." Clara's youngest brother was six, almost seven. "Are you hungry?"

"Starving. What are we eating? Or did you eat already?"

"Soup and sandwiches, and I've been waiting for you." They sat at the table and bowed their heads.

"It's your turn," Sally murmured, so Louisa said grace.

She'd barely said "amen" before Sally leaned forward like a coconspirator. "Did you have fun this morning?"

The pain she'd been holding back all morning burst

from its restraints and ran wild, spreading through her body like a raging prairie fire. "Oh, Sally, it's so hard. I gave her the dollhouse I made. I make up little games for her. I stand and watch how much Emmet loves his daughter, and I try to be grateful for what I have. But inside I die a little every day, knowing I can never have a part in it."

Sally sat back, her lunch forgotten. "I didn't realize it was so hard. Maybe you should quit."

"No. I intend to prove I can do this. I'm tired of being weak and fragile." She ignored Sally's mocking laugh. "I am holding on to the promise of that paycheck at the end of the two months. I'll give it to Mother to pay the bills and feel like I've done something useful for the first time in my life."

"Oh, Louie. You have contributed so much to our family. How can you think you have to prove anything?"

"I have contributed nothing but anxiety and medical bills."

Sally reached across the table and took Louisa's hands. "Oh, my dear, dear sister. No one cares about that. What we care about is your sweetness, which hasn't been affected by illness. We appreciate how patient you are no matter what you must endure. Do you know how many times I fell asleep listening to you sing? Or play the piano? I always knew things weren't all that bad so long as you could sing. That's worth more than anything money can buy."

Sing anyway. Sometimes it was hard, but knowing it encouraged others, Louisa renewed her vow to do so.

"Sally, you are far too generous, but I thank you. Now eat your soup before it gets cold."

They ate in companionable silence for a few moments, then Sally put her spoon down and stared at Louisa. "You gave your dollhouse away? I can't believe it."

Louisa shrugged. "I thought of keeping it to give to a niece, but I can always make another if you or Madge have a little girl. Ellie has no mother, so I thought it appropriate."

Sally looked as if she meant to say something, then changed her mind. Had she been about to point out that Louisa couldn't have children and Ellie needed a mother? If that was her intention she had, thankfully, thought better of it. If Emmet married again, he would want more children. He was very clear on that matter.

They had almost finished when Sally jerked her head up. Louisa smiled, knowing she was about to hear one of Sally's sudden brainstorms.

"I know what will cheer you up. Let's go to the orphanage. We can play with the babies when they wake up. And when the older kids come home from school, we can do things with them. You know, like play games, read and sing to them, help them with homework. Let's go."

Louisa wanted to say no. She wanted to retreat to her bedroom, wrap her arms around little Mouse and wallow in her sorrow. But there was no value in that. She would be cheerful despite her sadness. And making the children laugh would surely ease her own misery.

The afternoon passed quickly and pleasantly with the children and staff at the orphanage. By the time they returned home it was past supper time, but Mother was still away so the girls scrambled eggs and had them on toast for their meal.

They finished and sat back, relaying stories of the children when a knock sounded on the door.

Mouse leaped from Louisa's lap in a frenzy of barking.

Louisa laughed. "Some guard dog you are. We already know someone is there. Silly dog." She and Sally exchanged looks full of curiosity. Who could it be? Did it signal bad news? Perhaps Mrs. Roberts—she wouldn't consider all the things that could go wrong. "I'll get it." She crossed to the door, took in a deep breath before opening it. "Emmet? Is something wrong?" She cupped her hand to her throat in alarm. "Ellie? Auntie May?"

He reached for her, caught her elbow. "Everything is fine."

Relief made her legs wobbly. She welcomed his steadying touch. Almost immediately, a new kind of weakness claimed her heart and body as his touch reached into her inner being, uncovering wants she thought she had successfully buried, and laying claim to them.

"I thought I'd come here to do lesson preparation. Save you the trip to town."

She needed to step away from his touch. She needed to answer the man. She needed to bury her feelings. But she couldn't move, couldn't speak and, heaven help her, couldn't find the will to deny the longing in her heart... longing for love, home, family. A groan escaped her heart and pressed against her teeth as she fought against disappointment.

"I'm sorry." Emmet gripped her elbow more firmly. "Is my being here a problem?"

Sally had moved to the doorway. "You surprised her, I think. Come on in."

Emmet dropped his hand to his side and waited.

Feeling as if she had been set adrift in a vast ocean with no horizon in sight, Louisa blindly followed her sister, Emmet at her heels.

"We just finished supper." Sally scooped up the dirty dishes, carried them to the basin then wiped the table clean. "There you go. You can go over lessons here."

Emmet hovered behind a chair.

Louisa realized he waited for her to sit, or show any degree of civility. "Have a chair while I get my satchel." She scurried from the room, didn't slow her steps until she reached her room. She sank to her bed. *Oh, Lord God, I am trying to trust You but sometimes it is so hard.* Impossible. *With men this is impossible; but with God all things are possible.* Matthew nineteen, verse twenty-six. A verse Father had taught her, had repeated to her when she struggled to breathe through the worst of her pneumonia. She'd clung to the comfort of that assurance. *Thank You, Lord. I will trust You.* She rose from her bed, squared her shoulders, grabbed the satchel from the chair where she had tossed it and marched down the stairs to face Emmet. She faltered at the last step. *Gird yourself in God's strength,* she reminded herself briskly and lifted her chin a little higher as she entered the kitchen, where Emmet watched her, a worried look in his eyes. He'd guessed something upset her. She vowed he would never know what or why.

"I have the materials here." She sat across from him and pulled out the lessons. "Adele suggests we go as quickly with arithmetic as Ellie can handle. Success in this area will help her tackle the more challenging subject of reading." There were several sheets of equations then some problems, which would require Ellie to apply her knowledge of addition.

None of this required more than a few minutes. They could easily discuss everything before they began in the morning. So why did he insist on this preparation time? Why did he come out to the farm?

She answered the question herself. No doubt he was lonely.

I suppose the least we can do is make his visit more enjoyable. Surely that was their Christian duty. Grateful for the excuse, she relaxed.

"Would you like tea?" she asked.

"I don't want to be a nuisance, but I have to confess I get bored in town. Would you mind—" He ducked his head without finishing.

Louisa and Sally exchanged glances. Sally tilted her head toward Emmet, signaling that Louisa should help him.

"Please feel free to ask anything."

He raised his head, gave her a piercing look, and she smiled, knowing her assurance eased his tension. "Very well. I miss the ranch. I thought if you showed me the barn and we could walk around a field... Well, I would enjoy it immensely."

"Very well." Louisa refused to look at Sally, knew

she'd see a gleam of encouragement. But Louisa's wayward heart needed no encouragement. It needed a good stiff dose of reality. However, she didn't mind showing him around the farm. Even if most of it belonged to another now. He deserved kindness and friendship. That was why she would do it. No other reason.

She only wished her heart would obey her mind. Instead it sang a secret song of something beyond friendship. And beyond possibility.

"We can have tea when you get back." Sally tried to sound matter-of-fact, but Louisa heard the little note of happiness that her sister was stepping out.

"Shall we go?" Louisa headed for the door, paused to murmur for Sally's ears only. "It's only a tour of the farm. Nothing more. Remember, it can be nothing more."

Sally shrugged, totally unrepentant.

Emmet waited on the step and Louisa joined him.

"What would you like to see?"

"Everything. Do you still farm any land?"

"We kept only enough for a bit of pasture. We keep a milk cow and calf."

"What about winter feed?"

"We buy it. Or more likely, trade for it. Judd helped us find feed last winter." Such mundane conversation, but she welcomed it. A safe topic.

They went to the garden. The only thing visible was rhubarb. "There should be tiny plants poking through soon. We water it faithfully. Once they're up we'll have to fight off the hordes of grasshoppers." The insects were already beginning to hatch. Soon there would be thousands of them, eating anything that survived the winds and drought.

She led him to the barn. "Father had dreams of several cows and horses here."

Mice rustled across the floor overhead.

Emmet breathed deeply. "I love the smell of hay."

Curious about his life, she faced him. "Tell me about your ranch." It was only natural to want to know a little more about him. After all, she taught his little girl and spent several hours a day with him. Only she didn't want to know because of Ellie. She wanted to know Emmet. And no amount of reasoning and mental argument erased that truth. She wanted to know what he liked first thing in the morning, what his favorite time of day was, what tiny things gave him pleasure... She must stop this foolish meandering of her thoughts.

"My house is on a little hill. A creek flows by on the west side. In the spring the creek is full and noisy. Later in the summer it is slow and quiet. When I need to think, I have a place by the creek in a little grove of trees where I sit and watch the water. Deer often come to water at the creek."

"It sounds wonderful." She couldn't remember moving to the empty manger and perching on its edge, Emmet beside her, but that's where they were.

"It's nice all right."

"Tell me about your house."

He slanted her a teasing look. "I don't think you'd be impressed with it right now."

"Why not?"

"A widower and seven-year-old don't make good housekeepers." His eyes were so blue she thought the sky must be reflected in them. "What it really needs is a woman's touch."

"And more children running through the rooms?"

"That would be nice."

She pushed to her feet. "Let's look at the fields. Mr. Emerson planted the closest one last week, but we need rain to make it germinate."

He followed her. "The original house was log. But it was small so I added on—frame structure. It turned out rather nice, I think. The original is the kitchen and living room with a loft above. The addition is four bedrooms and a storeroom."

They reached the field, and Louisa scooped up a handful of dirt. It was so dry it sifted through her fingers. She shook her hand. "We need rain." She didn't want to hear about the four bedrooms that longed to be filled with children. She didn't want to hear about the house on the hill, the creek and the private spot in the trees.

But Emmet continued on as if she'd asked him to describe every detail.

And despite her denial, she wanted him to.

"Like I say, the house has been neglected since— well, since Jane died."

Tell me more, her heart begged. *Talk about something else,* her brain insisted. "What did you do with your animals when you left?"

"In the summer they graze the high pastures. They need little supervision, but I asked a neighbor to check on them. I'll have to bring them down to home pasture before the snow comes."

He'd have to leave by fall. That would be a relief to

her mental wrangling. Only, she counted off the months with a sick feeling. It was mid-May. When would he head back? September? Earlier if Ellie was ready to travel? It took all her inner strength to push her regret into submission and turn the conversation to something else.

"I visited the orphanage this afternoon. And it gave me an idea. There's one little girl there who is a little younger than Ellie and seems pleasant. I thought if you asked her to visit, it would provide Ellie with some company her own age."

Emmet faced her, surprise in his blue eyes. "I think that's a great idea, especially if you think this child is appropriate."

"Appropriate?" When did children have to pass inspection?

"I'm sure you realize I wouldn't want Ellie associating with a child who, for instance, had a foul mouth."

She chuckled at his expression. "You look ready to fight off any danger she might encounter."

"I am. If I'd been more vigilant, she wouldn't be where she is now."

"Emmet, accidents happen and sometimes illnesses. We do our best and leave the rest in God's hands."

"I try." He seemed to struggle with his conflicting need to be in control and desire to trust God. "By all means, invite this child to visit if you think it's appropriate."

She wanted to say something to ease his mind. Perhaps offer comfort, but she dare not let herself say all that was in her heart—a longing to stand at his side through accidents and trials, an ache to put a woman's touch to his neglected home.

Instead she steeled herself to speak calmly, as if nothing mattered but inviting a child to play. "I'll see to the arrangements."

Helping Ellie was the best she could do to satisfy her desire to help him.

Chapter Nine

Emmet left after he shared tea and cookies with Louisa and Sally. He walked back to town. He could have driven his truck, but he preferred to walk the three miles. It gave him time to think.

Trouble was, his thoughts made no sense. Why had he come out here? Lesson preparation wasn't the answer. Why had he told her all about the ranch? How the house sat on a hill? As he told about the rooms he'd added to the house, he imagined her in the house, filling it with love and laughter, faith and—dare he admit it? Yes, children. After Jane's death, or maybe even before it, he had vowed he would no longer dream such dreams. Jane had given him only one child, and although he loved Ellie, it was a disappointment. He longed for a large family. In part, he wanted to fill the hollowness in his heart he'd known since his parents died so suddenly.

Not a hint. Not a moment of warning. Here one minute, gone the next.

He had been alone. So alone.

The feeling had never quite left him. Not when

Auntie May gave him a home—a perfectly acceptable home. He had no doubt Auntie May loved him. His marriage had not robbed him of the feeling. Not that it was Jane's fault. She loved him decently enough. Having Ellie was the closest he'd come to satisfying the emptiness within himself. It was the best he could expect.

But in his mind he saw Louisa at the stove in the ranch house. Saw her bending over a child's bed. Saw her standing on the veranda, watching for him to return for supper.

He kicked a lump of dirt that poofed into a cloud of dust. All she'd done was help with Ellie's lessons. Yes, she was good with Ellie, but she'd given no indication that her interest in either of them went beyond her job as a tutor. And he would do well to keep that in mind. For the time being, this was best for Ellie. He would do nothing to change that. And when they left again, just the two of them, he would continue to do what was best for her.

And safest for him, a faint voice insisted.

Yes, what was best for him was keeping his heart's desires under lock and key. He'd already learned his dreams were empty. Led only to more hurt—watching Jane die and having to bury her was the second-hardest thing he'd ever faced.

Somehow he managed to guard his heart throughout the lessons of the next day, and then two days later, Louisa brought Leila to visit. He'd asked her to be present.

"After all, we're strangers to her. She'll feel better if you stay."

So Louisa had agreed. He couldn't tell if she welcomed the idea or not.

Leila edged forward when she saw Ellie. "You broke your leg?"

"Fell out of a tree."

Leila's blue eyes were wide with disbelief. "Your mommy let you climb trees?"

"Ain't got no mommy."

"Me too. I got no daddy either." She slid her gaze to Emmet and studied him long and hard, her eyes practically eating him up. She had long, blond, baby-fine hair tied back with a limp bow. Her fair skin was a marked contrast to Ellie's darker skin. In fact, compared with Ellie with her dark blond hair and brown eyes, she looked ethereal.

"You got any brothers or sisters?" Ellie asked.

He heard the hungry note in her voice and understood Ellie ached for siblings just as he had.

"I had a sister, Emmy. She died along with Mama and Papa."

Emmet shot a glance at Louisa, saw an echo of his shock and pain. Children should be spared such sorrows. But he knew they weren't. He wasn't much older than Leila when his parents had died. He leaned down toward Leila. "Honey, what happened to your family?"

She clung to his gaze, sucking up strength and demanding something more from him.

He only wished he knew what it was she wanted. He would gladly give it if it lay within his power. "They got sick and died. All except me."

"You don't have any relatives you can live with?"

"Only my grandma, and she is very old and lives across the ocean."

Ellie shifted in the bed, as if trying to move over. "You want to play dolls with me? Miss Morgan gave me this dollhouse."

Leila instantly brightened. "That's a nice dollhouse." She climbed up on the chair beside Ellie, and soon the girls were playing happily.

Louisa signaled Emmet to leave the room.

A minute later they stood in the kitchen, staring at the table.

"Poor child," Emmet murmured.

"I know. It seems so unfair they've lost their parents and I—" Her voice broke and she stopped speaking. "Sometimes," she whispered, "it's hard to remember to sing."

He clasped her hand, wanting more than anything to bring the music back to her voice. "Louisa, don't ever stop singing. What would happen to our world if all the songbirds grew silent?"

She gave him a look of pure disbelief. "I'm no songbird."

"Ah. But you are. Nicely disguised as a beautiful woman, but still a songbird underneath."

Her cheeks blossomed like June roses. Her gaze darted away and then returned, almost as hungry as the look in Leila's eyes. "I am not."

He didn't know if she meant she wasn't a beautiful woman or a songbird. Maybe both, which is exactly what he meant when he said, "You are indeed."

She eased her hand from his. When she pressed it to her waist as if she cherished the feel of his palm, he grinned. "The girls are enjoying each other." Their happy voices came from the other room.

"I thought they might."

He didn't want Louisa saddened again by thinking of orphaned children. Besides, he wanted to enjoy her company without the excuse of schoolwork. Just this once. Auntie May was outside puttering about her garden. "Do you want to see an old photo album?"

"Of you?" Did she sound eager?

"Maybe."

Emmet led her into the front room, waited for her to settle on the old sofa that had likely made the trek west with Auntie May's grandparents. His father's grandparents. He seldom thought that far back in his family tree.

He put a black photo album on her lap and sat close to explain the pictures. "My great-grandparents, before they moved west."

She bent over the picture to examine it closer, giving him plenty of time to study her—the tumble of dark curls, a profile that would be suitable for a cameo. She glanced up and caught his interest, and the pink returned to her cheeks. "You look like your great-grandfather."

He turned the page to pictures of the house they'd built in the British Territories, now Alberta. There were more pictures of his grandparents and great-aunts and uncles. Cousins back east he had never seen. He flipped the page, and his heart stalled. He'd forgotten this page.

She waited. Then prompted him. "Who are these?"

"My parents." His voice sounded distant and hoarse.

"And that would be you in your mother's arms?"

It was. He could only nod. She turned to the next picture. A little boy in a pair of knee pants, holding a cap. "You?"

"I was five. Still in short pants."

On the next page would be the picture Auntie May had insisted on taking. The two fresh graves.

Emmet took the photo album and closed it. He did not want to be reminded. That portion of his life was forbidden territory.

Louisa shifted, considered him long and hard. "Emmet, what happened to your parents?"

"They died."

"How?"

He shook his head. "It doesn't matter how, does it?"

"I think it does."

"I don't wish to talk about it." He stared at her, silently daring her to take this any further, informing her the subject was closed.

"As you wish." But her gaze remained demanding, sorrowful at the same time.

He didn't need sympathy any more than he needed reminders. "I better check on the girls."

She rose to follow him and laughed as they stepped into the room.

Leila had found an old red hat on the shelf and wore it. She had been twirling about and skidded to a halt at the sight of two adults. She yanked the hat off and returned it to the shelf. "I was only showing Ellie a little dance."

Emmet chuckled. "It's okay. Auntie May won't mind, so long as you don't damage anything."

Leila stared at the floor. A shudder raked her shoulders.

Emmet gave Louisa a help-me look. Why was Leila upset?

Louisa lifted one shoulder, then knelt beside the child. "Leila, what's wrong?"

"Nothing," she murmured.

"She likes that cup." Ellie pointed toward a chipped cup on the top shelf of the china cupboard.

"Is there something special about it?" Louisa asked.

"It reminds me of Mama."

Emmet could not take the way the child's voice cracked with emotion. "Would you like to have it?"

Leila's eyes threatened to consume her face. "It's not mine."

"I'll give it to you." He removed it from the shelf and handed it to her.

Leila shook her head. "Matron will be angry that I made you want to give me something. We aren't supposed to beg."

"You didn't—" He turned to Louisa for guidance.

"Maybe you can leave it here for now. But it's yours."

Leila took the cup and held it between her palms.

Emmet wondered if she even breathed as she studied the purple flowers on it. "Thank you. Very, very much. Mama would have loved this cup. She had a saucer with a crack that had these same flowers on it. She said her mama had given the cup and saucer to her, but all she had left was the saucer."

"What happened to it?"

The child's eyes filled with liquid, but she did not let

a tear escape. "I don't know. I only brought my clothes with me and my doll."

"You still got your doll?" Ellie asked.

Leila nodded, her eyes flashing mischief. "I keep her hidden under my underwear so no one will touch her."

Ellie wrinkled her nose. "Phew." Both girls laughed.

Louisa chuckled too, her eyes sparkling as much as the little girls'. She met Emmet's gaze. "No better place to hide something, you know."

He shook his head. "Makes no sense to me."

Still chuckling, Louisa waved at him to follow her from the room. She put the kettle to boil. Her shoulders quivered.

"You're laughing at me." He tried to sound regretful.

She faced him. It was plain as could be that she struggled to contain her amusement. "I'm laughing at the situation. I never realized how different boys and girls were."

"It's amazing. Surprising and interesting. Who'd think a chipped bit of china could bring so much happiness to a child?"

"Because it reminded her of her parents." Her eyes darkened. Delved into his heart, searching…for what? She opened her mouth. Seemed to reconsider. Closed it again. "I think it's good for her to have something that reminds her of them."

He knew then what she'd wanted to say and was grateful she had changed her mind. She'd considered saying something about the way he refused to talk about his parents. How could he possibly explain he didn't want to remember them? It brought only pain.

They sat at the table and had tea, listening to the giggles and whispers of the girls in the other room.

"It was a good idea to suggest Leila visit." He leaned across the table, as if about to share a secret. "You are very good with children."

She blinked. Seemed to pull back into herself. "I guess I remember my own childhood well."

He saw the silent challenge in her eyes and changed the subject before she could voice it. "Have you considered becoming a teacher?" Though she surely belonged in a home, with her own children. The thought tugged at his heart. But he wouldn't again picture her in his house. This afternoon's reminder of his parents and the pain of their death made him more determined to guard his heart.

"I can't afford to attend Normal school."

"I'm sure there's a way—"

"I don't wish to discuss it." Silent determination made her expression brittle.

Likely holding out for marriage. He wondered if he preferred to picture her married to someone, raising his kids, or unmarried and teaching. Neither sat very comfortably. But he would not follow his line of thought, knowing it went to places he must deny himself.

"It's time to take Leila back." She called Leila.

The girls whispered something and cast furtive looks at Louisa and Emmet.

"What are they up to?"

Louisa shrugged. "Secrets are very important to girls. Boys too, it seems."

It was a little dig about him closing the photo album,

refusing to talk about his parents. "Entirely different reasons, I expect."

"If you say so."

Leila took Louisa's hand. "Thank you for having me, Mr. Hamilton."

"Thank you for coming."

"Bye," Ellie called.

Emmet escorted Louisa and Leila to the door. He couldn't bear the thought of them leaving with constraint between himself and Louisa. "I have secrets for a very good reason."

She nodded. "I'm sure you do." She paused on the step, let Leila run to the car alone then turned to face him, her expression full of something far beyond curiosity. "Emmet, I don't mean to pry. But—" She shrugged.

"But what?"

"It's none of my business, is it?"

He wanted to say no, it wasn't. It wasn't anyone's business. But he couldn't deny her concern any more than he could deny the ache in his heart at keeping doors closed to her. It simply had to be that way. "What if I say I want it to be your business?"

"Okay. I don't know if I can explain it well, but I feel like whenever your parents are mentioned a huge lump of something chokes you. I guess I wonder why you don't want to get rid of that lump." She shrugged. "That's all."

That's all? That was like saying the sky was a little blue, the horizon was only a tiny distance away, the wind barely stirred the air. It wasn't little at all. The lump—as she described it—filled his insides. He couldn't pretend it wasn't there. He could only try to ignore it. He'd been trying for eighteen years, mostly with success—until he'd opened that silly photo album.

She touched his elbow. A thousand shivers raced up his veins, threatening to break the locks on a solid door. He feared what would happen should the door ever fling open.

"I can't. I simply can't." Did his voice sound as anguished as he felt? He hoped not.

"I'm sorry," she whispered. "The last thing I want is to upset you."

He nodded. Tried to say he wasn't upset. Failed. Feared his eyes betrayed his pain.

"Miss Morgan?" Leila called from the car.

"I have to go." Louisa sounded as if the idea hurt her deeply.

Louisa listened to Leila's happy chatter with only a tiny portion of her brain. The rest thought of Emmet. Why had she said what she did? Pushed him into a corner, forced emotions from him that obviously caused him such anguish. What made her think she had the right to probe at his wounds?

She wouldn't have thanked him for probing at hers.

Thankfully he didn't know her deepest wound. Nor would he ever.

She delivered Leila at the orphanage and spoke to the matron, assuring the good, solid lady that her little charge had been a perfect guest.

But she didn't immediately go home. She needed time to think. At first she thought of going to see Madge, but this was too deep, too personal to discuss

with either of her sisters. Or her mother. There was only
one source of wisdom and comfort for the confusion
she felt, and she pulled the car off the road at a dusty
approach and leaned back. *Oh, God. Help me. I feel
like I'm caught in a whirlwind. I don't want to cause
Emmet pain, and yet I know his past is really eating
him up. Help him find his own song. And Lord, while
I'm asking, please, please guard my heart.*

She sat for a few minutes, letting God's peace en-
velop her, then turned the car toward home.

The next morning she returned to the Hamilton
house, her emotions firmly under control, and she was
determined to keep them there. Emmet seemed relieved
that she was a little distant—a fact that bothered her
only slightly. She reminded herself it was far better to
be interested only in doing a good job. And expecting
nothing from him, apart from helping her teach Ellie.

They slipped into a routine. He spent less and less
time in Ellie's room helping with the lessons. That was
good, Louisa told herself repeatedly. Ellie was progress-
ing nicely. Flying through arithmetic and now able to
read at the beginning of her grade-two books. Louisa's
goal was to see her able to read at the level of her classmates before she finished her contract. She had four
weeks left. Once Ellie's cast came off, Louisa would
no longer be needed.

It wasn't a thought she allowed herself to dwell on.

"I wish Leila could come again." Ellie's words
brought Louisa back from her mental wandering.

"Ask your father. I'm sure he would approve."

"Daddy!" she yelled.

"I didn't mean this very minute." She had trouble

focusing on anything but her trembling heart when Emmet was in the room. But it was impossible to take back Ellie's call. Emmet bound through the door.

"Did you need me, Button?"

"Louisa said to ask you if I could invite Leila to come and play with me again. Can she?"

Emmet considered his daughter a moment, then shifted his gaze to Louisa.

She forgot to breathe when she saw the darkness in his eyes. What did he want from her? Whatever it was, she feared she could not give it.

"Would you be willing to bring her?"

Louisa couldn't for the life of her remember what they had been talking about and scrambled to think what he meant. Oh, right. Leila. "I think I could make arrangements for her to come after school."

"That would be nice."

Still he watched her. She gripped her hands together, determined she wouldn't touch him, ask what bothered him, offer to help in any way she could. Instead, she forced her thoughts to center on arrangements for Leila's visit. "Would tomorrow be good?"

"It would be fine."

Ellie cheered, freeing Louisa from the intense, demanding look in Emmet's eyes.

Ellie enjoyed the visit so much they arranged for Leila to come over a couple of times a week. Louisa liked seeing the friendship develop between them. It reminded her of the fun she and her sisters had shared growing up. But there was one big difference. The girls weren't sisters and would have to part in a few weeks.

What would happen to the friendship when Emmet and Ellie left? Would both little girls be hurt?

She expected Leila would be as heartsore as Louisa.

She renewed her vow to continue the work without breaching any more barriers. The lesson preparation did not require she and Emmet meet every evening, but they still needed to get together for planning a couple of times a week.

Emmet insisted on coming to the farm. A form of sweet torture. She couldn't—wouldn't fall in love. She told herself this every day.

Even so, she could not imagine the pain she must endure when they left. Knew it would rival the pain of learning she would never bear children.

Lord, I'm trying to trust You. But my emotions get in the way. Help me. Hold me up lest I fall.

She feared she would soon test the truth of those words.

Chapter Ten

"May I sit with you?" At Emmet's voice behind her as she edged into the pew after Sally, Louisa jerked about, her heart in her throat.

"What are you doing here?" she whispered. He never came to church, because he had to stay with Ellie.

"Auntie May said I would turn into a heathen if I missed church another Sunday. She volunteered to stay with Ellie. They had some scheme cooked up. I believe I heard something about a bed picnic. I was warned not to return before supper time, so I'm at loose ends. Any suggestions as to how I should spend the afternoon?"

Sally overheard. "Join us. Madge and Judd are coming. It will be fun."

"I'd like that."

Louisa kept her head down, giving a great deal of attention to settling herself, arranging her purse and Bible on her lap, all the time resisting an urge to check and see that her hat was still on straight. And not looking at Emmet as she fought a battle in her heart.

Having him sit beside her in church crossed some kind of barrier. She hadn't expected she would be so blindsided by his presence. Her defenses weren't constructed.

Sally nudged her, and she realized the pastor had announced the first hymn. Her beloved sister took the hymnal before them and turned to share it with Mother. That left Louisa no choice but to share Emmet's hymnal. She barely touched the edge of the book, and yet every cell in her body tingled with awareness as she tried hopelessly to remain indifferent.

And then he began to sing. A hoarse, gravelly sound. Not unpleasant any more than the sound of water bubbling over rocks in a sun-warmed stream was unpleasant. She'd heard him sing silly songs to Ellie. Heard him whistle while he worked, or walked away from her house. But hearing him sing in church, while sitting next to her, joined by a narrow eight inches of book...

Her throat tightened, and she couldn't get out the words of the hymn. She coughed discreetly. Let the others think a tickle in her throat had choked her voice.

Throughout the service she was acutely aware of Emmet. His solidness. The warmth of his almost-touching body. The silent in and out of his breath. Her own twitching nerves.

She forced her attention to the sermon. Heard every word, but for the life of her couldn't have repeated a one of them.

By the time the last "amen" had been uttered, the final benediction offered, the last relaxed sigh of the congregation released, Louisa felt ready to explode from her skin. But she calmly rose when the others did. Nodded and smiled at Emmet as if he were one of their old, familiar neighbors sharing the pew, and made her way demurely after him to the aisle.

He stepped aside to let the Morgan ladies go ahead of him.

Sally paused, turned. "You'll be out right away? Or do you want a ride with us?"

"I'll be out in a few minutes. I need to let Auntie May know where I'm going. Just in case she needs me." He shifted his gaze between Sally and Louisa.

Louisa told herself she didn't see a flicker of hesitation. As if he'd guessed at her uncertainty and hoped she'd echo Sally's invitation. But she couldn't. She dare not admit to anyone, including herself, how much she wished she could put her arm through his and draw him into her family circle.

"We'll see you in a little while then?"

Emmet nodded agreement to Sally's question. Outside he strode down the street without a backward look.

Sally pulled Louisa toward the car. Mother lingered, talking to Mr. Roberts. No doubt asking after his wife and the new baby.

"I've never known you to be so rude."

Louisa stared at her sister. "I was not rude."

"Would it have hurt you to extend just a hint of welcome to the man?"

Louisa pursed her lips. "Did you ever think I might not want him spending Sunday afternoon with us? Do you know how hard it is to see him every day, be constantly reminded that I can never have—" She wouldn't say she could never have him. "What he represents."

"That's your choice. No one said you had to turn into a prune-faced spinster. Why you've closed your heart to the possibility of love without once giving a man the chance to decide if he is willing to accept you as you are is beyond me."

Pain sliced through Louisa's insides, leaving a trail of tears. "Sally, I've never known you to be cruel like this."

Sally sighed. "Louisa, I am not being cruel. Only pointing out that you might have closed the door prematurely."

"You've heard him yourself." She could manage only a tight whisper. "You know he wants more children."

"You don't have to fall in love with him. But it doesn't mean you have to shut yourself up in a cold casket either."

Louisa could not speak. Could barely remember how to breathe. No, she didn't have to fall in love with him.

How she wished she hadn't.

Sally grabbed her arm. "Mother is coming. Put on a happy face. We're going to go home and enjoy the afternoon with friends and family. You think you can manage that?"

"Of course." Friends and family. She had to remember it was nothing more.

Emmet changed his mind about going to the Morgans a dozen times after he left the church. For days he'd been aware of constraint between himself and Louisa. It was his fault. No doubt she felt he'd put her off by refusing to talk about his parents. But he finally concluded it would be rude not to show up.

So he told Auntie May and Ellie where he'd be. Laughed at the way they obviously wanted him to hurry and leave. He caught a glimpse of dandelions, cats and something red and furry on the bed. They expected Leila to appear soon. "I'd have brought her from church if you told me."

Ellie shook her head. "You weren't supposed to come back until supper time. It's your day off."

Emmet couldn't decide if he appreciated that the pair had schemed to allow him to be away for the afternoon, or if he felt suddenly useless.

But at least he could join the Morgans and Kirks without feeling he neglected his duties. He decided to walk, hoping the time and activity would enable him to discipline his thoughts into submission.

His stride ate up the miles, but when he headed up the lane toward the house, his steps slowed. An afternoon of adult company sounded fine, though he thought only of one person—Louisa. But—he threw back his shoulders—he could spend a relaxing afternoon without forgetting all his hard-learned life lessons.

Mrs. Morgan waited in the open doorway as he approached. "We're always glad to have another young man join us. Poor Judd is sadly outnumbered, I fear."

"Not a problem for me." Judd stepped from the kitchen. "Though I admit I am sometimes baffled by the reasoning of the female mind."

Remembering Louisa, Leila and Ellie hiding something in an underwear drawer, Emmet laughed. "I've known the same confusion from time to time." He glanced past Judd's shoulder. Saw Louisa watching him. Caught a flash of awareness in her eyes before she ducked away to put a dish on the table. Dare he hope that somewhere inside, she allowed a tender feeling toward him?

"Come in. Dinner is ready."

He knew a jolt of gratitude that Sally's words prevented him from following that errant thought any further.

Sally waved him to a chair. The others took their places. Sally at one end of the table, Mrs. Morgan at the other. Judd and Madge side by side across from him. And to his left, Louisa. He wanted to glance at her, watch her face for hints as to how she felt.

He'd been so aware of her at his side during the church service that it was downright annoying. He could barely get his lungs to work for the tension of each moment.

So what, his brain mocked, are you doing here? Hoping to become immune to her?

Mrs. Morgan asked Judd to say the blessing. The food was passed. Simple, plain food, but more than adequate. Many survived—existed—on far less. The other day in the store, he'd heard terrible stories of people eating unusual things to keep themselves alive. One family had nothing but turnips to see them through the winter.

"Clara didn't come to church." Sally passed mashed potatoes to Emmet. "I wonder if her mother is doing poorly."

Mrs. Morgan answered her. "Mrs. Roberts is feeling better, according to her husband, and the baby is doing well."

"I suppose Clara is simply busy." Sally seemed content with the observation and the conversation shifted to other things, like who had moved on and what people were doing to cope.

Emmet hated to think of Louisa and her family struggling against the challenges of the drought and depression, and yet they didn't complain, only expressed concern for others.

"I bought four cows and calves." Judd was obviously pleased with his acquisition. "The man said he'd had enough of trying to eke out a living in this country and was headed west. Figured he could find work at the coast."

Emmet couldn't help but wonder how he would feed the critters, so he asked. Judd went into a very detailed account of his plans.

Madge sighed. "You should have never asked him. Honey, tell Emmet about how you worked on a ranch in the foothills." She grinned at Louisa, and the girls shared a moment of amusement.

Judd rattled his lips. "You're mocking me." His expression, though, said he considered it a privilege that his wife would tease him. He shifted his attention to Emmet. "I'll tell you later if you're interested. Madge, tell them about your baby chicks."

She leaned forward and explained in great detail how she'd put fourteen eggs to set and had ten healthy chicks.

Judd chuckled and whispered across the table, "If you think that's a lot of information, then don't ask about her garden."

Madge broke off midsentence. "Now who is mocking who?"

"Whom." Louisa corrected, and everyone but Emmet laughed.

Louisa broke off. "Sorry. I guess it's silly to a spectator, but we play these little games with each other."

"Speaking of games." Judd glanced around the table. "How about croquet after the dishes are done?"

"You're on." The three girls leaped to their feet and began gathering up the dishes.

Mrs. Morgan started putting things away, but Louisa caught her about the waist. "Mother, we have lots of help. You go nap and read your book."

Mrs. Morgan smiled at each of them. "I don't mind if I do."

Before she made it to her room, Madge whipped a tea towel around Judd's waist and secured it in his waistband. "You're the chief bottle washer."

Louisa tossed Emmet a towel. "Why don't you be the chief drier?"

Judd rolled his eyes. "They think they can soften us up so we'll be nice to them."

Madge planted her hands on her hips. "I believe you are my partner. Wasn't that part of our wedding vows?"

Another burst of shared laughter. This time Emmet joined in. He glanced at Louisa to gauge her reaction. Their eyes met. The air between them seemed to shift and buckle like shimmering heat waves. He forgot all his good intentions. He forgot to check the locks on his heart. He—

"Hey, Emmet. You going to dry this?" Judd nudged him, bringing him back to his senses. He carefully checked to make certain all the bolts were in place on those invisible doors as he turned away from Louisa's dark eyes and concentrated on drying dishes.

They finished up and carried a croquet set outside. Sally handed mallets to everyone. "Judd and Madge can challenge Louisa and Emmet. I'll be the referee."

"Referee? What kind of rules do you follow?" He'd played croquet a few times. One of the neighbors at his ranch liked the game and often invited others to join. It seemed like a gentle game to him.

"You haven't seen Judd play yet."

"Me?" Judd clutched at his chest. "I am a superb player."

The girls chortled.

Louisa fell in at Emmet's side. "I better warn you, Judd always has to win."

"Judd thinks he's superior because he's a man." Madge sounded as if it was a dreadful fate.

"I'm just a better player." Judd gloated, bringing another burst of denial from the girls.

Louisa leaned closer to Emmet to whisper, "Sounds like someone needs a little competition."

Emmet shifted so his mouth was close to her ears. So he could breathe in the sweetness of her. "We might just give him what he needs." And who—a distant voice demanded—would give *him* what he needed? He straightened. Forced the traitorous question into the back regions of his mind.

She laughed and took her place at the start. "Let the game begin."

Within minutes, it was obvious Judd had only one goal in mind—win by any means. Emmet was equally intent on proving his worth as an opponent. Sally was kept busy calling fair or foul and admonishing Judd to play by the rules.

After each turn Louisa and Madge stood back to watch Judd go after Emmet's ball, roqueting it out of the play area.

Emmet retrieved his ball and returned it to the imaginary yard line. "I hope you never decide I'm an enemy. You would stop at nothing to destroy me."

Sally warned Judd to stay within the boundaries.

Judd snorted. "I don't need to bend the rules to win. I'm just a better player." He swung his mallet with enough force to make Louisa shudder.

Emmet almost grabbed her to keep her safe from this attack. But the violence was restricted to the ball.

Judd leaned back, gloating.

"You've obviously had more practice, which doesn't equate to being better." Emmet lined up his shot and returned his ball to the playing area with precision. Only it encountered a lump in the rough yard and veered off course.

"Too bad," Louisa said. "But we'll still win."

Judd scoffed. "Not likely. Hurry up, Madge."

Madge sighed. "Louisa, I don't know why we're even playing. If these two want to go at each other, let them." She backed away, indicating she withdrew.

Louisa hesitated. Emmet wanted her to continue playing as his partner. He liked the sense that they fought a common enemy. Did she enjoy working together as much as he did? But Judd grinned at him— though it would better be described as a mocking sneer.

Louisa retreated to Madge's side. "This ought to be fun. I can't wait to see Judd defeated."

Emmet's chest seemed to grow several inches at her support of him.

"I wouldn't be counting my chickens before they hatch," Madge warned, which brought a burst of laughter from her sisters.

"You know a lot about hatching chickens, after all," Sally teased.

Louisa watched Emmet, her silent encouragement filling him with determination. She cheered as he played, sending his ball through a wicket.

Judd followed with a nasty hit. Emmet shook his head in mock sadness. "Where did you learn to be so competitive?"

"From my brothers."

As the pair continued to play, Judd explained. "Brothers teach you to play a game well. Then they teach you how to defend yourself." Wham—on Emmet's ball. "Then they teach you how to defeat your opponent."

Emmet knocked his ball back in. "You don't need brothers to learn how to play hard and fair."

"Nope." Wham again. "But without brothers, it seems to me you have a choice about how you play a game. With brothers, you don't."

"Don't we always have a choice about our actions?" He felt as if he was parroting something Louisa said, and he glanced in her direction.

Her eyes said she recognized the echo of her beliefs. For a moment their gazes held in an invisible bond, then Louisa turned away and wrapped her arm about Madge's waist. "I can see it's much better to have sisters. We are always so kind and helpful to each other."

"Yes, indeed." Madge placed her arm around Louisa's waist and giggled.

"I'm certainly glad for a family of girls." Judd came over and gave Madge a quick kiss. "Especially the middle sister." He returned to the game.

In the end, Judd won...by sheer determination, Emmet figured.

"I'll give you a chance to win the next round." Judd seemed eager to have another go.

Emmet handed the mallet to Sally and held his hands up in mock defeat. "I concede."

Judd did a victory dance and shook his hands together over his head.

Madge groaned. "It wouldn't hurt you to be a little humble about it."

He pulled her into his arms and kissed her.

Emmet turned away. Their love was so apparent. He'd tried love once. But he'd failed as a husband. He hadn't been able to protect Jane, keep her safe. Part of him wanted to yell a warning to these people. Love hurts. But perhaps they would be spared the grief he'd known.

Judd grabbed Madge's hand. "Mrs. Kirk, let's you and I walk home across the fields. What do you think of that idea?" The adoring smile blessed Madge with his love and devotion and left Emmet feeling alone and cranky.

Madge beamed her love back at Judd. "Whatever you say, Mr. Kirk." She ducked her head in mock submission, then laughed as they raced toward home.

Sally yawned. "I have a book to read."

That left Louisa and Emmet stranded in the yard.

"Shall we go for a walk?" He half expected her to demur, but instead she turned toward the trail that led past the barn and he readily fell in at her side.

The sun shone brightly. The sky spread out from horizon to horizon like an unbroken blue canvas. All in all, a beautiful afternoon. He didn't mind in the least sharing it with a beautiful woman.

"I've enjoyed the afternoon."

"I'm glad. I was afraid you might find my family overwhelming."

"Not at all." They paused to lean on a wooden gate. "You have what I've always wanted."

She looked as surprised as if he'd announced he carried rain in his back pocket. "Really? I can't imagine."

"Family. Siblings." His voice had thickened, but he couldn't help it. "I always felt lonely growing up alone." Abandoned.

She looked away, her gaze seeking the far edge of the field. "You know what I want?"

"No. What?" Whatever it was, he wished he could give it to her.

She paused for a beat. Two. Shuddered as if a chill had raced across her shoulders. She tried to speak, but her voice caught.

It obviously meant a lot to her. And his heart softened with such a protective urge that it was all he could do not to pull her into his arms and hold her close, keep her safe.

"For it to rain." Her voice rang with determination. "I pray for it every single day."

He knew without a doubt that wasn't what she'd started to say. Disappointment stained his insides. What was she afraid to admit she needed? For that matter, what made him think he could do anything about it? Keep her safe? What a bitter thought. He couldn't keep anyone safe.

She faced him squarely with a look of such fierce determination that he blinked. "We have no choice but to trust God. He will supply all our needs."

He wondered if she meant simply rain—or the lack of it—but her faith blared through him, seared away doubts.

"I do believe that." As he had never before believed.

Chapter Eleven

Louisa managed to walk back to the house with Emmet. Somehow bid him goodbye. Her lungs felt as tight as when she'd had pneumonia. Only she knew it was shock and sorrow, and her struggle to contain them, that caused her distress. She tiptoed into the house, not wanting anyone to see her. Her sister and mother knew her too well not to notice how stiff her face was as she held back her emotions. But the house was quiet. Mother must still be in her room, and Sally was likely reading in her room as well. She'd do the same, and she stumbled upstairs, Mouse whining at her heels.

The dog jumped to the bed, but Louisa's limbs were too stiff to be able to sit, let alone lie down. She stood in the middle of the room, as lost as if she had somehow landed in a foreign country. Nothing in her room seemed familiar. Maybe looking out the window would help. But she couldn't move.

Her insides groaned, but no sound escaped her lips. She couldn't find a word or sound to express the gut-wrenching way she felt.

He wanted more children. She'd almost confessed how much she wanted them too. How it was impossible. Caught herself just in time. She couldn't confess it to him. He would despise her inability if he knew.

She'd substituted her desire for rain at the last minute. But as she vowed she trusted God, tension had eased from her insides. Unfortunately the release had lasted only until Emmet said goodbye. Then it returned with wicked insistence. She counted the number of weeks until Ellie would have her cast off and this torture would end. It seemed an eternity away.

I must trust God. He would not send me more than I can bear.

Oh, but how much did He think she could take?

Strength slowly returned to her limbs. Overwhelming exhaustion followed. She sank to her bed, cradled Mouse in her arms and fell asleep.

The next day, still feeling as if she needed to sleep a week or longer, she returned to tutoring Ellie.

"My daddy had to take care of some business," Ellie said by way of greeting. "He won't be here today."

A reprieve. *Thank You, Lord.* Only, regret twisted with gratitude. She missed him.

She better get used to it.

The morning passed slowly. Although Ellie did her lessons well, Louisa found it difficult to concentrate until Ellie crossed her arms over her chest and glared at her.

"What's wrong with you?"

Louisa snapped to attention. "Nothing. Why?"

"Did I do something wrong?"

"Not that I know of. Why do you ask?"

Ellie's face crumpled, and tears flowed. "Why are you mad at me?"

"But I'm not. Why would you think that?"

"'Cause you act like it."

Louisa shook her head. "But I haven't said one cross word."

"You pretend you don't hear me."

"Oh, honey. I've been distracted is all. My mind has been on other things. I'm sorry. It's not your fault. Not for a minute."

"You sure?" Ellie's voice still carried her tears.

"Of course I'm sure." After that she devoted her attention to the child and, to her relief, found it helped her forget her problems.

As the days passed, she continued to find solace in teaching Ellie. But it only partially relieved the ache that grew like lengthening evening shadows inside her soul.

One afternoon, after a morning with Ellie, she made her way home but paused at the turnoff to Madge and Judd's house. Madge was the practical one. Perhaps she could help Louisa find a solution to her growing restlessness. She turned down the drive.

Madge saw her coming and hurried to meet her. "It's been a long time since you've been here."

Louisa laughed. "Not much more than a week. We all came last Friday."

"But you haven't paid me a visit." She drew Louisa's arm through hers. "Never mind, I know you're busy. Come see my garden." Plants were poking through. Madge glanced skyward. "Oh, for some rain."

The remark echoed Louisa's comment to Emmet. The darkness inside overwhelmed her. She sank to the grass beside the garden and buried her face in her hands. "Oh, Madge. What am I going to do?"

Madge sat beside her. "What's wrong?"

"Everything." She sounded like a spoiled child, but she didn't care.

"Maybe you'd like to be a little more specific."

She flashed Madge a trembling smile. "I don't know if I can be." Or perhaps she simply didn't want to confess the truth.

"It's about Emmet, isn't it?"

Louisa stared across the garden.

"I see how he looks at you. How you look at him."

She flinched. "I try not to—"

"What? Feel something for him? Louie, why not let yourself care?"

Louisa pressed her lips together and held back the pain. She didn't speak for a moment. When she did, her voice trembled like the last leaf of summer in a winter wind. "You heard him. He's always wanted a large family. I can't give him that."

"Judd wanted to go back to the mountains until he fell in love with me. He says after that, his priorities changed. He wanted a secure home. He wanted to be near family. Maybe Emmet is the same."

Louisa shook her head. "I would never be able to give him what he wants."

"On the other hand, maybe you can give him what he needs."

The idea scratched across her thoughts. If only she could believe it.

Madge went on. "Maybe what he's looking for is something that family represents."

"Like what?" What was there besides lots of joy as children ran about? Pleasure in watching them grow and develop? Sharing around a crowded table or in a circle in a front room? She didn't even have to close her eyes to imagine herself in a big living room made of logs, the windows overlooking a stream. It was winter. The stream was frozen and children skated on it. A baby cooed in its cradle. And Emmet played with a toddler. Her insides felt bitter at her foolish dreams.

"I would think that happiness, love, security, partnership are all things that don't require having children."

Madge's words were but meaningless letters of the alphabet. Louisa knew they held no answer for her. Emmet—if he ever thought of marrying again—wanted children. Lots of children.

Louisa sighed deeply. "I seem to have a natural aptitude for teaching, or so Adele tells me. I would go to Normal school if I had the money."

Madge didn't say anything. Louisa gave her time to digest the information, and when she still didn't venture an opinion, she turned to study her face. Madge wore a careful expression.

"What?" Louisa asked, knowing Madge wanted to say something.

"It's your life. And although I agree you would make a dandy teacher, I don't think you should choose to become one simply to avoid facing life."

Madge's evaluation of Louisa stung. "I am not trying to escape life. I have no intention of avoiding it. I spent enough years on the sidelines. But I think I would get a lot of satisfaction out of teaching children."

"I think what you mean is you would find it a substitute for having your own family."

Louisa shifted so she could lean very close to Madge. "I can never have my own family. You know that."

Madge stuck out her chin. Their faces almost touched. "No. You cannot have children. It isn't the same thing."

"I thought you might offer some words of comfort or wisdom. After all, you're the one who always knows how to solve a problem. Instead you mock me."

Madge chuckled. "I gave you answers. You just aren't willing to consider them." She tucked her hand around Louisa's elbow. "Now forget about it and come see what I've done in the house."

Louisa allowed Madge to drag her along. By the time they reached the kitchen her anger had evaporated. After all, she could hardly blame Madge for not understanding what it meant to never be able to have children. And despite Madge's argument that love would be enough, Louisa would never force a man she loved to make such a choice.

Madge pointed out the new curtains she'd made. "From an old dress Judd's mother gave me." Louisa noticed the vase full of wild buffalo beans and pussy willows.

"Now sit and we'll have lemonade."

Boots thudded on the step.

"Oh, good. Judd is going to join us." Madge looked toward the door, a look of such sweet expectation on her face that Louisa had to turn away. She would never be able to experience that emotion. *Lord God, help me be strong.*

"Hon, I brought company." Judd stepped into the room, Emmet at his heels.

Dismay jolted through Louisa. She half rose, intent on escape, but the men blocked the doorway.

Madge glanced at Louisa, silently signaling her to stay put.

Louisa sank back, her chest pressing toward her backbone.

Emmet saw her. Nodded a greeting. Hung his hat beside Judd's as Judd explained he and Emmet were taking down an abandoned building and using it to build a bigger chicken house. "The way my wife successfully raises chickens, the little shed she's been using is not going to be good enough." He pulled Madge close and kissed her nose.

Louisa couldn't tear her gaze from Emmet's. His look went on and on, silently laying claim to her thoughts even as she scrambled to put up barriers, to block the emotions that she feared tumbled from her eyes.

Then Judd pulled out a chair and indicated Emmet should sit.

Louisa sucked in air and shifted her gaze to the center of the table, where the vase of flowers stood on a lacy doily.

Conversation winged back and forth past Louisa. She nodded, smiled and made an occasional comment, but it wasn't until Judd and Emmet left to return to their work, until Louisa said goodbye to Madge and hastened homeward, that she could breathe without her eyes stinging. *Oh, God, help me.*

He wouldn't be here much longer. Somehow the idea offered no comfort, only an ache drawn out down a long empty road. She must make plans. Find escape from her memories. More and more she considered the possibility of attending Normal school. If only she had the finances.

Emmet did his best to be out of the way when Louisa came to the house. He sensed she didn't welcome his presence and the knowledge sliced through him, even as he assured himself it suited him. He didn't want to feel anything for her except appreciation for her work with Ellie.

Tomorrow he was scheduled to take Ellie to the doctor to see if her body cast could come off.

"I'm going to run and run and run as soon as it's off," Ellie said.

"You might have to take it easy for a little while and be content to walk."

"Nope. I'm gonna run."

Emmet knew there was a chance her leg wouldn't be better. She might have to wear the body cast longer. But he didn't have the heart to tell her so. If only he could make things work out the way Ellie wanted. He waited until Ellie fell asleep.

"Auntie May, I'm going out for a while." Waiting for tomorrow and the verdict filled his brain with sharp fragments of something.

He turned his steps down a familiar road. The one that led to Judd's. And past that, to the Morgan farm.

But he wouldn't stop at either place. He just needed to walk off his tension.

He passed the Kirk farm. Saw Madge in the garden. She glanced up and waved. He waved back and continued on his way.

Despite his resolve, his steps slowed as he approached the turnoff to the Morgan home. He'd have a quick glance and see if anyone was outside. Yes—a figure in the garden. Louisa. He would recognize her anywhere. Doing what she enjoyed. He grinned as he remembered her saying that's what she did for fun.

She straightened—her back to him—and stretched, then returned to her task.

It would be unseemly to pass without speaking to her. He allowed himself the convenient excuse as he headed her direction.

She heard his approach and turned. A flash of welcome lit her eyes, then she shuttered it.

But it was enough to make him feel welcomed, if only temporarily. It was enough that he knew he was right in coming here.

She waited for him to cross the last three feet. "I suppose you're excited about Ellie getting her cast off."

"Nervous, if you want the truth."

"Really? Why?"

"She's so eager. How will she deal with it if the doctor says she must wear it another month?"

"That's possible? I didn't know."

They perched on two of the five rocks at the end of the garden. Louisa smiled. "Not comfortable chairs, but Father put them here shortly after we moved. He said a person needed to take a break once in a while, but he didn't think we should get too comfortable." She studied him. "I know it sounds trite to say God is in control. But He is." She looked so serene. So positive.

"Aren't there times when you find that hard to believe?"

Something dark flickered through her eyes, and she nodded. "I'm grateful He doesn't change like we do. He's the same yesterday, today and forever."

He clung to the words and held her gaze. "Thank you."

Her smile flashed. "I only repeated God's word."

"I know, but I needed the reminder. Would you—" He hesitated. Would she think his request odd? Or too personal? "Would you pray with me?"

"Of course." She reached for his hands, stopped, but before she could pull them back to her lap, he took them and bowed his head. "God, I ask You to make things go well for Ellie tomorrow. Help me trust You more." It wasn't elegant, but he spoke what he meant. He continued to hold her hands, enjoying the strength and oneness the contact provided.

"Lord," she whispered. "I ask the same thing. Help Ellie's leg be healed. Help me trust You more."

He raised his head. Watched her slowly lift her face to him. Their gazes locked, searched—hers a little guarded, his anxious. Dare he dream that somewhere inside her heart lurked a tenderness toward him?

He would not dream such dreams. Allow such hopes. But he couldn't help himself. So he sat smiling at her, their hands still clasped.

"Would you come with us tomorrow?"

She blinked, sat up straighter, pulled her hands to her lap. "I don't know."

"Ellie would like it." He cracked a door inside him ajar and allowed a deep-throated admission out. "I'd appreciate it."

"Okay." She nodded slowly.

Her agreement eased his tension. He could face whatever happened with her at his side, knowing her faith would never waver. More than that, he was certain she shared his concerns, his—

He could not allow himself to take the thought to a conclusion. He would not think about what it would be like to have someone to share the ups and downs of every day.

"I'll see you tomorrow."

Doc came to the waiting room. When he saw Louisa he looked startled, then gave a flash of a smile before he turned to Ellie. "Well, young lady, I suppose you'd like to keep that cast a little longer."

"No, I don't. I want to get rid of it."

He chuckled. "Then let's see what we can do. We'll take some pictures of your leg. As soon as the films are developed, we'll know if the cast comes off or not. Emmet and Louisa, you can wait here." He called his nurse and they wheeled Ellie to the X-ray room.

Emmet leaned over his knees, his heels bouncing up and down in a frantic rhythm.

Louisa realized how nervous he was about Ellie. She could offer him no assurances about the leg. "She's in good hands. Doc has cared for me a number of times, and he is the most gentle, kind person one could ask for."

Emmet nodded. "I hope she's not scared in there."

Louisa touched his shoulder and got his attention. "We are talking about your daughter, aren't we? Ellie, the girl who climbs trees, rides horses and confronts challenges with a jutted chin?"

His gaze claimed hers. He read her encouragement, her comfort and perhaps a whole lot more that she didn't intend he should see. Then he chuckled. "Right."

She retreated back into the protection of her guarded heart.

He blew out a long breath. "It's me who's worried. What if her leg isn't better?"

"Then you take her back to Auntie May's house and continue to care for her as you have."

"It's that simple, isn't it?" He didn't seem relieved.

She touched his arm, feeling his tension beneath her fingers. "I'm not saying it's simple, only that if it's necessary you will do it. You will always do what is best for her."

He nodded and settled back, as if he had found his direction on a compass. "You're right."

Over the waiting room door hung a big clock that ticked the minutes off in merciless reluctance.

Emmet sprang to his feet and strode over to look down the hall. "What's taking so long?"

She wished she had words of comfort, but it did seem Ellie had been gone a long time. She hurried to Emmet's side to stare down the hallway.

He reached for her hand and squeezed. She squeezed back, as tense as he. What if something was wrong?

Without giving herself a chance to consider her actions, she pressed her shoulder to his, finding and receiving comfort from the touch.

A door opened. The nurse wheeled Ellie toward them.

Emmet rushed to Ellie's side.

Louisa wisely went to Ellie's other side. She must remember who she was and her role here, and not cling to Emmet so blatantly.

"What did the doctor say?" Emmet demanded of the nurse.

"He's reading the X-rays right now. He'll be with you soon."

"I'm tired of waiting," Ellie whined.

Louisa took Ellie's hand on her side, Emmet the hand on his side, and they leaned over the child.

"We'll know soon." Louisa tried to sound cheerful, but she was as anxious as the other two. She thought her muscles would snap like an overstretched rubber band by the time Doc strode back into the room.

"Good news."

The air whooshed from three sets of lungs.

"Her leg looks fine. However, she will have to be careful for a while. Now let's get that cast off and get her on crutches. She'll have to use them until I say otherwise. I'll have my nurse instruct her."

Emmet grabbed two hands—Louisa's and Ellie's—and raised them in a victory salute, then shook the doctor's hand.

Louisa couldn't stop smiling. Neither, she guessed, could Emmet and Ellie. It was good to celebrate such a wonderful occasion with them.

Doc and his nurse took them to a little room where they endured the nerve-racking ordeal of watching the cast being cut away.

When it was off, Ellie sat up for the first time in weeks. She swayed a little.

"Take your time," Doc advised.

But Ellie wasn't about to waste a minute of her first hours of being free. She made to spring from the bed, but Doc caught her.

"You have to use crutches for now."

The nurse helped her to the floor and showed her how to use the crutches. Ellie balanced on her crutches, her eyes bright.

"You are to use these at all times, young lady," the doctor warned. He stood to speak to Emmet. "She'll need time to build up the muscles to support that bone."

"She'll be careful." Emmet meant he'd make sure she was.

Louisa couldn't stop smiling. She'd never seen Ellie standing. Never seen her without the bulky cast. Something inside Louisa glowed with an emotion she wouldn't admit to. She looked at the thick mane of dark blond hair and thought how she'd like to brush it and fasten it back with a bow.

A troubling thought pushed at her joy, but she refused to give it any attention. Today was a day for celebrating.

Emmet guarded Ellie as she swung from the room. "Slow down."

Ellie sighed and rolled her eyes, which brought a tickle of laughter to Louisa's throat.

Emmet glowered at them both. "It's my job to take care of you."

"I'm being careful." Ellie slowed down measurably. "Can we go to the store and get a piece of candy? I want to go inside and pick my own."

"Seems reasonable." Emmet helped Ellie into the truck, held the door for Louisa then ran around and climbed in behind the wheel.

Louisa allowed her happiness at sharing this moment with them to balloon until it obliterated every other thought. This was a day to remember only with joy.

She and Emmet stayed on each side of Ellie as she negotiated the steps into the store. Joanie stood behind the counter.

"Hello, Louisa. Hi, Emmet. Guess you don't remember me?"

Emmet spared her a quick smile. "Last time I saw you, you had pigtails and a muddy face."

Joanie wrinkled her nose. "I was a tomboy, wasn't I? This is your little girl. I heard about her."

"Ellie, this is Miss Sharp."

Joanie snorted. "It's just plain Joanie. Nice to see you out of your cast, Ellie. How about a candy stick to celebrate? A treat."

"Thank you." Ellie hobbled to the display of candy.

Emmet angled against the counter, standing close to his daughter to guard her. Joanie stood by Louisa. "Tell Madge to come and see me. I've got some good news."

"Conrad has asked you to marry him? Finally?"

Joanie shook her head. "Not so far. He's a stubborn, stubborn man. I hope he doesn't expect me to wait forever. One of these days I'm going to find me someone else." She eyed Emmet up and down. "You looking for a wife, Emmet?"

Poor Emmet. He glanced toward the door. Louisa figured the only thing that kept him from running was his concern for Ellie.

Louisa chuckled. "She's teasing. She's only interested in one man. Conrad Burns. Only, his parents are both dead, and he's raising four younger siblings."

Joanie snorted. "You think he'd be glad of my help, but no. The man says he doesn't want to burden me with his responsibilities." She huffed around the counter. "No, sir. He'd far rather burden me with loneliness and impatience." She bent her head so low, it almost touched Ellie's. "This is a new flavor—green apple. I like it. Want to try it?" She held it up and popped it in when Ellie opened her mouth. "Good, isn't it?"

Ellie's eyes widened, and she nodded. "Can I have a licorice too?" She gave her father an appealing look. When he nodded, Joanie put one in a paper bag and handed it to Ellie.

A few minutes later they departed.

"I don't want to go home," Ellie said, craning her head from side to side to see everything. "Can we go by the school and pick up Leila?" School was almost over for the day.

Emmet hesitated. "I don't want you overdoing it."

"Please, Daddy, please."

Louisa turned to look out the side window to hide her amusement.

"Can we take her on a picnic? It would be so much fun to celebrate. After all, this is a very special occasion for me." Ellie's voice grew shrill with excitement.

Emmet groaned. "I don't suppose I could say no?"

Ellie quieted. "I suppose you could, but do you think it's necessary?"

Louisa grinned at Emmet across the child's blond head.

He shook his head in mock resignation, but his eyes glowed with joy. "Only if Louisa will join us."

"I'd love to." How could she refuse a part in this joy? "If we go by the farm I'll prepare food." There was bread enough for sandwiches, and no doubt Sally would have made more cookies. Simple but adequate. After all, it wasn't the food that was important, it was sharing this special occasion.

So they went to the school, where Ellie insisted on getting out and standing by the car. Several children raced by her and waved, then Miss Ross spotted them and hurried over. "You are back on your feet. What good news. This means—"

Leila saw Ellie and screeched, "You're all better!" She danced around Ellie, sending them both into a fit of giggles.

Adele stepped back. "You have two very happy little girls. Leila hasn't stopped talking all day about the possibility of Ellie getting her cast off." She beamed at both of them, then turned to Louisa. "Come by in the next day or two."

Louisa's balloon deflated. She had been pushing away what this meant…she'd no longer need to tutor Ellie. The child could go to school. Emmet and Ellie would likely return to their ranch. Her temporary happiness had come to an end. Now was the time she had dreaded. Had tried to prepare for. Somehow she would hold her head high and make it through. If only she hadn't agreed to accompany them on the picnic. But she had, and she wouldn't disappoint Ellie by retracting her promise.

Leila squeezed in beside Ellie in the truck and hugged her. "Now we can make a playhouse in the bushes like we talked about."

Louisa wanted to warn Leila that her days of enjoying Ellie's company would soon end, when Emmet took his daughter back to the ranch. However, the facts would have to be faced soon enough. In the meantime, let the girls enjoy each other.

The pair chattered away as they drove to the orphanage and received permission to take Leila for a few hours. Then they swung by the Morgan place so Louisa could pack a lunch.

Emmet and the girls waited outside so they could play with Mouse.

Mother was away visiting a friend, but Sally was home and helped Louisa prepare the food.

"It's nice to see Ellie up and about," Sally said. "How do you feel about it?"

"It's a joyous occasion. That's why we're celebrating with a picnic."

Sally nudged her, forcing her to meet her look. "I asked how you feel."

She met her sister's eyes without flinching. "Why, I'm happy, of course."

"You will be out of a job. More important, you will no longer have an excuse to see Emmet. Or Ellie, for that matter."

Louisa blinked away the sting in her eyes. "I've known from the beginning it was temporary."

"Does it have to be?" Although Sally's voice was soft, it was also prodding.

"You know it does." She stubbornly concentrated on packing cookies into a basket.

"Oh, Louisa. Stop running away."

"I have no intention of running anywhere."

"Except from your heart."

Let Sally think love could be enough. Let her believe other things didn't matter. May she never experience the pain of knowing otherwise. "I will celebrate the good news with Emmet and the girls. Then I will say goodbye as I planned." She grabbed the basket and marched for the door.

Sally called after her. "I will pray you get over your stubborn denial."

Louisa ignored her words and handed the basket to Emmet, who stowed it in the back and called the girls to climb in the truck. They bounced forward on the edge of the seat.

"Where are we going?" Leila demanded.

"A long, long ways," Ellie said. "I don't want this day to ever end."

Louisa tried to keep her attention on the familiar scene out the front window, but when Emmet groaned, she couldn't stop herself from turning toward him. His gaze caught hers and held it in a warm smile.

"I think we'll stay close to home. Don't you think that's wise, Louisa?"

Two little girls turned to her, silently imploring. She forced herself to turn from Emmet's gaze and consider the children. "I think Ellie should take it easy for a day or two. Wouldn't you agree?"

Ellie looked ready to deny the need, but Leila nodded. "I wouldn't want anything to happen to her. We'll be happy anywhere." She turned to Ellie and took her hand. "Won't we?"

Ellie studied the younger girl, and her expression softened. "Uh-huh."

Startled by how connected the two seemed, Louisa shifted her attention to Emmet. Was he aware of how close the girls had grown? From the speculative way he considered them, she thought he was starting to notice. She turned away. How could any of them escape this situation without pain? She could tolerate it, but the girls? It didn't seem fair. But hadn't she learned life wasn't always fair, if one judged it from an earthly view? She could only pray they would all be better and stronger for the experience.

In the meantime, she meant to do everything in her power to help the girls have an afternoon they would not forget.

"There." She pointed toward a little grove of trees. "That's a nice place for a picnic."

Emmet pulled to the side of the road and came around to help Louisa out. Her heart burst with longing as he took her hand and waited for her to gain her feet. Thankfully he didn't seem inclined to prolong the moment, and turned to lift Leila down then edged Ellie out. But he kept her in his arms.

"I think I better carry you across the field."

"I'll take her crutches." Leila gladly carried the burden.

Louisa grabbed the picnic basket and followed them. Ellie proudly clung to her father, while Leila bounced happily at his side.

"Stop. Shh." Emmet halted and held his finger to his lips.

"What?" Ellie whispered.

"A baby antelope. See it?" He pointed.

Louisa followed the direction he indicated and saw nothing but yellowed grass and gray rocks, then she noticed the shape of a tawny-colored rock. A little animal no bigger than a jackrabbit curled into a ball.

"Where? I can't see it." Leila wavered on tiptoes.

"You aren't tall enough." Emmet scooped her up in his free arm. Two little heads pressed to each side of Emmet's face.

At the sight, Louisa's mouth went dry as the grass at her feet. He deserved to have his arms…his home… his heart full of children.

Leila saw the baby antelope at last. "Ohh. Can we touch it?"

"Best we leave it be."

"But he's all alone. I bet he's afraid."

Louisa heard a note of longing that ached clear through her. This child knew about being alone.

Emmet's arms tightened around both girls, and she guessed he'd felt the same tug of loneliness in Leila's words. "The mommy will come back and get him after she's found her lunch."

Leila touched his cheek and turned his face so she could stare into his eyes. "You sure?"

He grew very sober. "I promise."

The two considered each other for several seconds. Then Emmet drew in a shuddering breath.

Louisa couldn't begin to understand what he felt. Disappointment that he had only one child when he ached for more? Pain that Leila had lost her family? She wasn't sure she even wanted to know, but she did want to help him and moved to his side. "Who's hungry?"

"I am," three voices chorused.

Leila did not ask to be put down, nor did Emmet make any indication he wanted to release her, so Louisa scooped up the crutches and followed them to the trees. They sat on the patch of green grass in the shade. Leila scampered to Ellie's side, and they were soon engaged in play that involved creating a family and a home from twigs and leaves.

Emmet kept his gaze on the distant horizon. Louisa wondered what he thought but was content to give her attention to the girls. She passed around the sandwiches and settled back with a sigh of contentment. Yet this would soon be over. She would not be spending quiet afternoons with Emmet and the girls. But for today, for this moment, she would not let the future steal from her joy.

Emmet chewed thoughtfully. "Good sandwiches. Thanks."

She chuckled. "They're only peanut butter and syrup."

His grin teased. "Maybe so, but the situation makes them special."

She nodded. "It's so good to see Ellie up and about."

"It's a huge weight off my shoulders, I can tell you." He grew somber as he watched the girls, and again she wondered what he thought. She squelched her curiosity. Before long, before she was ready to accept it, she would no longer be aware of his shifting expressions, have cause to wonder about his reactions or be aware of him watching her as he was now. She tried to keep her attention on rearranging the contents of the picnic basket, but forbidden, her gaze went to his. And her heart stalled at the insistent way he studied her.

"Louisa—"

Whatever he'd meant to say was cut off by Ellie's shriek. "Ants! Everywhere!" She flapped her hands over her legs and chest.

Leila sobbed quietly and stared at them crawling up her legs.

Emmet bolted to his feet, grabbed both girls and swiped his hands over their bodies until he was certain all the ants were gone. "You were sitting practically on top of an anthill. Why didn't I notice? You could have been bitten." He pressed both girls to his sides and hugged them.

Louisa wasn't sure who was more upset—the girls or Emmet. He blamed himself for being careless. She gathered up the rest of the picnic. "Seems you can't have a picnic without uninvited guests showing up."

Leila giggled. "Ants like picnics too."

Ellie sniffled, then seeing Leila's reaction, she straightened. "I'd say they do. Here's your old picnic." She tossed a bread crust at the ants. The girls laughed as ants clamored over it.

Emmet straightened. Seeing the harshness in his expression, Louisa touched his arm. "No harm done."

"I should have been watching more carefully." He scooped up both girls. "Let's get out of here." He glanced over his shoulder. "Can you manage?"

She nodded. Yes, she would manage. Somehow.

Ellie glanced back over her dad's shoulder. "I thought there were cookies."

Emmet chuckled. "I guess even ants can't dim your appetite."

"Nope."

Louisa's tension released. "We'll share them in the truck."

They ate cookies then drove back toward the Morgan place. Emmet stopped at the house. Louisa hopped out before he could climb from the truck and open the door. She hugged each of the little girls. Let her glance breeze by Emmet without meeting his eyes, then headed for the house.

"See you tomorrow." Emmet stood with one foot on the ground, the other still in the truck.

"Yes." Would she be saying her final goodbye then?

Her legs feeling much too long and decidedly wooden, she walked calmly indoors. Sally must have understood how fragile Louisa felt, for she squeezed her shoulder but kept her comments to herself. Somehow she made it through supper, helped with the dishes, carried water to the garden—said normal things, did normal things. But inside she was as lifeless as last year's brown, crackly grass.

She finally retreated to bed. Opened her Bible and read a few verses, as she had promised Father she would do. But nothing reached her soul. She had fallen in love with a man against her better judgment—and his little girl.

She must hold herself together until it was over.

The morning sun seemed weak. Or was it too bright? Louisa wanted to pull the covers over her head and ignore it. Ignore life. But she knew if she didn't show up at the breakfast table Mother would fret. *Are you sick? Should I call the doctor? I was afraid this would happen. I told you not to try and work.*

And if she let any of her emotions show, Sally would comment. *I told you it was impossible to lock your feelings up. Why don't you tell him how you feel? Once he knows the truth he won't care. Love is more than enough.* Sally was such a romantic.

So she rose, dressed, put on her happy face and went downstairs. Her smile was still firmly in place when she drove up to the Hamilton house. It faltered only slightly when she entered the house and heard voices in the kitchen.

"Come join us," Auntie May called.

Louisa trudged across the crowded living room to the kitchen. The three of them sat around the table. As usual, cats sat on the unoccupied chairs and crowded around Louisa's ankles.

"No more eating in bed," Ellie crowed.

"Coffee?" Auntie May asked.

Louisa politely refused.

"Have a chair." Emmet shooed a cat off the chair next to him and swept aside the hairs.

Louisa sat. How was she to say goodbye when everything in her called to say "I want to stay"?

Ellie rambled on about Leila and the games they could play now that she wasn't in a cast. Auntie May scolded a couple of cats for being too inquisitive about what was on the table. More than once, Louisa had wondered if she let them eat off the table like guests when she was alone. The clock over the table ticked loudly. Across the street a child called goodbye as he headed off to school.

Emmet looked at the clock. "I suppose it's time to start lessons."

"Aw. Do I have to?"

Louisa sucked in air. Now was the time. "I won't be tutoring you anymore, now that you can go to school."

Her announcement landed with a plop and lay silent and quivering as everyone stared at her.

Ellie let out a wail that sent half the cats scurrying into the other room. "I don't want to go to school. I want you to teach me."

Louisa widened her eyes to keep back the tears. "I'm going to miss teaching you." She reached for Ellie, wanting to hug and console her.

Ellie pushed her away. "You don't care about me. You were just being nice because you had to be."

"No, Ellie. That isn't true. You know it isn't."

"I hate you." Ellie struggled to her feet. Pushed away her father's helping hand. She staggered as one crutch went too wide.

Emmet scrambled to her side. "Take it easy, Button."

She shrugged away from him, made it to her room and slammed the door.

Incredible silence followed her departure, the only sound her muffled sobs.

Louisa pushed to her feet, backed from the room. "I'm sorry. So sorry." Then she fled.

Where could she hide? Where could she escape her feelings? She should find comfort in knowing that God was with her in this private torture. She had no choice but to seek His consolation.

She walked until she reached a dry, dusty slough. The willows surrounding it were verdant with new growth, and she turned aside into their shelter. She found a spot where the grass was flattened and sank down, buried her head in her hands and wept. *Oh, God, help me through this.*

Her tears were enough to water the drought-stricken land, but eventually they ended, leaving her drained but ready to march forward. Somehow she would get through this, and she would do so with grace and dignity because she trusted God to provide both.

Chapter Twelve

The next day, Emmet took Ellie to school, making sure Adele understood she was not to be too active.

"I'll keep her and Leila inside where they can play quietly."

He ached to stay. Ellie was his responsibility. It was hard to leave her in someone else's care. But he had no choice.

Just as he had no choice but to let Louisa go. She deserved more than a broken-down man with a seven-year-old child.

He strode out of town, the opposite direction he normally took. His steps pounded the truth from him. It wasn't what she deserved—although she surely deserved more than he had to offer—that made him let her walk away. Auntie May had lots to say about that. *Your child needs a mother. You need a wife. You can't pretend you're dead. You're a young man yet. What about your dream for a large family? Think what beautiful children Louisa would give you.*

He growled as he thought of the beautiful children.

Dare he allow himself to love again? Was it worth the risk?

He couldn't answer and scuffled his way back home, where he set about fixing the back fence. A job he shouldn't have neglected so long.

Auntie May came out at noon. "Lunch is ready."

He went indoors and sat at the table.

She eyed him as he ate. "Emmet—"

"No more. You've said all I care to hear. We'll be heading home any day now." Just as soon as the doctor gave his final okay on Ellie's leg. "I'm just waiting for her to manage without crutches."

In the meantime, he would make sure Auntie May's place was in good shape. He cleaned out the cellar. He organized the storage shed in the back corner. He pruned trees. He found some discarded cans of paint in the cellar, mixed them together to produce a puce green and painted the front door, the outside window trim and the back gate.

Ellie looked at it and gagged.

"Beggars can't be choosers," he grumbled, but he didn't know who was begging. Or for what.

Several days passed. Ellie sat one evening, her head hanging almost to her chest. He studied her with a watchful eye. Had she done too much? Had he neglected her again? So buried in his own misery and regrets that he didn't notice his own child's needs? Some father he was. He'd make a mighty poor husband, as he'd already proved. "What's ailing you?"

"I miss Louisa." Deep sigh. So dramatic. "Do you suppose she's mad at me 'cause of the mean things I said?"

"I don't know. A person should learn to guard their tongue."

Auntie May came into the room in time to hear Ellie's question and Emmet's reply. "Child, you could say you're sorry. Louisa doesn't strike me as the kind of person who would refuse to forgive."

Ellie perked up. "I will. Daddy, can you take me to see her?"

"Can't. I'm busy."

Auntie May snorted. "You're going to busy yourself right out of a life, if you aren't careful."

He shrugged.

Ellie knelt before him. "Please, Daddy. Please. I have to tell Louisa I don't hate her."

Emmet sighed. "You can be very persistent."

"It's important," she said with the dignity of being right. "Come on. Let's go."

"Now?" He kind of hoped he could put it off until she forgot.

"No time like the present," Auntie May said.

Yeah. Thanks, Auntie May. You're a great help. "Fine. Get your jacket."

"Daddy, it's warm out."

"Jacket or we don't go. You never know when it might rain." He didn't miss the way Ellie rolled her eyes, but he chose to ignore it.

They took the vehicle. No way could Ellie hobble that far. At least he was a good enough father to realize that. He kept his thoughts in negative territory in the hopes it would provide him an insurmountable barrier.

Ellie bounced forward on the seat as they turned toward the Morgan house.

"Their car is gone." His relief was bitter with regret. "I guess they're not home." But no. Louisa stood in the garden watching their approach. He told himself he wished she was gone. But his heart pressed against his ribs, urging him to hurry forward.

"I see her." Ellie had the door half-open.

He grabbed her arm. "Wait until I stop. And use your crutches."

Mouse saw the unfamiliar girl and bounced on her four paws, barking.

"Mouse, cease and desist."

Ellie giggled as the dog obeyed the order. It even brought a reluctant smile to Emmet's lips. Trust Louisa to teach her dog fancy words.

Louisa dusted her hands and brushed her skirt before she crossed to the edge of the garden. She looked as if she wanted to turn into a bird and fly away. He could hardly blame her.

Did she still sing anyway?

Ellie didn't stop until she stood facing Louisa. "I'm sorry. I didn't mean those awful words. I don't hate you."

Louisa pulled the child into her arms. "I know that. I forgave you as soon as you said it." She held Ellie. And if Emmet didn't miss his guess, those were tears glistening on her lashes. "I care about you. Very much. Never forget it."

Ellie nodded, her face awash. "I don't want you to leave."

"I'm here, aren't I? Any time you want to see me, I'm here." She lifted her face to the sky, seemingly unmindful of the tears dripping from her jaw. She swallowed hard. "Ellie, I love you. I will never forget you."

They clung to each other for another moment, and Emmet's eyes glassed with wetness. Not tears, he informed himself. Not tears. He wouldn't get emotional about this. But she loved his child. It felt like a kiss from heaven.

Ellie broke away. "Is this your dog? I saw her when we went on the picnic."

"She is. This is Mouse. Mouse, meet Ellie." Mouse held up a paw for Ellie to shake, bringing a burst of giggles from her.

"I've never seen your place before, except the front of the house."

"Would you like to look around?"

"Yes, please."

Louisa looked at Emmet for his approval. He nodded.

They had a long, detailed look at the garden. Stopped to inspect Sally's chickens behind the wire fence. Moseyed toward the barn. Inspected the empty stalls. Talked about the mice that made homes overhead. Ventured to the house, where Ellie had to hear stories about every room, every piece of furniture on the ground floor. Then, leaving Emmet in the kitchen, they climbed the steps. He supposed she received the same detailed information of the rooms up there.

Mouse sat watching him. Emmet scowled at the dog. "Why aren't you with your mistress?"

Mouse seemed to grin, Emmet thought, then snorted at his foolishness. *Well,* he excused himself, *what would you call it when the dog hung out his tongue and pulled his mouth back like a happy clown?* "Of course you're happy. You get to live with Louisa."

He jerked from his chair and stared out the window.

Finally the truth could not be denied. He wanted to share his life with Louisa. She cared for his child. No doubt of that. Did she have similar feelings for Ellie's father?

Dare he ask? Dare he risk letting himself love again?

He heard Auntie May's mocking voice. *Love isn't a risk. Love is an opportunity.*

Ellie and Louisa descended the stairs. He rushed forward, ready to catch Ellie should she stumble, but she had grown very agile on her crutches.

Ellie held out a sheet of paper. "Louisa gave me this."

It was a pencil sketch—a likeness of Ellie. "It's very nice."

"I'm going to keep it forever."

"We need to go now."

Ellie nodded. She and Louisa exchanged some secret understanding. "Thank you."

Louisa walked them to the vehicle. He paused with his hand on the door. "Thank you for easing her mind."

"My pleasure."

He searched her gaze. Was there a flicker of affection in those brown depths? He considered suggesting an outing. But he stalled. Couldn't find the words.

"Thanks again." As they drove away, he mentally kicked himself.

Later, he tucked Ellie into bed. "You're much happier now. I'm glad."

"Did you hear? Louisa said she loved me. Did my mommy love me?"

"Of course she did."

"I can't remember her."

"You weren't very old when she died."

"Daddy, why don't you marry Louisa? She'd make a good mommy. And she'd be nice to you."

Emmet chuckled. "You have it all figured out, don't you?"

"Yup." She rolled over, cuddling her doll in her arms. "You'll ask her, won't you?" Little cupid might be tired, but not too tired to press her point.

"I'll take it under consideration."

Auntie May sat in her rocker in the kitchen. How much had she heard? He wasn't going to ask. Nor was he going to give her a chance to say anything. "I'll be out for a little while." With no destination in mind, he hurried down the back lane and across the dusty prairie. But it didn't take long to realize he couldn't outrun his thoughts. For the first time in three years, he allowed himself to think of sharing his life with someone other than Ellie. Sharing with an equal, a woman, someone to love.

The idea excited him.

The idea scared him.

It hurt to love. No, it hurt to lose, and loving came with that built-in risk.

He sucked in air—dry, dusty. Just as his life would be if he continued alone. Without Louisa.

He made up his mind. He would speak to her. Ask if she had a little tenderness in her heart for him. Enough to consider marrying him.

It took him three days to get his courage in place.

Three days of facing his inner demons. Three days

of dark looks from Auntie May. Three days of persistent prodding from Ellie.

Finally he could take the tension no longer and headed to the Morgan place. He hoped they'd all be away. He hoped they'd all be home. No. He only wanted Louisa to be there. He hoped he would be able to speak when he saw her.

He turned into the laneway. Three women in the garden turned to face him. Great. All of them. He didn't want to see anyone but Louisa.

They seemed to hold a brisk discussion, then Louisa crossed toward him. "Hi," she murmured when she was five feet away.

"Hi." That was it. He could think of nothing more. Not one word.

"Is Ellie okay?"

"Yup." Absolutely brilliant.

"Is she liking school?"

"Think so."

Louisa nodded encouragingly. No doubt wondering why he had driven all this way to say four words.

He looked away. Perhaps he could think more clearly if he studied the windows on the house. Two beats. Nothing. Three tea towels whipped about on the line. He stared at them. His thoughts flapped about as uselessly. Time to act. "Louisa, would you like to come for a drive?"

"Now?"

Of course she was confused. Suddenly he knew what he wanted to do, where he wanted to take her. "Want to see if water is running over the dam?" The railway had a dam to the north to catch and hold water for the water tower. In good years, it ran over the spillway each spring.

Her eyes sparked with interest. "Okay." She called over her shoulder, informing her mother and Sally of her plans.

He jumped from the truck and escorted her around to the passenger door, made sure she was safely seated before he clamored back behind the wheel.

"When was the last time you saw the dam?" he asked.

"A couple of years ago. The last time I saw it overflowing was three years ago."

They turned off the road on a sandy trail. The dam was five miles from the road. The trail was rough, at places only two parallel tracks running through the grass. "Doesn't look like it's used very often. It used to be a favorite picnic spot when I was a kid."

"I keep forgetting you grew up here."

"Look. Crocuses." He pulled to a halt and looked at the field dotted with them. The flowers had faded on many, leaving only feathery plumes that caught the sun in silvery threads. But there was still a scattering of purple flowers. "It must have been a purple carpet a few weeks ago."

"I wish I'd brought paper and pencil. Can I get out and look at them?"

"Certainly." He pushed his door open, intent on helping her, but she was already out of the truck and running across the field. She paused often to bend and examine a plant.

He stood at the verge of the field and watched. She was so full of life.

She straightened, grew very still. Signaled him to be quiet then pointed. He followed the direction she indicated and spotted a burrowing owl, standing on spindly legs beside a hole in the ground, watching with big-eyed caution and curiosity.

Louisa backed up slowly, quietly until she reached Emmet's side. "I don't want to disturb her. She probably has babies."

"Let's go then." He reached for her hand. Changed his mind. He would wait until he spoke to her before he could feel free to touch her.

They arrived at the dam a few minutes later.

"The water is very low." She sounded so regretful, he wanted to paint clouds in the sky then pull them down and empty them in the dam.

They got out and walked around.

"We used to row a raft across here." Now it was dry, hard clumps of clay. Very real evidence of the drought. As if he needed anything to prove it. The drifting soil, the parched grass were sufficient. "Come on. Let's go to the top of the dam." A road ran along the top, but they walked.

She breathed deeply. "I love the view from here. It's like you can see forever. Funny how everything looks different when you can see it like this. The colors fade to pastels, the shapes soften. Nothing looks as bad as it does close up."

"I guess that's so." He indicated they should sit. It was a perfect place to voice his question.

"A little like life, wouldn't you say?" She sat with her legs curled under her.

"Sorry?"

"Everything—even the bad stuff—will be part of the beautiful picture when viewed from a distance."

"It's nice to think that is so."

"I believe it. Because of Romans eight, twenty-eight. 'We know—'"

He joined her. "'—all things work together for good to them that love God.'"

She turned to him as he repeated the words and smiled. Her eyes darkened with what he knew to be joy.

Now was the perfect time. He shifted so they faced each other. He held her hands. Drew her close. Watched her expression grow cautiously interested. He admired the perfect shape of her face, her porcelain clear skin, her dark brown eyes framed with thick lashes. Her mouth, so pink and kissable.

He bent his head and caught her mouth with his own. Felt her quick indrawn breath, felt her kiss him back.

And then she jerked away, her head down, hiding her face.

"Louisa, I'm hoping you have some idea of my feelings for you so you won't be surprised when I ask, will you marry me?"

She jerked her hand away. Put both behind her back. Stared at him. Emotions chased across her face in rapid succession. He tried to catch and analyze all of them. Certainly surprise. He understood that. Then was it shock? Was his confession of having regard for her that unexpected? Then confusion mixed with...pain? Why pain? Had he properly voiced his feelings?

"Louisa, I love you. I want to marry you."

She bolted to her feet. "No. You can't love me. You

can't want to marry me. I can't marry you." She rushed down the trail toward the truck.

He hurried after her. "I can certainly love you. And marry you, if I so desire."

"I can't marry you." She flung the words over her shoulder. Reached the truck and planted herself on the seat, facing straight ahead, her expression stony.

He climbed in beside her. "Louisa."

She held out her hands. "Stop. Say no more. Take me home."

He didn't make any move to start the truck. "Can you at least tell me why?"

"I will never marry. You hear me? Never."

"But—"

"Please take me home."

He started the truck, drove toward town. But her rejection twisted and turned, flapping against his thoughts. "Never marry? I can't see it. You're a beautiful woman with a beautiful heart. Okay, I understand if you don't care for me." No, he didn't. What about all those fun times they'd shared? The special moments? The quick exchange of smiles at something Ellie said or did? Had he read more into it than he should have? He couldn't believe that.

She didn't reply.

"Louisa, what's wrong?" It had to be something more than lack of feelings for him. Didn't it? Besides— a fledgling hope—she hadn't said she didn't care for him. Only that she would never marry.

"There is nothing wrong." Her voice was so tight, he figured the words had to edge out sideways. "Except

I've decided I like teaching and want to make it a career."

He tried to shift his thoughts of her to include this bit of information. Yeah, she'd make a good teacher. But a better wife. However, her interests obviously didn't include marriage and motherhood. He had misinterpreted her kindness for something more than interest in teaching Ellie. He'd deceived himself in believing she had some regard for him. Worse even, he'd opened doors he'd vowed would remain forever locked.

He dropped her at the house, muttered goodbye and drove away. How many times did life have to up and smack him in the face for him to learn his lesson? Three years ago he vowed he would never love again. He should have listened to himself. Instead his pride had been kicked about. His love had been tossed aside as if worthless.

By the time he reached home, he had made up his mind. As soon as the doctor okayed it, he was returning to the ranch. And he would never open his heart again.

Now all he had to do was face Ellie and Auntie May.

The latter was easy. She took one look at his face. "Oh, you poor boy." She hugged him and patted his back.

He allowed it, but his hands hung at his sides. He couldn't remember how to lift them. How to hug her back.

He simply did not have the emotional strength to do so. Feared he would break in half if he let himself feel anything.

Explaining to Ellie was much harder.

"She said she didn't want to marry me."

"You must have asked her wrong."

His smile struggled to his lips. "I did the best I know how."

"Maybe if I ask her?"

"No, Button. She was pretty clear that she doesn't intend to marry. We have to accept it."

Ellie went to bed without being asked and turned on her side, refusing a good-night kiss when he went to tuck her in.

He couldn't blame her. He'd do the same if he could. Turn his back to life, curl up in a ball and refuse to let anyone near him.

But he didn't have that choice. He loved Ellie and would devote his life to making her happy and keeping her safe.

Chapter Thirteen

"Something is ailing you," Mother said, worried lines creasing her forehead. "I think it's time to call the doctor."

"No, Mother." Louisa forced firmness into her voice. "I have no need of a doctor. I'm just a little blue at not having my teaching job anymore."

"If you say so. But you don't look well. Does she, Sally?"

Sally shook her head. "You really don't. Are you sure you're okay?"

"I'm fine." The doctor could offer no cure for how she felt. "I think I'll go talk to Madge."

"You do that. But don't overexert yourself."

With Mother's needless warning echoing in her ears, she tromped across the dusty trail to Madge's place. She wasn't ill. She was heartbroken and she knew of no cure. By the time she reached the doorway, tears flooded her eyes.

Madge took one look at her and pulled her inside. "Louie, what's wrong?"

Louisa could only shake her head as tears spilled

down her cheeks. Madge opened her arms, and Louisa went gladly into her sister's embrace. She soaked the shoulder of Madge's dress before she cried herself out.

Madge led her to a chair and eased her down. "Now tell me what this is about."

She sniffed. "Emmet asked me to marry him."

Madge smiled. "That sounds like good news to me."

"It's not. I had to say no."

Madge puffed out her cheeks. "Does he love you?"

"He said he did. And he kissed me." She pressed her fingertips to her lips. "It was sweet." She might never have a husband or children, but she had the memory of that kiss and would cherish it to her dying day.

"Then you didn't have to say no."

Louisa scowled at Madge. "Why must you insist on ignoring the facts?"

Madge grinned, as if Louisa's protests were laughable. "You would be surprised at how strong love is. Tell him the truth. Give him a chance to say if he loves you enough to want you despite your barrenness. If he loves you half as much as I think, I doubt it will be a barrier."

Dare she allow herself this hope? "I don't know if I could stand it if he withdraws his offer of marriage." Better to hold on to that dream.

"Would you prefer to live the rest of your life wondering if you missed the chance to be his wife, and a mother to Ellie?"

Louisa tried to convince herself the memory of a kiss, an offer of marriage would be enough. She knew, however, that compared with the reality of true love, they were but paper flowers left too long in the sun and would soon fade and grow brittle. They were dead.

"I'll have to think and pray about it."

"I'll pray for you. We both know God is able to do abundantly more than we ask or think."

"Thank you for that reminder." Louisa clung to the words, hung on to hope as she returned home. Rather than go directly to the house, she stopped in the garden to pull weeds and chase away grasshoppers—a losing battle, but one none of them was willing to abandon.

Lord, God, my savior, friend and guide. I need You to show me what to do.

She plucked a grasshopper from a tiny lettuce plant, tossed the insect into a bucket and examined the plant. Damaged but still lots of growth potential. Her mouth watered at the promise of fresh salad in a few weeks. She went down the row, rescuing plant after plant, then started on the row of potatoes. Meager as it was, this garden was so important to their survival. The gardens they'd grown when Father was still alive, before the drought hit and the Depression made life so difficult, had been lush and bountiful. Yet she and the others were grateful for every bit of food they could eke from this land.

She sank to the ground and stared at the tiny plants as something scratched the back of her thoughts.

Would she destroy this garden because it didn't measure up to the ones before the drought?

No—never. She tended it all the more carefully.

And yet it was only a garden—a bit of soil, a few plants. Here today. Gone tomorrow.

Like the lilies of the field.

If God so clothe the grass, which is today in the field, and tomorrow is cast into the oven; how much more will He clothe you, O ye of little faith.

Lord, I know You love me and will take care of me. That isn't the question.

Was it possible to believe that God had sent Emmet here to love her? Or was she wishing for something that was simply not so? What if she told him her problem and he backed away in horror and disappointment? How would she survive such a reaction?

Yet, how could it be worse than her rejection of his love?

Give him a chance.

Lord, would it be wrong to give him a chance? If so, stop me. Otherwise, I am going to tell him.

Nothing happened except more grasshoppers invaded the garden. She picked them off and pulled more weeds.

She returned to the house. Her peace must have been evident because Mother's tension released when she saw her. "Your talk with Madge seems to have done you good."

"It did. So did having a soul-searching talk with God."

Mother hugged her. "He gives us peace that passeth understanding, but too often we don't take it."

"Mother, I want to thank you and Father for raising us to trust God."

Mother's eyes sheened with unshed tears. "I couldn't ask for anything better than my daughters walking with God."

Sally demanded details. "This has something to do with Emmet, doesn't it?"

Louisa told her what happened. "I'm going to tell him the truth tonight."

Sally clapped her hands. "About time."

Mother dabbed at her eyes. "I'm so happy for you. Since the doctor said you would never have children, I've prayed you would find a man who would love you for who you are. I worried you might shut your heart to love. This is an answer to prayer."

After supper, Louisa brushed her hair into submission and held it in place with matching silver combs. She wore her second-best dress and added a lace collar for good measure, but decided to forgo the gloves.

She stood before the door, ready to leave, then spun around to face Mother and Sally. "I'm scared."

They rushed forward, patting her arms and hugging her. "No need to be afraid. We'll be praying for you."

She tucked courage under her heart and pushed confidence into her limbs. She whispered a little prayer and drove toward Golden Prairie.

Her emotions bumped along in time to the rough road. Elation and hope, followed by fear and doubt. At times it seemed her heart stuck to her ribs, unable to function, then it took off at a gallop, leaving her breathless.

She laughed—a sound of self-mockery—as she drove down the street. Nothing like being one hundred percent sure of her actions. But she was going on faith here. Following what she believed was a God-given opportunity.

Pulling the truck to a halt before the Hamilton house,

she sat and stared. The formerly faded wooden door was now a sickly shade of green. Not particularly an improvement, to her way of thinking. What did she do next? She really ought to have planned this out better.

The door eased open.

She held her breath and tried to guess if Ellie, Auntie May or Emmet would step into the opening. Or perhaps it was only a neighbor leaving after a visit.

Emmet stepped into the light and stood watching her, the interior dark behind him, the setting sun highlighting his face. From this distance she couldn't see the color of his eyes, couldn't use that to judge his reaction to seeing her. But she took courage in the fact he didn't slam the door on her.

Instead he closed it with particular care and walked toward her. A crow flew overhead, cawing. Hopefully not a mocking warning of what was to come.

She pushed her fears and doubts aside as he reached the gate.

"Can I help you?" Guarded—but of course he would be.

"I'd like to talk, if you don't mind."

"You were pretty clear about what you felt."

"That's just it. I didn't tell you everything, and I think you deserve to hear it."

He studied her a moment, revealing nothing.

"Please let me explain."

"Very well. Do you want to come in?"

She glanced past him. "It's rather private."

"Ellie and Auntie May went to visit one of her old friends. Why don't we sit in the backyard?"

"Fine."

He held the door for her, and she stepped to the ground and followed him around to the back. He'd done a lot of work since she'd been here. "You fixed the fence and cleaned up some of the junk."

"I put a bench against the shade in the hopes that Auntie May would use it once in a while."

They both laughed somewhat nervously.

She sat on the bench at his invitation and waited, hoping he would sit too. But he stood, one boot resting on a bucket Auntie May had filled with dirt and planted with beans. And he waited. She felt his impatience even though he didn't indicate it, either by speech or restless movement.

"I'm not sure where to begin." She had rehearsed what she would say, but it had been much easier when she was alone. "I didn't want to hurt you by saying I couldn't marry you, but I felt I had no choice."

A muscle in his arm jerked.

"Not about hurting you. I don't mean that. But I felt I had to say no, even if it was the hardest thing I've ever done." She lifted her face to him, let her love and hope and desperation show, not wanting to hide any part of the truth. "Emmet, your love is the greatest gift I could ever hope for. I love you too—"

He dropped to her side. "Then why did you say no?"

"Because there are things about me you don't know." Her voice broke, and she couldn't go on.

He draped an arm over her shoulders and pulled her close. She didn't resist. The weight of his arm anchored her. Made her realize their love was worth telling the truth.

"Remember, I told you I'd been sick."

"Pneumonia? Right?"

"When I was younger. Last year it was influenza. Only for me, it was more. I had a raging infection throughout my body."

His arm tightened about her.

"The doctor said I was fortunate to survive it."

He rested his cheek against her head and made a rough sound in the back of his throat—a sound that indicated sympathy and pain at her suffering. "I'm glad you did."

She nodded, reveling in the way her cheek brushed against his shoulder. "I'm glad too. But I lost something in the illness."

"So long as you're alive."

The words gave her needed courage. "The infection left me barren." Blunt, but she had no idea how to couch it in gentler terms.

"What?"

Her pain erupted. She'd never told Mother or her sisters how much she'd lost when she lost the ability to have children. "All my life I dreamed of having a houseful of children." Tears gushed like a bottled-up waterfall. Her chest heaved in shudders. "Now." She could only manage one word at a time. "I." Sob. "Will." Sniff. "Have." Swallow hard. "None."

She felt him stiffen. Knew the news had shocked him. She waited for him to pull her close, dry her tears, assure her over and over it didn't matter. Love was enough.

He bolted to his feet and put a distance of two strides between them. "You can't have children?"

Her tears dried at the roughness in his voice. "Never."

He spun away, but not before she saw the look in his face. "To never have children—" He shook his head as if the idea was impossible to fathom.

"I'll see myself out." Never mind that she was already outside. She marched around the house. Cringed at the sound of something crashing.

It was what she had always feared. Expected, even. She shouldn't be surprised.

No, she wasn't surprised. She was devastated. He didn't want a barren woman.

Who was foolish enough to think love could be enough?

Emmet let her go. He didn't know what else to do. He'd seen the agony, heard the sobs, watched the tears flow. And he could do nothing to stop it. He couldn't marry her now and every day face the undeniable fact he couldn't protect her from this pain. He kicked the wooden bench, neatly removing one arm.

He knew how hard it was to live with failure. It had been his job to protect Jane. He'd failed.

Just as he failed his parents.

Everything stopped. His parents had died in an accident. An auto accident on a hilly road. He shook his head. He wouldn't think about it.

Just as he wouldn't think about Louisa and what she had lost. And how powerless he was to protect her.

He picked up the pieces of the shattered bench and repaired it.

By the time Ellie and Auntie May returned, there

was nothing to indicate anything unusual had happened. Nothing but the acid burn in the pit of his stomach and a deep ache in the back of his brain.

Louisa made it home by instinct alone. She had no memory of the trip. The only thing she recalled was stepping into the house and knowing she would never be the same.

Sally and Mother waited for her return and rushed to ask how it went. One look at her, and they didn't need to voice the question. Mother reached for her.

"Louisa, come sit."

Sally closed the door, then helped Mother guide Louisa to the living room.

Louisa sat because they said she should.

She wasn't the least bit thirsty, but when Sally placed a cup of water in her hand she drank because she lacked the energy to argue.

"What did he say?" Sally asked.

"I can't remember." She didn't need to recall the words. His actions, his expression had said it all. "Having children is very important to him. I knew that. Why did I think it wouldn't matter?" She choked on her emotion and swallowed hard.

Mother sat at her side, rubbing her hands. "I can't believe this. I thought better of Emmet." She said it over and over, until Sally reached across and squeezed both pairs of hands.

"Sometimes things just don't work out the way we want."

Mother nodded. "But it isn't Louisa's fault."

Her mother's support was welcome, but it didn't change the facts. "He can't help what he wants either."

"I suppose." Mother rubbed Louisa's back. "I hope you aren't going to let this set you back."

"What do you mean?" She glanced at Sally, but her sister shook her head. She didn't know either.

"You've been so sick in the past. I can't bear the thought this might affect your health."

The words shook Louisa from her state of shock. "I'm not going to go into a decline, if that's what you mean. When Doc told me I was barren, I decided I would never marry, so this is but a little bump in what I had planned." Only she hadn't planned anything. She'd simply ridden along on necessity and opportunity. She'd taken the job tutoring Ellie only for the money, not out of a great passion or plan.

All that was about to change. It must. She had to have something to aim at, some direction or, indeed, her mother's fears might come true.

"I'll be fine. Yes, it's a disappointment, but don't we all have to face them? I will pray about my future, and once I'm sure of what I want to do—what God wants me to do—I will begin making plans."

"There's no need. You always have a home. You know that."

"Yes, I do. And it is a great source of comfort, but I believe I'd like to do something with my life."

Sally chuckled. "You're not interested in becoming a cat lady?"

Louisa pushed at her sister. "I might have cats, but I think I'll aim a little higher." She knew what she'd like to do, but she wasn't sure how to make it happen.

Over the next few days she worked hard to get her feelings under control. She smiled to prove she wasn't upset and to keep her mother from worrying. Yes, she'd be okay. Did she have a choice?

She would move on.

For three days she planned and prayed, then she went to talk to Madge. "I want to become a teacher."

"Great. Glad to hear it."

"You don't think I need to stay home and take care of Mother?"

Madge sighed, as if Louisa's question signified faulty reasoning. "Mother will be okay. We'll see to it. Sally can get a job if necessary. Haven't we always managed?"

"Yes. And of course, once I start work I'll be able to help even more." Though there were teachers who didn't get their promised wages. The funds simply weren't available. However, that was a problem she'd deal with when she confronted it. "I don't have the money." She'd received her earnings for tutoring Ellie and given the funds to Mother. It had paid off the doctor's bill and eased Louisa's mind on that matter. "I could borrow the amount, but I only know of one person who could afford to lend it to me."

"Emmet?"

Louisa recoiled in horror. "I wouldn't ask him even if he had it." She hoped she could avoid him until she made her escape. "I mean Uncle Peter."

"But Mother—"

"I know. Will you help me ask her if I can write him?"

"You could write without her permission." Madge's tone indicated she didn't think it was a good idea.

"No. I don't want to upset her. Besides, I really want her blessing."

So Madge came over for afternoon tea. Sally had also promised to support Louisa's cause.

Louisa waited until the ordinary things had been discussed—the weather, the gardens, who had moved away, the houses the bank had foreclosed on, who was having a baby. She wondered if Mother would ever run out of topics.

Finally, Mother glanced around the table. "So what brings the three of you together in the middle of the week?"

The girls tried to look offended.

"Do we need an excuse to get together?" Madge demanded. "I'm here so often, I'm surprised you don't ask how Judd manages on his own?"

It wasn't quite true, but Madge did pop over often.

Mother fluttered her hands. "All of you have a let's-ask-Mother look. What is it you want to ask me?"

Sally and Madge turned toward Louisa, effectively informing Mother who wanted to ask something.

She swallowed hard, silently said a quick prayer and smiled, hoping to disguise the anxiety that suddenly threaded through her insides. Not until now did she realize how badly she wanted this. "Mother, I discovered how much I enjoy teaching, and Adele says I have natural talent for the task. I want your approval to go to Normal school. My earnings will help out once I get a job."

Mother studied her fingers a moment before replying. "I have no doubt you would make a fine teacher. My concern lies in the unsavory conditions some teachers must endure. I've heard stories of rural teachers practically starving to death, having to share tight quarters—" She fluttered her hands again. "I don't think you are up to that kind of hardship."

Louisa figured she could put up with almost anything she made up her mind to. She was learning that she could live and thrive despite a broken heart. How could physical challenges be any more difficult? "I would make sure I take a position that offers decent accommodations."

Mother nodded. "I suppose I must content myself with that. Very well, you have my blessing."

"Thank you."

A heavy, waiting silence descended over the table.

"There's something more?" Mother asked.

Louisa nodded. "I want to ask Uncle Peter if I may borrow the money from him to attend Normal school." She saw the beginning of a refusal on Mother's face and rushed on. "I know of no one else I could ask for money. And I intend to pay it back. Mother, please say it's okay. You must understand that I can't stay here and watch everyone else marry and have children while I sit around doing nothing but growing old. I need to do something."

Mother considered Louisa for a moment, gave the other girls a studied look. "It seems you are both in support of her idea."

Sally and Madge nodded.

"I confess my only objection to Peter is he kept himself distanced from the family. I know your father was hurt by it, although he insisted Peter had his reasons. I suppose I have been somewhat unforgiving toward him. I just never realized it. You go ahead and write him. Perhaps I'll include a little note of apology as well."

Relief fell from Louisa's shoulders. "Thank you, Mother."

She wrote the letter that very afternoon. Took it to town and mailed it, carefully avoiding the street where the Hamiltons lived. Not that it stopped her from thinking of the occupants. How was Ellie managing schoolwork? When would she see the doctor again? Would they leave as soon as Ellie didn't need crutches?

She stumbled. Blamed the rough road. Knew it was the weakness of her limbs at knowing Emmet would soon leave and she would never see him again.

All the more reason to move on with her life.

She delivered the letter to the postal wicket and released it with a degree of relish.

The first step in her future.

A future without Emmet and Ellie.

Chapter Fourteen

Emmet took the note Ellie brought home from Miss Ross. "Are you in trouble?"

Ellie shrugged, her gaze direct and challenging. She'd been moody for days. Since Louisa had said she wouldn't marry Emmet, but he refused to acknowledge it had begun then. Even as his own unsettled misery had begun at the same time.

He could live without her. Without marriage. Even if he had to remind himself how okay he was a thousand times a day.

He'd gone for walks. Heard the birds in the trees singing as if everything in the world was right. *Sing anyway.* Louisa's words mocked him. What did birds know about loss and pain and failure? They just laid eggs and were oblivious to the rest of the world. He wished he could find the same freedom.

The next afternoon, in response to Adele's request to meet her, he went to the classroom. Last time he'd been here he'd been with Louisa. He remembered noticing her generous smile, her chocolate-rich eyes, her—

That was then. This was now. No point in looking backward. It would only make him stumble.

Adele waited for him in the classroom and indicated he should sit in the front desk. He already knew he needed a shoehorn to pry himself in and out. Louisa, on the other hand, had slipped in with the ease of a child. She was slender as a willow branch. Moved as gracefully as one waving in the wind.

Enough. He had to stop seeing her in every corner of his house, remembering her in every corner of his life.

"You wanted to talk about Ellie?" He realized he sounded cross. He'd have to watch that. It wasn't Adele's fault he kept thinking of Louisa and resenting he couldn't erase her from his mind.

"Ellie has regressed. I'm wondering if there is something wrong to cause this."

"Regressed? How?"

"A number of ways. For instance, she says she can't read."

"She can read. I know it." Louisa's drawings and cards had made it easy for Ellie to learn. Too bad she hadn't made it easy for Emmet to forget.

"She says she can't remember. I'm afraid there's more. She is uncooperative and says things like her father generally lets her do as she pleases. Reminds us all that she doesn't have a mother, so she should be excused. I'm very sorry she is motherless, but I'm afraid I can't excuse bad behavior because of that."

"Of course not." But he had no idea what to do. He wasn't going to marry just to give Ellie a mother. Besides, he seriously doubted it would solve the problem.

"I think you need to talk to her. See if you can find out what's going on. Perhaps review her skills at home."

"I'll do that. For sure." He left a few minutes later, feeling as if he failed even at being a father. What did God expect from him? How could he find a degree of success? He didn't know.

The only thing that made sense was to return to the ranch as soon as Ellie was ready to go.

That night he pulled out the reading cards. "Let's play a game."

"It's Louisa's game."

"She gave it to you. It's yours."

"I don't want to read."

"Miss Ross says you need to practice at home." He shuffled the cards and passed them out. Ellie half-heartedly played. In the end he had the vast majority of matched cards.

"Miss Ross is right. You're being uncooperative. What's wrong?"

She shrugged. "I miss Louisa. Not that you care."

He scooped her up, sat with her on his lap and rocked back and forth, finding a modicum of comfort both in the warmth of her little body in his arms and the rhythmic motion. "Button, I care very much that you're hurting. But what can I do?"

"Ask her again."

"It's not that easy." He couldn't ask her. It made him feel as if he'd swallowed battery acid to think of her pain. And he'd never be able to make things better for her. He'd never be able to take care of her as he should.

The words struck a chord so deep in his thoughts that it startled him. It was as if he'd heard the words before.

Of course he knew where they came from. When Jane died, he'd beat himself up mentally that he hadn't been able to protect her. But even then, they had a familiar ring. As if he'd heard them or said them before. But when? It didn't make sense, and he pushed the silly idea away.

Somehow they struggled through the next few days, Ellie barely making an effort to read or cooperate at school. He could hardly wait for the day he took Ellie to visit the doctor again. After that, Lord willing and the creek don't rise, they would head home. He'd originally planned to stay until Ellie finished the school year, but now it seemed a futile reason.

Finally the day to visit the doctor arrived. They drove to the office. Neither of them spoke. Emmet had no idea if Ellie worried about whether or not she would lose the crutches. Lately it had been hard to figure out anything when it came to Ellie.

Lord, help her be okay.

He marveled often that he turned to prayer even in his disappointment. Of course Ellie wasn't part of his disappointment. He could and would continue to pray for her well-being.

They walked into the office, and Doc waved them into the examining room. The nurse led Ellie to the X-ray room, and Emmet sat and drummed his fingertips together and tried not to remember the last visit to this room. Louisa had sat right beside him, waiting while the X-rays were taken. She'd smiled and laughed. He couldn't remember what he said. But he'd never forget the way he felt. As if music filled him. How could she be so cheerful, so gentle, so serene while all the time holding such a painful secret?

How could she say sing anyway? He wasn't sure he'd ever sing again. Certainly, he'd never feel music in his soul again.

Why was he feeling sorry for himself? He had a precious little girl and a ranch. Once he got back on familiar ground, both he and Ellie would feel better. Except—he could no longer deny the nagging question—how could he watch Ellie, keep her safe and at the same time run the ranch?

The doctor led Ellie from the other room and held up the X-ray.

"Good news all 'round. This leg has healed nicely." He nodded satisfaction. "Nicely indeed. Young lady, you can throw away your crutches."

Ellie handed them off to the nurse hovering at her side and marched around the room, as if to prove to everyone she needed them no more.

"She's okay?" Emmet wasn't ready to believe it.

"Should be as good as new, though it will likely take a few weeks for her to get her strength back." He turned to Ellie. "No more climbing trees. Okay?"

Ellie nodded. "Only little ones."

Doc laughed. "You got yourself a little tomboy."

"She needs to be. Ranch life requires she know how to ride and sometimes fend for herself."

The doctor gave him a few more instructions before they left.

"Thanks, Doc." On the way out, Emmet dropped the money for the visit on the desk. They returned to the truck. "Do you want to get a candy or ice cream?"

"I guess."

Hardly the enthusiasm one might expect, and no comparison to their last visit.

Ellie would get over her disappointment as soon as they returned to the ranch, but Emmet knew the rest of his life would be but a pale shadow of the few weeks he'd enjoyed Louisa's company.

They stopped at the store. Joanie saw her without crutches and cheered. "All better. I expect you're pretty happy about that."

"I guess."

Joanie blinked. "Wow, kid. Try to contain your enthusiasm."

Ellie shrugged. "What's so special about getting better?"

"Sure beats lying about in a body cast."

Ellie sighed. "It wasn't so bad."

Emmet knew what she meant. Being in her cast meant Louisa came every day. They both missed her visits. Not that he would wish Ellie back in a cast for such selfish reasons. "Pick out a candy stick."

Ellie didn't take any time making her selection. She took a licorice-flavored stick, stuck it in her mouth and headed back to the truck.

"She's just—" Emmet shrugged. He couldn't begin to explain Ellie's behavior. He dropped two pennies on the counter and left the store. They drove home without speaking. The only sound was Ellie slurping the candy.

Auntie May looked up as they entered the house. "Well, well. No more crutches?"

"Nope." Ellie crossed to her room and flopped on the bed.

"Shouldn't she be happier about this?" Auntie May asked. "Something wrong?"

"She's homesick. I'll take care of it." Emmet strode into the bedroom and closed the door. He sat on the edge of the bed. "Ellie, I know what will make you feel better."

"Humph."

"We're going home."

She didn't move. Didn't respond. Had she heard?

"We're going back to the ranch. You can ride your pony again—"

"I don't want to go home."

"Of course you do. Things will be better once we get back there."

"No they won't." Her voice rose to a screech. "Things will never be better, and it's all your fault. It's your fault Louisa doesn't come to see us anymore. Everything is your fault." She flipped to her stomach and buried her face in the pillow.

"Ellie?" He touched her back.

She shrugged from his hand. "Go away. Leave me alone. It's your fault and I'll never forgive you."

He stared at her a moment as the words raged through his mind. *It's your fault. It's your fault.*

Ah. The words hurt, they tore at his thoughts, they blasted at doors, they pounded at a memory.

Why couldn't he keep his loved ones safe? Why did he always fail?

Just like Mama.

He dropped his hands to his sides and stared into nothing. Where did that thought come from? How could this be like his mother's death? And how could it be

his fault? He was only nine years old at the time of the
accident. He remembered so little about it. Shock had
dulled his memories.

Auntie May had always assured him it wasn't his
fault.

Why would she say that unless there was reason he
might believe he was to blame?

He fled the room, passed Auntie May without looking at her. He barely realized she watched him, her expression wreathed in sympathy. He flung out the door
and strode away, down the back lane, out of town,
across the prairie, as if he could run from his failure,
his haunting accusations.

At the top of a rise, four miles from town, he ran out
of steam and sank to the ground, panting. Had he done
something that caused his parents' deaths? His mother's
death?

Why hadn't he dropped Ellie and rushed to rescue
Jane?

Was he doomed to be responsible for the death of
loved ones all his life?

He sat staring across the undulating prairie, time and
place forgotten. If only his thoughts would stop twisting
and knotting. If only they made sense. Instead, words
of blame and failure and fear tangled into a painful
ball. *It's your fault. I can never keep anyone safe. I've
failed. I'll fail again in the future.* He shuddered as the
words reverberated through his brain. Why did he hear
an echo of a voice not his own? Why did he feel sick
inside?

Nearby a bird sang. Endlessly. As if mocking Emmet. Or trying to drive a message home. But what message?

Find the truth.

Right. He'd love to. But who could provide it?

Auntie May must know what happened and could perhaps explain why Emmet had such a sense of dread as he thought of his parents. He must talk to her.

Until he did he was stuck in this black vacuum, always feeling as if he couldn't keep his loved ones safe. It was what made him turn from Louisa—knowing he couldn't protect her from her pain.

He returned home. Ellie was up but wouldn't talk to him, though she had plenty of dark glowers to share.

This was not a conversation he wanted Ellie to hear, fearing what he learned might confirm her feelings that he was to blame, so he waited until he was certain she was asleep. "Auntie May, can I ask you some questions?"

"Of course, my boy. Whatever you want."

"Let's go outside."

She followed him out the door and sat on the bench. Right where Louisa had sat to tell him her terrible plight. He steeled himself to forget that moment.

"Emmet, you look worried. How can I help you?"

He pulled over an empty bucket and tipped it over to sit at her knees. "What happened to my parents?"

She pressed a palm to her throat. "Oh, my. What a question."

He waited as she stared out across the yard, sorrow and regret chasing across her face. Finally she sighed.

"I've always wondered how much you remembered.

Was grateful you seemed to have forgotten. Yet I wondered if someday it would come back."

"What would come back?"

She brought her gaze to his and looked deeply into his eyes. "What do you remember?"

He shook his head. "Very little. Something about a car accident. That's all."

Her eyes clouded, and she nodded her head. "They died following a car accident. You were with them."

He jerked back. "I was?" A twisting road. Hills. His papa talking and laughing. "Papa liked his new car. He wanted to show Mama how well it handled on the road."

She nodded and waited, letting him find his words. All he found was a blank. "I don't remember."

"You realize I wasn't there. I can only tell you what the neighbors who found you said." At his encouraging nod, she went on. "Your father had indeed bought a new vehicle. Shiny and new. I suppose he wanted to take you both out for a drive. Or perhaps he had business in the next town. We'll never know."

Emmet remembered being excited. "We were going out for dinner at a restaurant."

"I see." She waited again, but still he remembered nothing. "The people said they didn't know if he was going too fast, or swerved to avoid something. All they could say for sure was the car went off the edge of the road and rolled. Your mother was thrown out and hurt. Your father was hurt badly as well. You had some cuts and bruises."

He glanced at the scars on his arm. Was that when he'd received them?

She touched the scars with her fingers. "It was a wonder that's all you got." Drew in a long breath. "Your father went for help and left you to watch your mother." She paused. "When they returned with your father—" She choked and paused another beat. "You sat with your mother's head in your lap. But she was gone."

He nodded, the memory edging closer. "I didn't know she was dead. I thought...I thought..." His throat tightened, and tears stung his nose. "I thought..." His voice fell to a whisper. "I was supposed to keep her safe. I thought I had."

She nodded, tears trickling unchecked down her cheeks.

"Papa told me to keep her safe." His father had pulled Mama from the rocks where she'd been tossed. He'd pressed back her hair and moaned. "Come here, boy." Emmet staggered to his side, the pain in his limbs drowned by a clogging fear. Mama didn't look like Mama. She looked like a beat-up doll.

"Sit here." Papa shoved him down by Mama's side. Lifted Mama's head to Emmet's lap. "I'm going for help. You take care of Mama. Don't let her die." He took a step away, then turned to speak to Emmet again. "Don't you let her die. Hear? It's your job to take care of her."

"I tried." He spoke aloud now.

Auntie May cupped her hand to his head. "There was nothing you could do."

"Papa came back."

All the time Papa was gone, he talked to Mama. "I'll look after you. I'll keep you safe." Over and over he said the words. He didn't know what else to do except pat her cheeks. "I'll look after you."

Papa limped back into sight, two men with him. Papa dropped down beside Mama. He called her. Shook her a little. Touched her cheek. Pressed his fingers to her neck. Then turned to Emmet. "She's gone. She's dead. I told you to look after her. What's wrong with you? You failed me, boy. You failed me."

One of the strangers pulled Papa away. "It's not the boy's fault."

Papa wailed like an angry bull Emmet had once seen. It was a very frightening sound.

The other man pulled Emmet away from Mama. "No. I'll take care of her. I will." He fought the man to escape, but he couldn't get away from this stranger.

Papa bellowed again. His eyes looked funny. He broke free of the constraining arms and knelt next to Mama. Tears flowed down his face. That frightened Emmet as much as holding Mama's head. He'd never seen Papa cry. Didn't know he could.

Papa lifted his tear-stained, gray-skinned face to Emmet's. "You let me down, boy."

Suddenly Papa fell to the ground. Emmet thought he wanted to lie down beside Mama. He wanted to die too. But the stranger took him away. Only later did he realize Papa had died as well, as seriously injured in the accident as Mama.

He hung his head and spoke quietly to Auntie May. "You knew Papa blamed me. That's why you kept telling me it wasn't my fault."

She stroked his arm. "It wasn't your fault. Your father was wrong to blame you. I was glad that you seemed to have blocked it from your mind." She made shushing, comforting noises for a few minutes. "You didn't remember it, but I think it has affected you anyway."

He jerked his head up. "What do you mean?"

"My boy, sometimes I think you try too hard to make sure everyone is going to be okay. Seems to me you tend to blame yourself if things go wrong." She leaned close and cupped his face between her palms. "There is so little in life that we truly have any control over. Ultimately, we must trust God. He holds us in the palm of His hand. Holds our loved ones too. Emmet, life is not your responsibility. Only loving and caring is up to you."

He didn't answer. Couldn't. How could he take a lifetime of self-blame and erase it in one thought?

Auntie May pushed to her feet. "You need to think about this. And while you're thinking, pray for God to help you sort out what you have charge of and what He has charge of. Might surprise you what you learn." She patted his head, then went inside.

Emmet continued to sit, his mind staggering with memories, regrets and yes, like Auntie May said, self-blame. He couldn't begin to sort out his thoughts.

Chapter Fifteen

Louisa received a reply from Uncle Peter within the week. "Come immediately," it read. Instructions on how to find his home were included.

She showed Mother and her sisters the letter. "I want to go right away. On tomorrow's train."

Mother shook her head. "It's not enough time to plan."

"What's to plan? I'll take enough clothes for a few days. I'll talk to Uncle Peter, and if he agrees to lend me the funds, I'll return to prepare for school." She couldn't wait to put distance between herself and Emmet. It was impossible to avoid him, as she'd discovered when she went to check the mail.

She'd seen his truck coming down the street and barely had time to duck out of sight around the corner of the hardware store. She peeked around the building to observe. Ellie had climbed from the truck without crutches. Joy flooded Louisa's heart. The child was all better. She'd be able to run and play now.

Emmet followed. He didn't look particularly happy. Perhaps he had decided it wouldn't be fair to pull Ellie from school a second time in order to move her back to the ranch. No doubt he was regretting the delay.

But the near encounter convinced her she must leave as soon as possible.

Sally and Madge sided with Louisa. "It will do Louisa good to go to the city."

Mother acquiesced. "No doubt you are right. I'm just being selfish, not wanting to let go. But you proceed with your plans. I'll pray for a satisfactory outcome."

So Louisa sent a wire to Uncle Peter saying she would arrive on the train the next day, and she packed a small case for her visit. That night she fought a battle with fear and regret.

Oh, God, I am running from the man I love. But what choice do I have? He doesn't want me. Help me find a future full of promise and possibility.

The next day Louisa stepped from the train in Edmonton. They'd lived there seven years ago, and she tried to tell herself it was like coming home.

"Louisa." She turned at the sound of her name and stared at Uncle Peter. He was so much like Father that Louisa stumbled as her eyes filled with tears.

Uncle Peter caught her and steadied her. "It's so good of you to visit."

She nodded. He might change his mind once she'd told him the purpose of her visit.

He waited until they were in his charming home and had been served tea by his housekeeper to say, "I'm most happy to have you visit, but it is a surprise. I suspect there is a reason behind this rare pleasure. What is it?"

Louisa set her teacup aside, clasped her hands in her lap and prayed for uncommon courage and courtesy. She began by telling Uncle Peter of her experience in tutoring Ellie. "I enjoyed it and seem to have a little aptitude for the job. I'd like to attend Normal school."

"That sounds like a wonderful thing."

She twisted her fingers. It was hard asking for money.

"Can I help in any way?"

He sounded so much like Father, she had to swallow twice before she could answer. "I wondered if you could lend me the money to go to school." It sounded so brash said out loud. She couldn't meet his eyes.

"Is that all? Why, of course, I'll gladly finance your education. It's the least I can do."

"I'll pay you back."

"Nonsense. You'll do no such thing. I've never had children. Something I wish could have been different. You and your sisters are the closest I will ever have. It's my privilege to help any way I can."

She met his eyes, smiled. The two of them shared something—no children. It made her feel they had a special connection.

"Now you must stay and visit a few days…unless you have a young man waiting for you back home."

"No. No, I don't."

"I hear regret in those words. Is it regret that you have no young man or regret that he has designs on another?"

She smiled. "The former." So far as she knew, Emmet didn't have another woman in mind.

"Good. Because if it was the latter, I'd wonder if the man was blind."

Louisa's cheeks warmed, and she knew she blushed under her uncle's praise.

She spent two pleasant days in her uncle's company, finding him extremely easy to talk to. It amazed her he'd never married, and finally she said so.

"I love a woman."

"But why—?" She broke off. It was none of her business.

"Why aren't I married? Why doesn't anyone know?"

She tried to pretend she wasn't curious, but he chuckled.

"Your father knew, but he kept his promise to never tell. Come, I'll introduce you to the one who has my heart."

She climbed into his car with him, expecting they would visit a cemetery. Instead they left the city and drove to a picturesque estate. A stately brick building set in a beautiful parklike setting.

He stopped in a gravel lot and led her inside. He greeted several women in nurses' uniforms as he led her to a room that looked like a well-fitted guest room in a fine house, except for the bed that was raised, as Ellie's had been.

In the bed lay a little gray-haired woman.

Uncle Peter crossed to the side of the bed and bent over. "Hello, Carrie Ann."

The woman's eyes lit up like dawn.

Uncle Peter held her hands. "She can't talk, can't feed herself. Can't sit up. My sweet, Carrie Ann had a stroke when she was but eighteen. A blood vessel ruptured in her brain, the doctors decided. I loved her before this unfortunate accident, and I will love her every day of my life." He stroked her hair back. "Sweetheart, this is my niece, Louisa. The oldest of the girls that I've told you about. She's come to visit us."

Tears pooled in Carrie Ann's eyes, and he wiped them away tenderly.

If only Emmet had that kind of love. A love undiminished by unfortunate circumstances.

If only.

Louisa wept.

Uncle Peter pulled her into his arms, while still holding Carrie Ann's hands. "Don't be upset. I've regretted not one moment. Carrie Ann's sweetness has been a blessing."

Carrie Ann tried to say something, but all that came out was unintelligible mumbles.

"She says not to cry for her."

"I'm not crying for her. I'm crying for me. I love a man, but he can't see past my health problems." The whole story tumbled forth, every pertinent detail. She even confessed her barrenness.

Uncle Peter made soothing noises and held her. Just as her father would have. Such sweet comfort.

"If he is worthy of your love, he will change his mind. If he doesn't, he is not worthy."

Louisa calmed, stood. "I'm sorry. I've made quite a spectacle of myself. It's just, you remind me so much of Father."

Uncle Peter caught her hand. "That is the best compliment I've ever received."

Over the passing days, she grew extremely fond of

Uncle Peter. "The one good thing out of Emmet's rejection is that I have grown to know you. How did we miss all those years?"

"It is my fault. I wanted to protect Carrie Ann. And myself from people's pity, so I distanced myself from the family. It wasn't until your father died that I realized what I had lost. And by then it was too late."

"It's not too late. I admire you so much for how you have stayed at Carrie Ann's side. I hope I can find the contentment in my situation that you've found."

"Child, I would spare you the sorrow, but it isn't in my hands."

"Nor mine." She tried to prepare herself to return home, but dreaded confronting daily reminders of Emmet.

When Uncle Peter suggested, "Why don't you stay longer? Get to know Carrie Ann," Louisa readily agreed.

Emmet had not made any further plans about returning to the ranch. He couldn't. It was as if his life had hit a bump in the road, and he couldn't seem to get over it or around it or through it. He'd prayed, asking God to show him the answers. Auntie May was right. He wasn't to blame. He had been only nine years old.

But a persistent voice mocked, *What about Jane? You weren't a child then. And what about Ellie's accident? Where were you when that happened? Not protecting your child. That's for sure.*

And Louisa. How he missed her. Like a giant toothache that wasn't calmed by warm oil or a clove. He couldn't possibly protect her from something that had already occurred.

He wandered up and down back roads, praying and begging for an answer.

It was almost supper time when he turned his steps toward home. As he neared the yard, he heard Ellie and Leila playing. At least Ellie had found solace in her young friend.

One more loss she must endure when they left. Seems everything he did had a hurt associated with it.

The girls had the dollhouse and dolls out playing with them. Ellie guarded that gift carefully. More proof of her fondness for Louisa. Oh, if only he could prevent his daughter from experiencing further pain.

The girls arranged the family of dolls in the various rooms, having them talk in individual voices.

"Take the mommy out," Ellie said. "These children cannot have a mommy."

Leila removed the paper doll. Ellie stared at the remaining family. Took out all except the father and a girl doll.

Emmet stood in the back of the shed, unobserved, to watch and listen, sensing Ellie expressed her own life.

"Why did God take my mommy?" Ellie seemed to be speaking to the dolls. "Does He hate me?"

God hated them. Is that what Emmet thought? God was punishing him for not obeying his father, not keeping his mother safe?

Leila touched Ellie's hand. "God doesn't hate anyone. My mama always said He loves us all. No matter what."

Ellie considered the information. "But He took your mommy and daddy and sister. Why?"

Leila tilted her head. "It's awfully sad. But Matron says none of us are smart enough to know God's mind and understand Him. Bad things happen and we don't know why. But I'm glad God loves me."

Oh, for the innocence and trust of children.

But the words spoken by a child painted his thoughts. He couldn't keep people safe. Accidents happened. Illnesses happened. There was the uncertainty of weather and financial markets. But whatever happened, he could trust God. Even when he couldn't understand or make sense of it.

"I wish I could have a family like this," Leila said, putting the entire family into the playhouse. Her voice dripped with such sadness, it brought a sting to Emmet's eyes.

Ellie reached over and took two dolls—little girls, from what Emmet could see. "These two are sisters forever. Just like I wish you and me could be."

The girls bent to touch their foreheads together.

Emmet closed his eyes against a flood of pain, then called to the girls and entered the yard.

Both girls rushed toward him. Ellie flung herself in his arms and sobbed against his neck. He welcomed her gladly, even though he suspected she sought only temporary comfort. She would no doubt revert back to blaming him for driving Louisa away. When Leila hung back, he opened his free arm to her. With a strangled sob, she went to him and both girls snuggled close.

Oh, if only he wasn't a man alone, he would adopt this little child. The pair could be forever sisters. It tore at his insides to know he must leave Leila behind. How would the child survive without a family to love her?

She'd shown herself remarkably strong in face of her trials. He could only hope and pray she would continue to be so.

"You two can write each other. And maybe Leila can come and visit when she's a little older."

Two pairs of arms tightened about his neck.

After a bit, Leila lifted her head. "I wish you could be my daddy."

He knew his smile was very shaky as he studied her. "I would like that. But you need a mommy too."

At that, Ellie insisted on being put down. She pulled Leila to her side, and they returned to playing dolls. He suspected they both purposely kept their backs to him.

Leila stayed for supper and then he took her home, letting Ellie ride along. The pair whispered and giggled together on the trip.

Later, after he'd returned, put Ellie to bed and retired to his own bed, he lay staring in the darkness.

God, I have a long way to go yet, but I think I'm ready to start a journey of trust with You. I want to take the journey hand in hand with Louisa.

Would she forgive him for turning away from her pain? All he could hope was she would give him a chance to explain.

He waited until Ellie went to school the next morning, then headed for the Morgan place.

Their vehicle was missing. But perhaps she was home alone. That would be good. But no one came to the door to answer his knock.

His nervousness tripled. He had to speak to her as

soon as possible. Perhaps Judd and Madge knew of her whereabouts. He jumped into his truck and raised a cloud of dust in his hurried departure.

At the Kirk place, he veered toward the barn where Judd stood in the doorway, a hunk of iron in his hand.

"What brings you out here in such a rush?" Judd asked.

"I need to see Louisa."

Judd leaned against the door frame and studied him. "You hurt her. I don't much appreciate that."

"I'm sorry."

"Yeah? That girl is well worth loving even if she can't have children."

"I don't care about that. I was only upset because—" It sounded stupid now, but he explained it as best he could. "I know now I have to trust God for things like life and death and everything in between. I want to tell Louisa. Hopefully she will give me another chance."

"I certainly hope you mean what you say, but I'm not sure—"

"I love her, Judd. I want to marry her."

Judd laughed. "I was about to say I'm not sure where she is."

"What?"

"She left a few days ago to visit an uncle. She plans to go to Normal school and become a teacher. Hear she was good at the work."

"Yes. But—you don't know where she is?"

"No. But Madge does. Let's see if you can convince her she should tell you."

Emmet followed Judd to the house.

Madge glanced up, and when she saw Emmet she frowned. "I'm not sure I want you here."

Only his determination to find Louisa and explain his reasons for turning away from her gave him the courage to face her displeasure. "I need to talk to Louisa."

"Seems to me you've said and done enough already." She stepped closer.

He gave a wary glance toward the big wooden spoon she shook at him. "I'd like a chance to change all that."

Madge hesitated. "How is that possible? You made it clear you want nothing to do with a woman who can't give you children."

"That wasn't my intention."

She crossed her arms, the spoon clearly evident in her grasp. "So what was?"

"She cried when she told me." His words were hoarse as his throat tightened. "I couldn't bear her pain."

Madge's expression softened. "So what's changed?"

"Me. I realized I can't protect everyone I love from life and its challenges." He wouldn't tell her more. That confession belonged to Louisa. "I think she would want to hear what I have to say." He didn't care that he sounded desperate. "I'm prepared to plead."

Madge turned to Judd and they communicated silently, then she moved to Judd's side and wrapped her arms around his waist, the wooden spoon hanging from her free arm. "I'm prepared to give you one chance, but if you hurt her again…" She brandished her weapon.

"You'll have the whole family to answer to," Judd added.

For a moment, Emmet hesitated. "I can't be responsible for her response."

Madge snorted. "I think you'll find my sister most reasonable."

The next day, address tucked in his pocket, he headed for Edmonton. He didn't explain to Ellie where he was going or why. Just in case Louisa rejected him.

God, I'm trusting You.

Of course, as Leila said, he couldn't begin to understand God's ways. That's why trusting was hard. And required faith. If he knew everything and understood all the reasons, there would be no need to trust anything but his own wisdom.

Louisa sat in a wicker rocker on the veranda of Uncle Peter's home. She had enjoyed every minute of her visit and planned to extend it until she must return home to pack for Normal school. Uncle Peter said but of course she would live here while she attended classes. She welcomed the idea. God willing, she would even find a job in the city when she graduated.

She turned her attention back to the sketchbook before her. Her intention had been to draw the flowers surrounding the veranda. Clematis crept up the side, almost blocking the view of the street. Yellow rosebushes stood grandly on each side of the entrance.

In the trees around the yard, birds sang. She'd identified the song of the vireo and even caught a glimpse of the shy bird. She'd seen an oriole, a tanager, robins, several species of sparrows and two kinds of hawks. She'd begun a journal of bird sightings, sketching them as often as possible. Maybe when she was a teacher, she would use this information.

Most of all, she enjoyed listening to the birds sing. She was getting her own song back, though it had a mourning quality to it. She would never stop missing Emmet. But she was learning to find peace in the midst of her pain.

One thing she had decided she would do was to pray for both his and Ellie's happiness. *Bless Emmet with happiness and peace. Bless Ellie.* She wasn't yet able to pray that Ellie would be blessed with a mother. But perhaps someday she would be able to.

A vehicle stopped nearby. She paid it little attention. Uncle Peter had gone to his office, and she knew no one who would call on her in the city. Perhaps one day she would feel ready to contact old friends, should there be any left living nearby. For now she was content to heal and prepare for the future.

A step sounded on the sidewalk, and she jerked about to see who approached the house. Through the canopy of leaves she almost thought it was Emmet. How many times would she look up at a man his size and build and feel her heart explode with hope?

She watched the man draw closer. Reach the step and mount to the porch. "Emmet?" Was she dreaming?

"Louisa. I've found you."

"I didn't realize I was lost." It was a silly thing to say, but she couldn't let herself believe he'd come for any special reason. "What business brings you to the city?"

"I'm not here on business. I'm here to see you."

She sat with her feet curled up beneath her and

now dropped them to the floor. "Is something wrong? Mother? Sally? Madge? Did Madge get hurt helping Judd?"

"No one is hurt." He snagged a chair from the opposite side of the veranda and pulled it close. He sat facing her. "I've come to see you."

She stared. She would not hope. She would not try and guess what he wanted.

"Louisa, I want to explain."

"No need." She did not want to hear how he simply couldn't give up his dream of a big family. Something she could not give him. *No excuses, please. Please do not say it's not personal. Because it is.*

"You once asked me about how my parents died. You even suggested there was a big lump of something that stopped my heart. You were right. I just didn't realize it." He told the story of his parents' death. Of feeling he was to blame. His father's unfair accusation.

Long before he finished, she leaned forward, pressing her hands to his.

"I realize that I have always held myself responsible even for things I have no control over." He looked into her eyes, searching beyond the surface, exploring her heart.

She too sought the deeper meaning in his words at seeing his eyes fully unshuttered for the first time ever. Hope sprang fully bloomed, even though she warned herself she still could not give him what he wanted.

"Louisa, when you said you couldn't have children and I saw the pain in your face, heard it in your voice, I knew what a disappointment it was for you. I knew I couldn't fix it. All I could think was how could I see this pain in you every day and be able to do absolutely nothing about it? I failed before I started." He shrugged. "Talking about it, I realize how little sense it makes, but it made so much sense to me at the time. I couldn't think of how I would live with a pain I couldn't fix."

"I'm sorry, but I will never be able to give you the large family you've always wanted." She sat back slowly, pulled her hands to her lap.

"I don't care about that. Don't you see? It isn't not having a large family that matters. It's knowing I can't keep this pain from you." He grabbed her hands, knelt at her feet. "I love you, Louisa Morgan. So much that your pain seemed unbearable. But I realize I have to leave life and death and a whole lot of other things in God's hands." He told her how he'd overheard Leila and Ellie playing, and the words Leila spoke that made him realize he could do nothing but trust when life seemed unexplainable.

She chuckled at the picture he created of the girls playing with the dollhouse. "I'm so glad they are getting pleasure out of it."

Emmet still knelt before her, and she wished he would sit down again. He was making her nervous.

"Louisa, I love you. You are worth more to me than a dozen children. I want to share my life with you. I want you to be my wife and Ellie's mother. Please say you'll marry me."

She studied him, watched his eyes flash from blue to green. "Are you sure? There will never be children. The doctor was quite certain of that."

"Louisa, I would rather share my life with you than with anyone else. We have Ellie. We can love her."

She had to be sure. She had to know he was certain. "Ellie will be an only child."

"We'll see she has lots of companions."

"No sons. No babies. And me, an unhealthy specimen."

He lifted his head and roared with laughter. "You are anything but a weak, shrinking violet. You are strong as steel." He touched her chin. "Gentle as velvet. I know what I want, and it is you. Marry me?"

She smiled from a heart overflowing with assurance of his love. Free to open her own store of love, she spoke words that she had for so long ached to say. "Emmet, you are all I need. You are my sunshine and my rain, my heart's joy and contentment. You have filled my life to overflowing with love. If you are one hundred percent certain this is what you want, then yes, I will marry you, Emmet Hamilton. I love you and will do my best to make your days happy and—"

"My heart glad." He finished, pressing her palm to his chest. "Together we will face life walking at God's side. Whatever comes our way, we will stand together."

"Strong in God's strength."

His murmur of agreement burred against her lips as he pulled her into his arms. He kissed her soundly, as if to make sure she understood all he felt.

By the time he finished and pulled away, she had no more doubts. They sat side by side, holding hands and kissing often as they discussed their future.

"I want to go back to the ranch." He sounded doubtful.

"I can hardly wait. Do you mind if I make the house ours?"

"It's been a long time since anyone has done much in the house. I'm afraid you will find it sadly in need of a woman's touch. I hope you will make it yours in every way."

"Ours."

"Ours," he echoed, kissing her again for good measure.

Uncle Peter returned a while later and stared at the pair of them.

Louisa jumped to her feet and introduced them.

Uncle Peter gave Emmet a hard look. "I'm not sure you're welcome here. You're the young man who broke my niece's heart."

Emmet faced the older man with dignity. "I don't blame you if you think I should be shot for that, but I plan to do my best to make up for it in the future. Louisa has agreed to marry me."

Uncle Peter's brows knit together. "Louisa, is that true?"

"Yes, Uncle Peter." She knew her happiness sounded in her voice. "It's an answer to a prayer."

"I have grown rather fond of my niece." He indicated they should all sit, and for an hour grilled Emmet on his plans, as if he hoped to detect some note of falseness in his affection.

Louisa's insides glowed with happiness at the way Emmet continued to speak of his love for her and how they would find their joy in loving each other and Ellie.

Finally, Uncle Peter relented and turned to Louisa. "I only regret that this means you won't be spending the winter with me."

"Uncle Peter, you must promise to come and visit us often."

"And you must come here as much as you can."

She looked up into the face of the man she had come to love like a father. "Will you come to my wedding and give me away?"

His eyes glistened. "I would consider it an honor." He kissed her cheeks. "Now go entertain your young man."

Emmet and Louisa had agreed to get married and return to the ranch as soon as school ended in June.

Emmet spent the night in one of Uncle Peter's guest rooms, and he and Louisa returned to Golden Prairie the next day.

"We need to speak to Ellie before we tell anyone else." Louisa wanted the child's approval.

"She'll be ecstatic. In fact, she figured I didn't know how to ask you. Blamed me that you said no." He grabbed her hand and pulled her to his shoulder, keeping one hand firmly on the steering wheel. "I never told her that I turned you down too. I'm sorry. I never meant to hurt you."

She kissed his chin. "I forgive you. I believe God used our time of separation to help each of us grow in faith."

They arrived back in town just as school got out and waited for Ellie outside the school. She saw Louisa and squealed. "You've come back." She shot a glance at her father and grinned. "Ohh."

Louisa chuckled. Ellie was much too smart for a seven-year-old. She and Emmet would have their hands full as this little one matured.

They had agreed to wait until they were alone to talk to her. They returned to the house and slipped to the backyard. Auntie May, smart woman that she was, stayed out of the way.

"Sit down, Ellie, we want to talk to you."

Ellie gave each of them a hard look and refused to sit. "Are you getting married?"

Louisa laughed at her demanding tone.

Emmet answered her. "Yes, we are."

Ellie squealed and threw her arms about Louisa. "I knew you'd be my mommy the minute you said you loved me." She squinted at her father. "I didn't know if you'd ever get it right."

Louisa grinned at Emmet, who shook his head sadly. "What did I tell you?"

Ellie backed away. "Can I have a sister?"

Louisa staggered back. She hadn't known Ellie would have the same dreams as her father.

Emmet caught Louisa's hand and pulled her to his side. "Ellie, Button, we can't promise a sister. Our future is in God's hands, but there might never be a baby."

Ellie made a noise of disgust. "I don't want a baby. I want Leila for a sister."

Louisa glanced at Emmet. At the look on his face, she knew he'd already thought of this.

"I'll see what we can do."

Ellie raced away to play.

Emmet took Louisa's hands. "What do you think of adopting Leila?"

She grinned. "I think it's a most excellent idea." Two little girls was more than she'd dreamed possible.

He caught her chin then and turned her face toward him. "You are one special lady. Have I told you that?"

She giggled. "Not recently. Besides, I don't think I'll ever grow tired of hearing it."

"You are special and I love you."

"I love you too," she managed before he kissed her.

Epilogue

Emmet checked the back of the truck, making sure all the gifts and extra furniture that Mother Morgan had donated, plus clothes for his growing family, were all secure. He tightened the ropes holding the canvas tarp in place. "It looks like it will hold until we get home."

He faced the crowd. Auntie May. Louisa's mother and sisters. Judd, of course, who had given him all sorts of advice for a married man. As if Emmet hadn't been married before. But this time was different. He was different. He had begun a walk of trust. And Uncle Peter, standing close to Mother. Louisa had commented how protective he was of her, and hoped they would now become friends.

"Are we ready to go?" Ellie demanded.

"We're ready."

Louisa circled her family, giving each a hug and receiving a whispered goodbye and, he suspected, a parting word of advice. Who'd have guessed everyone had so much to say about marriage and ranching? He couldn't remember such generous tidbits when he married Jane. Of course, he'd married away from home.

He followed at Louisa's side, getting hugs and good-byes. He paused before Auntie May. "I can never thank you enough for raising me."

She chuckled and patted his face. "I wish I could take credit for the man you've become, but we all know I can't. Now you behave. You write often. Send pictures and don't forget to visit."

"We plan to come back for Christmas, and all of you are welcome to visit us anytime."

They had been married only a week. He hated to take Louisa from her family, but it was time to start their life together—with his two daughters. Leila's adoption had been easy and rapid. The judge signed the final papers two days ago.

"Let's go home." He helped Louisa into the truck and lifted two chattering little girls in beside her.

Judd joined him at the window. "The way you're loaded down, it reminds me of the people moving out of the country, sick and tired of drought and poor prices."

Louisa leaned over to speak to Judd. "The difference is we're not running from the drought. We're headed to the future, with two precious little girls and a man who loves me. It's more than I asked or dreamed for."

Emmet leaned over and kissed her.

Leila clamped a hand to her mouth to hide her giggles, and Ellie sighed. "Guess what we'll have to put up with the whole trip?"

Emmet chucked her under the chin as the others laughed. "You'll have to put up with it a lot longer than that."

Ellie groaned, but her grin said how much she didn't

mind. She reached for Leila's hands. "This is the happiest day of my life."

Three voices repeated her words in unison.

The happiest day of their lives. A great way to start the future.

They called a final goodbye and headed west.

* * * * *

Dear Reader,

Happy fifteenth anniversary to Love Inspired Books. I am thrilled to have been writing for Love Inspired Historical since it began, and especially during this special year. I love the quality of the stories that come out under this line. Congratulations to everyone involved—authors, editors and especially our faithful readers.

In *The Cowboy Father,* I address a difficult and painful subject. Many women long to have children, but are not able to conceive. Nowadays there are alternatives, but not too far in the past, there were few alternatives. And barrenness was a shame. To many it signified punishment or disapproval from God. So how does a Christian woman who firmly believes in God's love deal with barrenness? How can she reconcile God's love with her condition?

I tackle that problem in this story, and I pray that all of us will learn the same lessons of trust and hope that Louisa and Emmet learn. I hope I did not trivialize their pain in creating a compelling love story. It was always my intention to give the subject the respect it deserves.

I love to hear from readers. Contact me through email at linda@lindaford.org or lindaford@airenet.com. Feel free to check on updates and bits about my research at my website, www.lindaford.org.

Blessings,

Linda Ford

Questions for Discussion

1. Louisa has endured a number of trials. What are they? How has she responded?

2. She has made a conscious choice to trust and rejoice despite these challenges. Has she found it easy?

3. Emmet has had his own trials. What are they and how would you describe his response?

4. How have family dynamics played a role in each of their lives? Do they continue to do so?

5. What part of his past has Emmet shut up? Why? Why does he need to address this for him to go forward? Or does he?

6. Little girls play a role in this story. How would you describe each? What lessons do you think they can learn from each other?

7. Who in the story has had the greatest impact on Louisa's attitudes (good or negative)? On Emmet's?

8. Is there a particular scene that spoke to you about a personal need?

9. All of us have events in our lives that impact us. What events have greatly affected who you are and how you deal with life? Can you learn any-

thing from how Louisa and Emmet reacted, or the choices and decisions they made?

10. What do you see as the theme of this story? How is the theme shown?

11. What advice would you give both Emmet and Louisa in order for their marriage to succeed?

12. If you were to write a chapter in their lives ten, fifteen, even fifty years down the road, what would it include?

13. How would you like a future chapter in your story to read? What can you do to make that happen?

FIREWORKS
Valerie Hansen

Chapter One

"Forget the former things; do not dwell on the past."

—Isaiah 41:18

"Really? You need me?" Bethany Brown clapped her hands, feeling more like a giddy child than the twenty-two-year-old she was. "Thank you for asking. I'd love to help out."

"We'll see you at nine sharp, then," the fire chief said. "Sorry about the short notice, but one of our regular auxiliary ladies fell and broke her arm yesterday and had to cancel."

Bethany grinned broadly. "No problem. I've already helped decorate the bank's booth. I don't have any other plans for the day except to enjoy the food and see the fireworks later."

"Good. And don't worry. You won't have to sell our baked goods alone. Stan said he had enough staff lined up to help on all but the first shift."

"Stan Ellison?" Her heart began fluttering as if it

had suddenly become a demented butterfly. "He's in charge?"

"This year he is. Why?"

"No reason. I just wondered." She hoped her flushed cheeks weren't giving her away because she didn't want to start rumors. It was bad enough that Stan and her sister, Amy, had been the talk of the town the previous summer.

She sobered. Poor Stan. He'd suffered so. And all because of Amy's foolish idea that she was pretty enough to be a success in Hollywood. As far as Bethany was concerned, any woman who would abandon a great guy like Stan to pursue a chance in a million of becoming a movie star was off her rocker.

And cruel, she added to herself as she watched the chief walk away. What Amy had done to Stan was a crime, pure and simple. She had not only broken his heart when she'd jilted him, she'd caused him to shut down his emotions where other women were concerned.

"Especially me," she murmured, disgusted and disheartened. There had been a time when she and Stan had been pals, special friends who had confided in each other. But all that had changed after Amy had packed her bags and left High Plains so abruptly.

Worse, as Bethany had attempted to help Stan heal his broken heart, she had grown more and more enamored of him. The excitement she'd started to feel every time they had met had become so telling she'd eventually had to distance herself. It was either do that or take the chance she might speak out of turn or even be so foolish as to throw herself at him.

"Which would be a terrible mistake," she insisted, shaking her head. "It would make him think I'm just like my sister."

Nothing was further from the truth, Bethany assured herself. She wasn't self-centered, nor was she the kind of woman who used others. When she made a promise she kept it.

"And speaking of promises…" She glanced at the clock atop the new town hall building across from the park. It was nearly eight-thirty already. In half an hour or less she would be in close proximity to the one man who could make her knees tremble and send shivers up her spine by merely passing her on the street. What was she going to do; how was she going to keep her sanity when they were cooped up together in the tiny food booth for three hours?

Her grin returned. It grew so wide, so joyful, it made her cheeks hurt. Perhaps this unexpected chance to help the fire department raise funds was going to be the answer to her prayer about how to break down the walls around Stan's heart. It certainly had possibilities.

Chapter Two

"You got *who* to help me? You mean Mrs. Beth Otis?"

"No, no. Bethany Brown."

Stan Ellison knew that the grimace on his face was telling, but he didn't care. There were some things a man shouldn't have to accept, even if his job security might depend upon it.

Anybody who had a clue about his past would never have assigned Amy Brown's sister to work with him. Never. Which was just one more reason why he felt the department should have hired a chief from High Plains instead of bringing in a man who had no idea about the internal politics of the small town.

"She said she was free this morning and I see here she's helped us out before," the chief reminded him as he checked the paperwork on the clipboard he held. "Besides, who better to take the money and make change than a bank teller?"

"Right." There was nothing more Stan could say. Not a thing. He was stuck and he knew it.

He muttered to himself as the chief hurried away. "Okay. I can do this. After all, Bethany isn't responsible for what her big sister did. She's actually not a bad kid."

If only her appearance didn't tie his gut in knots, he added, chagrined. Poor Bethany was really a pretty girl, which was part of his problem. She and Amy shared many of the same features, from their long, silky, reddish hair and hazel eyes to their stature and even the graceful way they moved. Catching sight of Bethany from a distance never failed to make his heart race and his throat go suddenly dry, thinking for an instant that Amy had returned.

He knew he didn't still love Amy, not after the way she had treated him, but there was enough emotion left over to make him decidedly uneasy with regard to her slightly younger sister.

Looking up, he realized with a jolt of awareness that it was happening again. Bethany was approaching and his pulse had quickened at the mere sight of her. This was not good. Not good at all.

He forced a smile and tried to act nonchalant. "Hey, kiddo. I heard you got drafted. Sorry about that."

She smiled so broadly in return that Stan's cheeks warmed.

"No problem. You know how I love cookies. There's no booth I'd rather work at than this one."

"You plan to eat up all our profits, is that it?"

She giggled. "Don't worry. I'll pay for whatever I nibble on."

"Aren't you afraid of getting fat?"

"Like Amy always said she was, you mean? Nope. I figure if the Good Lord wants a few curves on me I'm not going to argue. Besides, He made chocolate so He must want us to enjoy it."

"I've never heard anybody put a spiritual spin on food before," Stan said with a smile.

"Not all food," Bethany replied. "Just chocolate."

"I stand corrected." He backed away to give her plenty of room to squeeze between the tables and join him before he pointed to a folding chair. "You can sit over there and manage the cash box if you want. The chief said you'd be best at it because you're used to handling money."

"Well, I can count—as long as I don't run out of fingers and toes. That has to be a plus, right?"

"Right."

Something about her attitude, her very presence, cheered Stan so much he was flabbergasted.

Chapter Three

There was no way Bethany could ignore Stan's presence. Even when she wasn't looking directly at him she could tell exactly where he was in relation to her chair. If they hadn't been outside under the clear blue sky, with only a leafy cottonwood tree for dappled shade, she didn't think she could have tolerated that degree of closeness.

She surreptitiously watched him greet and joke with locals as well as welcome visitors who had come to High Plains to celebrate July 4th in the riverfront park. That summer tradition was one of Bethany's favorites. There would be live music in the gazebo, games for the kids, free watermelon, hot dogs and soda pop for supper and then a fireworks show that rivaled those in the big, nearby Kansas cities like Manhattan and Council Grove.

Right now, however, there was only her and Stan, bordered by three long, rectangular tables that held the baked goods, which had been donated for the fundraising effort.

Bethany stood, reached into her pocket and handed a dollar bill to Stan.

"What's this for?"

"Brownies. Two of them." She placed a couple of the chocolaty treats on a paper napkin. "I figure I may as well do it up right. These have been calling my name for the past hour and I'm through resisting."

I wish I could say I was through resisting you, she added silently. As of this morning, before she'd been asked to help in the booth with Stan, she'd assumed that she was well in control of her feelings, no matter what kind of temptation presented itself.

Now, however, she could tell she'd been kidding herself. The way she saw it, she would probably still have a stupid crush on Stan Ellison when they were old and gray. There they'd be, she imagined, sitting in rocking chairs on the porch of the rest home and trading barbed quips as always. Only, by then, neither of them would remember why they were at odds in the first place.

The silly picture in her mind made her giggle. Stan cocked his head and peered over at her. "You okay?"

"Oh, sure. I was just daydreaming."

"It must have been funny because you got a strange look on your face just before you laughed."

"Really? Well, well."

"You aren't going to tell me about it, are you?"

"Nope," Bethany said. She took a bite of one of the brownies, rolled her eyes and slowly licked her lips. "Umm, this is soo good."

The witty retort she'd expected in reply didn't come, so she glanced at Stan quizzically. He had an odd expression on his face and his cheeks were slightly flushed, the way a teenage boy's might be if he were bashfully interested in a girl. Either that, or the poor man was having an attack of indigestion.

The workings of her stressed-out mind and heart were getting so ridiculous and so funny she wondered if she was about to break into hysterical laughter. She wouldn't be surprised if she did. And then what could she say to him? How would she ever explain her true feelings? What had begun as a friendship and had deepened due to empathy, was now a full-blown crush.

Perhaps it was even more than that, she added with a sigh. Perhaps, in spite of all her self-recriminations and inner warnings, she had actually let herself fall in love.

Affection was not the problem, Bethany insisted. The real trouble lay in the man she had chosen to care for. Of all the eligible bachelors in High Plains, she had picked the one man who would be the least likely of any to return her love.

Chapter Four

As far as Stan was concerned, he would rather have been charging into a burning building without any of his protective equipment than be stuck for three hours making small talk with Bethany Brown.

He'd been on edge from the second the chief had told him exactly who he had recruited to help in the booth. And as soon as Bethany had arrived, his nervousness had increased until he wondered how much more tension he could stand.

Checking his watch, Stan discovered that his troubles would be over in fifteen minutes. He almost cheered.

"You look awfully pleased all of a sudden," Bethany remarked.

"Just glad we sold so much already."

"Oh. I thought maybe you were happy I'd be gone soon."

What could he say? The expression of hurt in her lovely eyes cut him to the quick. Made him want to tell her the truth in spite of everything.

"It's not that," Stan said, hoping to sound believable. "I really do appreciate all your help."

"But you wish I was Amy, right?"

"No. No way." His brow knit. "What makes you think that?"

She shrugged. "Just a wild guess. I know she caused you pain and for that, I'm sorry. Please try to remember that I'm not my sister. Not even close."

"I know that."

"Do you? Sometimes I wonder."

She blinked and shaded her eyes as if the bright sun was causing them to water. Stan knew better. Bethany had obviously been hurt by Amy's actions, too. That was something he hadn't considered before, partly because she had never given any sign of being so upset. Then again, perhaps he'd been so caught up in his own suffering he hadn't considered how Bethany might feel.

"Tell you what," he said. "How about letting me buy you a burger as soon as our shift is over? You need some real food."

The shock on her face was telling. Not only was she touched, she was as surprised by the offer as he was. What had come over him? Was he crazy? He'd spent the past three hours waiting for their parting and yet he'd just opened his mouth, stuck his foot in it and prolonged the agony.

Hoping she might turn down his offer, he held his breath. Her jaw had dropped and she was staring at him.

"Food? You and me? Together?" she finally asked.

"Don't feel pressured. You don't have to accept. I just thought…"

"I'd love to!"

Okay, Stan mused. *Now you've done it. She's not only going to let you buy her lunch, she's excited about the prospect. Terrific.*

Considering the situation, he nevertheless knew he'd done the right thing by asking. Bethany was sweet. A really lovely person. If her every move, every feature, had not continued to remind him of the woman who had broken his heart, he might even have been interested in her romantically.

Stan shot a quick, unspoken prayer heavenward. He had been asking the Lord for emotional healing, for a new, fresh start in life, but he had not imagined that God might require him to forgive Amy first. That possibility was starting to appear evident. If he could find it in his heart to befriend Bethany, in spite of what her sister had done, perhaps that would lead him to finally release his anger.

Was it anger? he wondered, surprised by the conclusion. In the past he had seen himself as a victim of an untruthful woman, but *anger?* Really?

As he mulled over the situation it became clear that that was part of his problem, all right. And now that he was aware of it, how was he going to cope?

The grinning young woman beside him was his answer, at least for now. He smiled back at her. "Here comes our new crew. Give the money box to Maya Logan and let's go check out the food at the Community Church booth. I'm starving."

Chapter Five

Bethany was so elated she felt as if her feet were not touching the ground. This was the stuff her dreams were made of. She couldn't seem to stop grinning so widely that she felt foolish.

It would complete the reverie if Stan would hold her hand, she mused, but under the circumstances she figured she'd better just take what had been offered and thank the Good Lord. She still couldn't believe it. Her. And Stan Ellison. Together. *Hallelujah.*

She smiled up at him. "In case I haven't already told you, thanks for the offer to feed me."

"You're welcome."

The moment she decided to pursue the conversation on a more personal level, her mouth dried up like the white, fluffy seeds that were drifting down from the cottonwood trees that lined the river. Many questions pressed to be asked.

Bethany shaded her eyes with her hand, looked up at him and settled on a simple, "Why?"

"Why what?"

She could tell from the way his brow wrinkled that

he was confused and she hoped that that was all that was bothering him. "Why ask me in the first place? I mean, you and I haven't had a lot to do with each other for the past year."

"You were away at college," he said flatly.

"Only as far as Manhattan. I came home every day and on the weekends."

"Did you? I hadn't noticed."

Blushing, she decided to let herself say what she was thinking—at least in part. "Fine thing. Makes me feel invisible."

"I didn't mean it like that." He continued to stroll with her toward the big Community Church building.

Bethany kept pace by taking two steps for every one of his longer strides. What she yearned to do was insist on further explanation, but in her heart of hearts she feared she would not like what she heard. Since he had already denied comparing her to her sister, what else could she say? It was evident, at least to her, that that was exactly what the man had been doing, even if he failed to realize it.

The three-story, white-painted Community Church sat at the east end of Main Street, on a low hill next to the High Plains River. The edifice dated back to the mid-1800s and was the focal point of much of the town's history. It, and the old town hall building nearby, was part of the heritage that so many current residents shared, even if they were not direct descendants of the Logan or Garrison families who had originally settled the area.

The row of temporary booths and vendors ended where the church lawn began. It was there that the ladies' society had set up their outdoor kitchen. The pastor, Michael Garrison, was greeting everyone and passing their orders to the cooks.

Bethany saw his eyebrows arch as she and Stan approached. Little wonder, she thought, since she had poured out her heart to the pastor after her sister had jilted Stan so cruelly.

"Afternoon, folks," Michael said with a grin. "What'll it be?"

Bethany's quick wit made her think, *everlasting love and marriage.* She said, "A burger with the works, please."

"Same for me," Stan echoed as he got out his wallet.

All she could do was stare and grin and give thanks that he could not read what was really going on in her active imagination. It was bad enough that *she* knew.

Chapter Six

Sighing unobtrusively, Stan carried a tray with their food to one of the picnic tables that had been set up under the shady cottonwoods between the church and the river.

Bethany followed with their drinks and chose to sit across the table rather than beside him. He wasn't sure whether that was good or bad. Either way he'd have to pay closer attention to her than was comfortable for him.

She swung her slim, jeans-clad legs over the bench and met his gaze. "Isn't this a beautiful day? I was afraid it might rain and ruin the fireworks show tonight, but so far, so good."

"Yeah. I'm glad, too. Although I wouldn't mind a little rain on the prairie grass on the other side of the river. Every once in a while we have a wayward spark land over there and start a spot fire."

"I forgot about that. Do you have duty tonight?"

He nodded. "Yes. I'm stationed on an engine across the river. We'll crew a couple other units here in town while the show goes on, too. May as well be ready if there's trouble."

"I really admire what you do," she said, taking a bite of her burger after bowing her head over it for a moment.

"Thanks. I see it more as a calling than a job."

"I know. I wish working in the bank felt like that to me. There's nothing very noble about passing out money."

"I suppose not, unless you were to give out samples to the needy," he said with a chuckle.

"Oh, that would be nice. I can see the headline now—*Local Bank Employee Arrested for Giveaways.*" She laughed. "I don't think my boss would approve."

"Probably not." Pausing, he ate a bite, then took a drink before continuing. "You could join the Fire Department Auxiliary. They do a lot of community service."

"Like what?"

"Well, they collect food and supplies for victims. And they make up these cute teddy bears to give to children who are involved in accidents or fires."

"Hmm. That sounds like a worthy cause."

"It is."

He decided to keep to himself the fact that he often spoke to the auxiliary and also taught classes in CPR. Here he sat, trying to think of ways to avoid Bethany in the future, and he had just invited her to become part of another segment of his life. What was wrong with him? He supposed he could back off those volunteer duties if she did decide to participate, but that didn't seem right, either.

Changing the subject, he asked, "How are your folks doing in Florida?"

"Fine. Dad plays golf all the time and Mom has gotten involved in a book club at the senior center in their neighborhood." She glanced at the children running and playing nearby. "They sound like kids at a picnic when I phone them."

"That's good."

"Aren't you going to ask about my sister?"

"I wasn't, no," Stan said with a scowl.

"You should."

"Because she's never going to disappear from my life and you need to know that she's miserable. At least I think she is. Oh, she puts on a big, important front and brags about her success, but I don't believe a word of it. I can tell how she really feels."

"I'm not interested."

He felt about an inch tall when Bethany reached across the table, lightly patted his hand and said, "I don't believe *you,* either."

Chapter Seven

Bethany could have kicked herself. The expression on her companion's face was unreadable, yet she knew without a doubt that her outspokenness had hurt him.

Well, everything she'd said was true, she argued. Then again, many unhappy things were. That didn't give her the right to bring them up or be so brutally honest. Stan had not asked for that kind of open dialogue and she had overstepped the bounds of their tenuous relationship.

"I'm sorry," she said softly. "I had no call to judge you that way."

He shrugged. "You're probably right—in both instances."

"That doesn't excuse it," she replied. The bright sun was not the main reason why she was having trouble seeing through unshed tears but she tried to blame it anyway, as she dashed them away. "Whew! I could use a little more shade."

"Right. You don't want to burn."

"I never do," Bethany said. "It was my sister who was always worried about getting freckles." Sobering and staring over at him, she shook her head. "You know, you and I are never going to be able to have a conversation without mentioning her once in a while. It's inevitable. The more I try to keep from talking about her, the more she comes up."

"I know what you mean."

"You do, don't you? It must be awful for you, living here and always running into people who remember how close you two once were."

"I really don't want to discuss it," Stan said.

"I know. I don't, either. But think about it for a minute. Please? Maybe, if we hash it all out, we can put it behind us and not be so tense all the time."

"I'm not tense."

Bethany covered her mouth but a giggle erupted just the same. "Oh, right. You get this look on your face like you just sucked on a sour lemon every time the subject of Amy comes up."

"Isn't there a saying that if life gives you lemons you should make lemonade?"

"Yes. All you need to do is add lots of sugar."

"I've tried," he admitted ruefully. "I really have."

She sobered. "I know you have. I have, too. But there's still this place in my heart that can't help being so mad at her I could scream." The moment those words were spoken she saw his countenance change. It was as if he were both pleasantly surprised and shocked.

"No way," he drawled, frowning and staring at her.

"Yes, way. Did you think that just because I'm a Christian I never get angry? Please. Don't imagine that I'm some kind of modern-day saint. I was so furious when Amy dumped you I could have smacked her. If I'd had the chance, I might have actually done it, too."

"Wow."

"Yeah, wow." She began to smile again. "Some loving sister I am, huh?"

"Sounds to me like you'd make a loyal friend."

A grin split her face and her cheeks flamed. "That, Mr. Ellison, is *exactly* what I've been trying to tell you."

Chapter Eight

Stan couldn't decide whether to laugh, cry or run. He chose "none of the above" and simply stared at her. She was right, in a strange way. They had once considered each other friends. And after he and Amy had fallen in love, poor Bethany had kind of been shoved aside.

"We did have some fun in the old days, didn't we?" he remarked.

Laughing lightly, she nodded. "Yes. Only I hate to refer to last year as the old days. It makes us sound ancient."

"There are times when I feel as though I've lived a hundred years."

"And you looked it, too, for a while," Bethany quipped. "I must say you look much better lately. I think you're going to live."

That made him smile. "Thanks. I agree."

"Good, because I've missed you."

"You have? How?" He figured she'd mention not seeing him in church or at the high school football and basketball games. He never dreamed she'd take the innocent question personally.

"Days like this," she said wistfully, sighing and gazing at the placid river as it flowed beneath the two-lane bridge. "We used to have so much fun just hanging out and talking."

"I don't know what we'd talk about these days," Stan countered. "Except you-know-who. And I think we've already exhausted that subject, don't you?"

"I suppose so. No use beating a dead horse, as my granny used to say."

"Speaking of horses, do you still ride?"

"Not often." She smiled at him. "I think the last time I was on a horse was the time one ran away with me on the church youth trail ride out at the Circle L ranch. You rescued me. Remember?"

"Yes. And I wasn't even wearing a white hat."

"You were still my hero," Bethany said softly. "You still are. Every time I hear the fire siren go off I pray for your safety."

"Really?" Stan was touched.

"Yes, really. Oh, not only for you, of course, but you're always the first one who comes to mind."

"Thanks. We can always use prayer. The job is mostly boredom punctuated with sheer terror. We never know what we'll find when we arrive on the scene."

"At least High Plains has escaped the kind of terrible tornados that hit Manhattan last year. I couldn't believe all the damage. It's a wonder more folks weren't hurt or killed."

"I know." He glanced up at the clear Kansas sky. "This is a beautiful place to live except for the storms we sometimes get. I suppose there's no place that's totally free of drawbacks."

"I suppose not. I do wonder, though, how people who lose everything manage to cope. I suppose the strong sense of belonging helps. This community is like one big family."

"Yeah," Stan agreed, chuckling. "It has just as many odd relatives as most families do, too. Take you and me, for instance."

Bethany arched her brows. "Oh, yeah? Speak for yourself, mister. I am as ordinary as apple pie."

"And as sweet as the ice cream on the top," he said.

"But not nearly as chilly, I hope." She blushed and averted her gaze.

"No," Stan said as he reached for her hand and touched it briefly. "You're one of the warmest-hearted people I've ever known."

To his astonishment, she pulled away, got to her feet and said, "I should be going. Thanks for lunch," and abruptly walked away.

As he began to gather up their trash and carry it to a nearby receptacle, he wondered what had spurred her to act so unexpectedly. He couldn't recall saying anything offensive.

Puzzled, he started for the fire department to ready his gear for the evening's duty. For once, it was Bethany who haunted his thoughts rather than her sister.

Chapter Nine

The tingle of Stan's warm, gentle touch lingered on Bethany's hand and in her mind the rest of the long day.

She hadn't known how to react when he had so innocently complimented her and patted her hand. The action had come as such a surprise her only instinct had been to flee. It was one thing to daydream about receiving affection from her sister's former beau but quite another to actually have it happen.

He hadn't meant anything by it, she kept telling herself. After all, they had barely spoken for a year—until this morning when fate had thrown them together.

More likely, God had been in the details rather than fate, she reasoned, which didn't help calm her one bit. She had prayed and prayed for a reconciliation with Stan and it had come, so what was she so afraid of?

When wandering among the booths and greeting friends had grown tiresome, she'd headed for her apartment on Third Street. The neighborhood was peaceful as always. It was she who was a ball of nerves.

She was almost to her own building when a small, wiry boy raced by on a pint-size bicycle. He came so close to hitting her she had to step off the sidewalk. As she did so, she lost her balance and ended up sitting on the grass verge with an "Ouch!" and a thud.

The freckle-faced boy spun the bike in a circle and returned. "Sorry, lady."

"It's okay." Bethany was dusting off her hands and mentally checking to see if she really was all right when a black-and-white dog galloped up, planted its front feet on her lap and gave her cheek a slurp.

"Charlie, down!" the boy yelled.

Laughing, Bethany held the eager dog away. "He is down. And so am I. That's the problem." She was ruffling the dog's fur and pushing him off at the same time. "Hello, Charlie. Pleased to meet you."

"I'm Tommy Jacobs. Charlie's my dog," the child announced proudly.

Her brow knit as she got to her feet. "Jacobs? I don't place that name. Did your family just move here?"

"No." He made a face. "I don't got a family. I'm an orphan."

"Oh. Then you must be living with Brandon and Beth Otis. They said they were getting a new foster child."

"I ain't stayin'. Not if they won't let Charlie sleep with me," Tommy declared.

"It would probably help if you washed him before you asked to bring him inside," Bethany said. "How long has it been since he had a bath?"

"I dunno."

The idea that struck her next was so absurd she almost dismissed it. Then, she realized that this was a chance to do some good within the community, exactly the way she had insisted she wanted to.

"Tell you what," Bethany said with a smile. "I live right up the street and I have the perfect place where you and I can give Charlie a bath. What do you say? Will you let me help get him clean enough to sleep inside?"

"He won't stay that way. He loves mud." The boy giggled. "So do I."

"Well, at least he'll be pretty fresh today. It doesn't look like it's going to rain anytime soon and we can dry him with a hair dryer."

"Why do you want to help?"

"Because," she said. "Just because."

That simple explanation seemed to sit well with the boy because he nodded and put one foot on the pedal of his bike, getting ready to ride. "Okay. But if Charlie doesn't like the bath he doesn't have to stay."

"It's a deal," Bethany agreed. "I'll wash, you rinse, and we'll be done in two shakes of Charlie's tail."

Besides, she added to herself, if she was fussing with a soapy dog and a little boy, she'd have less time to spend thinking about Stan and wishing that she had let him continue to touch her hand. After the way she'd acted, chances were good that he'd never try again.

Chapter Ten

The Independence Day engine crew consisted of Stan and two volunteers without much practical experience. Both younger men were trained in first aid but had not yet finished their studies in firefighting.

He briefed them before sundown, then stationed one at each end of the engine. "Your only job is to watch for sparks and let me know. The sooner we can have water on the hot spots, the less chance of it getting away from us."

"I thought they were gonna shoot the shells over the water," one of the rookies said.

"They are. But you never know when one might go astray. Just keep your eyes open and pray nothing lands on those spectators across the river."

"Yessir."

Thinking of the people already gathering on the church lawn and in the town park by the gazebo, Stan immediately pictured Bethany. She'd be there, of course. She'd always loved watching the fireworks. They all had, although Amy had usually wound up complaining that the show was lasting too long. Bethany, on the other hand, had greeted each colorful explosion with a squeal of joy or a similar expression of delight.

He remembered their last 4th of July together. Several couples and other twentysomething singles had gathered as a group to watch the show. He had already begun to wonder why Amy was acting so strange, but she hadn't yet informed him that she was leaving High Plains, for good, less than a week later.

"It's getting chilly and the mosquitoes are eating me alive," Amy had complained. "I want to go home."

Stan had taken off his jacket and placed it around her shoulders, barely noticing that Bethany, too, was probably cold. The way she'd been jumping around and cheering, however, she'd undoubtedly been warmer than her sister.

"Warmer in more ways than one," he told himself. Bethany was right about being different from Amy. Her face glowed with enthusiasm no matter what she was doing. And she greeted the people she met as if they were the most important individuals in her life. At least that was the way it had always seemed to him.

That was part of what he was just now realizing he had missed. Bethany's smile. And her eagerness, openness, regarding life's challenges. If he could ever get to the point where he saw her as herself rather than as a replica of her sister, then perhaps he'd stop being so tense around her.

The first fireworks salvo boomed just as the last rays of sun disappeared. The shell reached its apex and exploded in a flash of colorful, twinkling lights.

"One down, many to go," he told himself. The days

when he could sit back and enjoy the show had ended
when he'd joined the fire department. Although he
did still appreciate the pyrotechnics, he couldn't help
watching each launch and wondering how many live
sparks were going to land in the dry, prairie grass.

"Ranchers need all the feed they can get in weather
like this," he called to the nearest rookie. "Keep a sharp
eye out."

"Hey, man, I am, I am. There's nothin' out there but
weeds and coyotes."

Peering into the distance, Stan held his breath. *Was
it? Could it be?*

"There," he shouted, pointing. "I see a flicker."

"Where?"

"Just grab the nozzle and head that way. I'll charge
the hose," Stan shouted. "Move it. Now!"

Above them, more fireworks exploded. The show
continued. But in the prairie grass there was a different kind of show going on. One that could easily turn
deadly if everyone didn't do their job.

Chapter Eleven

Between Tommy's wild handling of the hose and
Charlie's shaking, Bethany and the boy had ended up
almost as wet and soapy as the dog.

She smiled, remembering their shared laughter and
how much fun she'd had. During their short time together, she had learned that Tommy was only six years
old. This wasn't his first foster home, nor was it likely
to be his last in view of the fact that he refused to go
anywhere without his best friend, namely Charlie.

The first salvo of the fireworks show had already
been set off by the time she'd showered, changed, dried
her long hair and returned to the park. She peered at
the land across the river. There was Stan's fire engine,
parked just where he'd said it would be. Her heart did
a little flip and landed in her throat.

Maya Logan, the woman who had relieved Bethany
at the baked goods booth, hailed her. "Hey, over here.
There's room on our blanket."

"Thanks. I forgot to bring a chair or anything."

"No problem." As Bethany sat down, Maya scooted
over and gestured toward the little girl who was curled

up, asleep, beside her. "Layla wore herself out playing. I tried to keep her awake to watch but even all this booming and commotion isn't enough to do that."

"So I see. How did the sales go after I left?"

"You mean after you and Stan left, don't you?"

"We happened to walk off together, that's all. There was nothing to it."

Laughing, Maya raised an eyebrow. "Oh? That's not the way I heard it."

Bethany was shaking her head and trying to squelch another huge grin. "Okay, okay. So he bought me a burger. That doesn't mean it was important, except to my empty stomach. It was just lunch, not a real date."

"If you say so. I also heard that you two were seen having a very engrossing conversation. Why did you suddenly jump up and run off?"

Bethany rolled her eyes dramatically. "I don't believe this. Doesn't anyone in High Plains mind their own business?"

"Nope. Never have and never will. Folks in a small town like this look after each other. We can't help it if that shared concern sometimes comes across as nosiness or gossip."

"You can say that again." Settling back and crossing her legs, Bethany sighed. "I wish Stan was as serious about me as the rumors make out."

"You might grow on each other if you give it half a chance."

"I doubt it. He still hasn't gotten over what my selfish sister did to him. I'm afraid that his memories of Amy will always be between us."

"Where is he tonight?" Maya asked, just as another

burst of brightness opened in the sky like a summer flower.

"Across the river, manning that engine," Bethany said, pointing. "The regular firefighters and the volunteers are all working, just in case there's a spark."

"Good thing, too," Maya told her. "Look."

Bethany's breath caught. Her pulse began to race. The revolving lights atop Stan's engine had just come on and there was a flurry of activity beside the pumper. Shadowy figures were running. She thought she could hear shouting above the already noisy crowd in the park, too.

"Dear Lord," she breathed, barely whispering. "Help them. Be with them. And keep them all safe."

The deepest regions of her heart added, *Especially Stan.*

Chapter Twelve

"Get ahead of it and cut it off before it runs all the way to the gully," Stan yelled.

The rookie just stood there, aiming the spray of water into the air so it fell like misty rain.

Recognizing that the younger man was not going to function properly under the stress of a real fire, Stan left the pump panel and raced to the nozzle.

His terse, "Give it to me," was not a polite request. It was an order that no man in his right mind would have disobeyed.

Taking full command, he narrowed the stream and directed it at the base of the fire, keeping the flames confined to a small area and quickly gaining the upper hand. By the time he had the perimeter of the spot fire under control, another engine had crossed the bridge and was coming to his aid. Together, the two units mopped up and stood prepared to take on other falling embers.

By the time the show ended an hour later, Stan's initial surge of adrenaline had waned and he was exhausted. He was also sooty and coughing from being so close to the fire. All he wanted to do at that point was go home and crash, but his job required that he first clean and prep the equipment so it would be ready if something else occurred.

He supposed he shouldn't have been surprised to find Bethany waiting for him at the firehouse, especially since it was located so close to her apartment. But he was.

"Nice show," she said, waving and approaching. "We were all impressed. I think there were more people watching you work than the fireworks."

"Just doing my job."

"Somebody wasn't. We could tell."

"That kind of thing can happen with rookies," Stan said. "No matter how much training a man has had, some guys freeze when they're needed most. The only way to weed out those people is to let them face real situations. With professional backup, of course."

"In that case, I'm glad it was just a small grass fire instead of a burning building!"

"No problem," he said with a smile. "You were praying for us, right?"

She made a face. "Right. But I think the Lord still expects you to fight the fire yourself."

"So that's why He gave me this bright, shiny engine. Imagine that."

"Don't make jokes," Bethany said wryly. "You know what I meant."

"Sorry. Yes, I do know. And we all thank you for your prayers." He paused, studying her wide, hazel eyes and concerned expression. "I'm glad you're still speaking to me."

"Speaking to you? Why would I not be?"

He shrugged, turning aside to cough for a moment. "I don't know. You sure had a burr under your saddle when you left after lunch. I've gone over and over everything I said and I can't for the life of me figure out why you took off the way you did. Care to enlighten me?"

"You're coughing and all smoky and sooty. You need your rest a lot more than you need to stand around talking."

He started to take a few steps closer to her, noticed how she immediately tensed, and stopped moving. "Don't be afraid to say whatever's on your mind, Bethany. I'd lots rather hear the truth from my friends than face nasty surprises like…"

"Like Amy gave you. I know."

"Well?" He waited, weary yet eager to hear her thoughts, to find out more about her feelings toward him. When he saw her countenance change he knew that that was not going to happen. Not tonight.

"Good night, Stan," she said. "I just stopped by to make sure you were all right. Take care of that cough, okay?"

"Okay. See you around." As he watched her turn and walk away he was struck by a sense of loss that took him by surprise. He wanted her to linger. To continue to keep him company. To lend her uplifting presence to an otherwise tiring evening.

That was a bigger shock than having her show up there in the first place.

Chapter Thirteen

The thrilling fireworks display had been nothing compared to the brightness and awesomeness of Bethany's continuing thoughts the following week. They mostly centered on Stan Ellison, of course. She was disgusted to find that she was spending an inordinate amount of time dwelling on him, even inventing scenarios in which they not only talked, they hugged and kissed!

Embarrassed even though no one else was privy to her thoughts, she finished dressing, grabbed her shoulder bag and headed for work. Living so close to High Plains Bank and Trust, she often walked the three blocks rather than drove, especially on beautiful summer days like this one.

Two doors past the bank entrance was Elmira's Pie Diner, the perfect place to grab coffee and a Danish if she chose not to have breakfast at home, which was about half the time.

The scalloped edges of the red-and-white-striped awning above the doorway were flapping slightly in the warm breeze as Bethany ducked inside and tossed her head to flip her long hair back. "Whew! Good morning, Elmira. Guess I should have worn a ponytail today."

"Morning. What'll it be? The usual?" the middle-aged matron behind the counter asked.

"Supersize the coffee, please. I need to stay awake at work today."

"Big night last night, huh? Have a date?"

Bethany shook her head and raked her bangs off her forehead while she looked for change in her purse. "Nope. Just not sleeping well."

The older woman laughed lightly. "Then maybe you needed a lively date to tire you out. My Harold used to take me dancing twice a week when he was alive." She sighed. "I still miss his company, even after all these years. I've got a houseful of cats but it's not the same."

As she picked up her order and paid, Bethany smiled. "I've never been fond of cats but I have been thinking of getting a dog for company."

"They're no good for conversation unless you talk to yourself a lot," Elmira said. "You need a husband, girl."

"Like a fish needs a bicycle."

Elmira cackled. "You make that up?"

"Nope. Can't take credit. I think I saw it on a T-shirt one of the teenagers was wearing during the picnic on the fourth."

"Those fireworks were sure something, weren't they?" she asked as Bethany carried her breakfast to a small, round table nearby.

"Yes. I've always loved watching that show."

"It was quite a show the fire department put on across the river, too. My heart was in my throat when

I saw that fire start. This time of year, dry as the grass is, it could have burned all the way to Manhattan if they hadn't gotten it under control so fast."

"I know. It's a good thing they were prepared."

"Sure was." Elmira began filling a big box with assorted doughnuts as she talked. "I was so impressed, I promised the firemen free treats all week long. "She grinned. "They've been taking me up on the offer, too."

"Really?" The hair at Bethany's nape prickled as if she were about to face danger. Or Stan Ellison. Or both. The chances of him being the one to pick up the free doughnuts were slim, yet considering the way her life had been going lately, she would not have been surprised to look up and see him standing there.

She blinked and stared at the door. Stan *was* entering. This was the first time in a year or more that she had run in to him in Elmira's. And now, here he was. Big as life and twice as handsome. *Oh, dear.*

Chapter Fourteen

Stan had looked through Elmira's window and spotted Bethany before he opened the door. The sight of her had almost caused him to delay his entrance. Almost, but not quite. After all, he wasn't afraid of her. She confused him. Or he confused himself where she was concerned. He wasn't sure which.

The little silver bell over the door tinkled. Marvelous aromas of fresh baked goods and hot coffee greeted him. So did the smiling face of the proprietress and the only current customer.

He nodded. "Good morning, lovely ladies."

Elmira giggled. Bethany simply lowered her lashes and took a sip of coffee from the steaming take-out cup. Stan could tell she was blushing.

"I see you have our reward ready again, Miss Elmira," Stan said, reaching the counter and eyeing the doughnut-filled box. "I do wish you'd let me pay you for it, though."

"Nonsense. I want you boys to get so used to eating my treats you'll crave 'em every day. I know what I'm doing."

That made Stan laugh. He snuck a peek past his left shoulder at Bethany. She was doing her best to feign disinterest but he knew her well enough to be able to tell that she was paying close attention.

"I'll take a large coffee, too, if you'll let me pay for it. The stuff the guys brew at the firehouse is thick enough to stand a spoon in."

"Coming up. Black?"

"Yes, please. No cream or fancy stuff. Just plain coffee." Paying, he carried his cup to Bethany's table and stood across from her. "Is this seat taken?"

"No, but…"

"Good, because there isn't another place in the whole diner available and I'd hate to have to stand up to drink this."

He chuckled at her puzzled expression. In view of the fact that they were the only customers, his comment was ludicrous. It was meant to be. He was at his best when he and Bethany were trading quips. The serious moments were the difficult ones.

"All right," she said, smiling up at him. "Since we have no choice, I suppose it would be neighborly for me to invite you to sit with me."

"Absolutely." Sliding into one of the red padded chairs, he rested his forearms on the table, cupped his hands around his coffee cup and looked at her. As expected, she frowned.

"What?"

"Nothing. Just taking in the scenery."

"I said you could sit with me, not study me like a bug under a microscope."

Stan laughed softly. "I'd rather think of you as a butterfly, if I have to pick an insect to compare you to." To his delight, Bethany picked up the analogy and took it one step further.

"Sometimes I feel like a caterpillar that hasn't transformed yet."

"Ah, but you have," Stan said, realizing the deeper truth of his statement. Bethany had gone from a gangly teenager to a beautiful young woman and he had been so obsessed with her sister he had almost missed noticing the transformation. Now that they were getting reacquainted, he could see that she was not at all like Amy except for a few external similarities.

It suddenly struck him that he was seeing her through new eyes. He had prayed to be freed from his thoughts of Amy but he had never dreamed that the Lord would replace those affectionate feelings with an attraction to Bethany.

I'll have to be really careful, he told himself.

If there was any chance that his heart and mind were playing tricks on him, he'd have to really watch his step. The last thing he wanted to do was hurt Bethany the way Amy had hurt him.

Chapter Fifteen

Bethany was so reluctant to leave Stan, she was late for work…three days out of the past five, if anyone was counting and seeing a pattern. She had begun arriving at the pie shop earlier and earlier in the hopes of encountering him. To her delight, he had joined her nearly every morning.

Lunch had often provided similar opportunities, once they had discussed their plans. Because Stan carried a pager and radio that kept him in touch with the fire station, he was able to get away even on the days when he was on duty.

She fidgeted, anticipating his arrival. When he finally did walk through the door she could tell from his expression that something was bothering him.

Smiling, she gestured to a chair at her table. "Have a seat. I had to go ahead and order or I wouldn't have had time to eat."

"That's fine. I can't stay today, anyway."

"Why not? What's wrong?"

As he pulled the other chair closer and sat down, he reached for her hand. The gesture was so unexpected, so wonderful, Bethany hardly heard what he was saying. She blinked to clear her head. "The weather?" She glanced out the window at the bright sunshine. "It looks fine."

"I know. And right now it is," Stan told her, still grasping her fingers and holding them gently. "But the reports don't look good. We could be in the middle of a bad storm in a few hours. The chief wants us on standby."

"You can't stay a little longer? We could share my sandwich. I got a Reuben, just like you like."

"It's tempting, and I don't mean the sandwich," he said, making her heart race even faster. "But I have to get back to the station."

"Be careful," she said tenderly, gazing into his eyes and willing him to understand how much he meant to her.

"I will. And you do the same. If the storm is as strong as predicted, the whole town might be in trouble. You should head home early if it starts to look serious."

"As long as we have electricity, you know the bank will have to stay open. I can just hear my boss yelling if any of us asked to leave before closing time."

"All right." He got to his feet, letting her hand slip through his fingers. "Just keep your eyes open and listen to a weather alert radio if you have one."

"I do at home." She shrugged and stood so she could remain closer to him. "The way the high plains affect the paths of storms there's no telling what will actually happen. If I get home before it starts to rain too hard, I'll be sure to keep my radio on and watch the sky."

"Is there a storm cellar at your apartment?"

"No, but there are no windows in the laundry room in the basement. If I think I need more shelter I'll go down there."

"Okay. Just..."

"What?" Her heart was already pounding when he grasped her shoulders, then leaned closer and placed a kiss on her cheek. After that, she figured it was a good thing he was supporting her. If he had not been, her knees might have buckled. *And there I'd be, in a heap at his feet. Some butterfly,* she reflected, almost smiling at the vivid image in her mind.

The expression on Stan's face grew so poignant it left Bethany breathless. In seconds, she understood the change in his character because he bent closer and kissed her again. This time, it was not a simple peck on the cheek.

This time it was a real-life, knock-your-socks-off, write-home-to-Mother lulu. If this kiss had not left her speechless, she might have told him so.

Chapter Sixteen

The afternoon seemed to race by at the fire station. Stan and his fellow firefighters had checked and re-checked their gear and emergency supplies. There was no way to tell what or how much would be needed beyond normal but they tried to cover all contingencies.

He'd been listening to the NOAA weather announcements and still knew no more than he had when he'd warned Bethany. The conditions were right for a thunderstorm with strong winds and hail. Beyond that, it was anybody's guess.

High Plains had suffered more than one tornado in the past, including the devastating one that had practically leveled the town in 1860. After that, its founders had rebuilt, mainly in brick and stone. Many of those sturdy edifices still stood, including the bank and trust where Bethany worked.

The same rookie who had frozen while fighting his first fire on July 4th stuck his head in the door. "Hey, Stan. What's the word?"

"It doesn't look good. You going to be okay?"

"Me? Sure. I've got the system down pat now. You put the wet stuff on the red stuff and the fire goes out."

Stan had to chuckle. "Right. Simple, but correct."

"How's the storm looking?"

"Nasty." He swiveled his desk chair and stood. "As long as it isn't as strong as the one that hit here in the mid-1800s we should be fine."

"Yeah, I heard about that one. Guess it kind of snuck up on them, huh? We're smarter these days. We've got weather satellites to keep us posted."

"Yes and no. Just because we know trouble is coming doesn't mean we can avoid it completely. According to historians, that twister came from the southwest, the same direction as this storm. That doesn't mean it's going to be as bad as it was in the old days, of course, but I've weathered a few pretty nasty ones myself."

"Well, we can always take cover like everybody else."

Stan shook his head, amazed at the young man's naive attitude. "We may duck when the worst comes through but believe me, kid, we won't be hiding our heads while there are folks who may need our help."

"I knew that. I just thought…"

"No. You weren't thinking. This job is not nearly as glamorous as it looks in the movies or on TV. It's hard, dangerous, grueling work. We risk our lives every time we roll to a scene. And most people expect it, so we get very little praise. Don't plan on being on the front page of the newspaper or getting decorated for heroism by the mayor or governor."

Shrugging and turning to go, the rookie gave Stan a

look that said he didn't believe a word of what had just been said.

Well, so be it. All Stan cared about, then and in the future, was doing his job to the best of his ability and serving his community.

That, and making sure Bethany stayed safe through it all, he added, chagrined. Since he was stuck there, on duty, there wasn't a thing he could do to help her, to look out for her personally.

He closed his eyes and shot a quick prayer heavenward. "She's special, Father. Watch over her and keep her safe. Please? I—I really care for her."

The moment the words were out of his mouth he realized that they were inadequate. He more than cared for Bethany. Heaven help him, he'd fallen in love with her.

Not because of Amy? he asked himself. *Are you really sure?*

It didn't take him more than a heartbeat to answer, "Yes."

Chapter Seventeen

On her way back to the bank after lunch, Bethany ran into Tommy Jacobs and Charlie. The boy was on his bike as usual, with Charlie running along beside him.

"Hi," Bethany called, waving. "How did your foster parents like the way we washed your dog?"

Tommy pouted as he skidded to a stop at her feet. "Dumb old grown-ups. They didn't believe me, even after I showed them how clean the white fur on his tummy was."

"I'm so sorry. Maybe I should have written you a note to prove we really washed him." She eyed the gamboling dog with its lolling tongue and twinkling dark eyes. He didn't look as if he'd rolled in the mud in the past week but there was really no way to tell since the majority of his hair was black.

"It's okay." The wiry child shrugged and prepared to ride off.

"Be careful out there," Bethany warned, eyeing the darkening sky to the west. It was impossible to see all the way to the horizon due to the two- and three-story buildings that blocked her view, but she could see enough to tell that Stan had been right about the impending storm. If there was one thing that was predictable on the plains, it was changeable weather.

"I know how to ride good," Tommy insisted.

"I don't mean about your bike," she said. "I mean look out for lightning and rain. There's supposed to be a storm coming."

"I ain't afraid. I like to play in the rain." He grinned. "So does Charlie. We love mud."

"I can see that by looking at your sneakers." Bethany returned his smile. "Just keep an eye on the sky, okay? You wouldn't want your dog to get hurt, would you?"

The boy shook his head so hard his hair ruffled. "Nope. I take good care of Charlie and he takes good care of me, too."

"I'm sure he does." She paused to check her watch. "Uh-oh. I'm late for work again. Gotta go. Bye."

"Bye," Tommy called after her.

As she passed through the front door of the bank she looked back and saw him riding off, standing on the pedals, leaning the bike back and forth and making noises to pretend it was really a motorcycle.

Kids. They could always find fun in the smallest pleasures.

Fun? Pleasure? Oh, yes. She instantly relived Stan's surprising kiss. Her lips still tingled and her breathing grew a bit unsteady. That long-awaited kiss had not been the way she had always imagined it would be. It had been a thousand times better.

Only one element of their relationship continued to bother her. Everything seemed to be happening too fast. Yes, they had already been well acquainted when they had renewed their friendship, yet there was still the specter of Amy hanging over their newfound affection.

How could Bethany be certain that Stan was not thinking of her sister when he kissed her? How would she ever know? He had remarked often about the family resemblance, so perhaps, even if he truly believed he was interested in her, he still yearned for Amy.

Disappointed at the way her mind had twisted an awesome occurrence, Bethany sighed. Of all the men she could have fallen for, why did her heart have to belong to Stan Ellison?

Because, truth to tell, it always had.

Chapter Eighteen

Stan was pacing the floor, watching the sky and listening to radio reports. The eye of the storm had passed Council Grove and was bearing down on High Plains at forty miles an hour. The wind was already blowing so hard it was starting to strip tender, green leaves from the cottonwood trees and whip the smaller branches wildly. Trash was blowing around as refuse cans were knocked over. This didn't look good.

He checked his watch. The bank would soon close. Perhaps Bethany would stop by the fire station on her way home. Chances were she had walked to work, meaning she wouldn't have the protection of a car if hail started to fall while she was en route.

Making a snap decision, he leafed through the phone book for the bank number, then quickly dialed.

"Let me speak to Bethany Brown," he said as soon as the operator answered.

"I'm sorry. Our teller stations are closed for the day," the woman said pleasantly. "Would you like to leave a message?"

"No. I want to talk to Bethany and I want to do it

now," he said forcefully. "This isn't bank business. This is the fire department calling."

"Oh, dear. Is there a problem at her apartment building?"

"No. Just put her on the line, will you? She is still in the building, isn't she?"

"Yes, sir. One moment, please."

He heard the breathlessness in Bethany's voice as she picked up an extension. "Hello?"

"It's me. Stan," he said. "I think you should stay right where you are till the storm passes. It's getting awfully close and you don't want to get caught outside if it starts to hail the way I think it's going to."

"What have you heard?"

"Council Grove got hammered with nickel- and quarter-size hail even though the main part of the storm missed them. We could have it much worse."

"Are you sure?"

"Nobody can be positive. I'd just feel better if you promised to stay there a little longer. You don't have your car, do you?"

"No. It was beautiful this morning. I always walk on pretty days."

"Must be the butterfly in you that craves the sunshine," Stan said, hoping to distract her by mentioning their earlier conversation.

"Must be." She paused, then continued, "How long do you think we should stay inside? I want to be able to tell the others and let them make educated decisions about whether or not to head for home."

"We should be through the worst of it in less than an hour," Stan said soberly. "I'm not trying to be an alarmist. I just know from experience how bad some of these storms can be. I was caught in a dandy when I was a kid. Remember?"

"Vaguely. I was too little to take anything seriously back then. Maybe that's why you're so uptight about the weather now."

"Maybe. Or maybe I'm just more prudent than some folks." He glanced through the window at the street. "Looks like traffic is about the same as always. People are acting way too nonchalant. I hope they're not sorry."

"So do I," Bethany replied. "Okay. I'll stay here for another hour or so, but after that, I'm going home. The probability of High Plains being hit by hail or a tornado should have been resolved by then."

"Call me before you go outside? Promise?" He gave her his private cell number and was relieved when she took the time to jot it down and repeat it back to him. "And, Bethany?"

"Yes?"

Stan hesitated. "Never mind. We'll talk later. Good bye."

He'd been going to express his tender feelings, maybe even tell her that he loved her, but something had stopped him. It was one thing to think about it and quite another to actually say the words. Besides, that kind of confession should be made face-to-face. That way, if she didn't take it well, he'd recognize the truth and know whether or not she returned his love.

The possibility that she might not gave him actual, physical pain.

Chapter Nineteen

Bethany stood at the wide front window of the bank and watched the rain falling. Thunder rattled the whole building and lightning was flashing so often it seemed almost continuous. The wind velocity was building. Sheets of falling water were sometimes so dense she could barely see the park across the street.

The distant sky was as dark as evening, yet the sun would not set for four more hours. Worse, there was a band of light near the horizon, signaling the presence of a wall cloud above. Bethany knew that was a bad sign. Clouds like that often spawned tornados.

Most of her coworkers, except for the bank manager and one other teller, had already taken the chance that they'd beat the worst of the thunderstorm and had headed for their homes. Bethany wished she'd done the same.

Perhaps there was still time to make a run for it, she reasoned, remembering all the previous storms she'd experienced. Just because there was rain falling and perhaps hail to follow, twisters weren't inevitable.

Nothing was that predictable, especially not during the spring and summer.

The promise she'd made to Stan nagged at her. "All right," she muttered, disgusted with herself for heeding his dire warning when she could have been snug and safe at home all this time. "I'm leaving, whether he likes it or not."

She raised her voice to get the bank manager's attention. "I'm going to make a private call, then you can unlock the door and let me out. Okay?"

"Is it safe?" the portly man asked, frowning and mopping his brow as he peered past her. "It looks pretty nasty out there."

"It's pouring rain but that's all. And that seems to be letting up." She used her own cell phone to call the number Stan had given her. As soon as he answered she spoke without giving him a chance to argue. "This is Bethany. I'm going home. It's not raining as heavily as it was and I'm worn out from the waiting."

"Not yet. Don't go yet."

"I promised I'd call and that's what I'm doing. Don't worry. I'll give you another call when I'm safely inside my apartment."

Suddenly, the line went dead. She stared at the little phone. Was it an accidentally broken connection or had Stan hung up? If he was miffed, that was just too bad. If she wanted to go home, she was going to do so. Period. End of discussion.

Bethany closed her cell and slipped it into her purse as she grabbed a light nylon jacket, draped it over her head and headed for the door. "Okay. I'm ready."

The manager seemed unduly nervous as he fiddled

with his ring of keys. "I don't know. I think we should go with our first instinct and stay off the streets." He pointed with a shaky hand. "Look."

Her eyes widened. Although the rain had slacked off for the moment, the wind continued to blow. Across the street in the park, people were scattering. Many umbrellas had been blown inside out by the gale and others looked as though they were about to collapse or be torn from their owners' grasps.

A police car with its red-and-blue lights flashing cruised to a stop directly in front of the bank. Bethany couldn't tell who was behind the wheel but she immediately recognized the man who jumped out of the passenger side and ran toward her.

"Hurry! Unlock the door," she shouted at the manager. "Let him in before he gets blown away."

The heavy glass door was nearly snatched out of their hands when it finally swung back. Stan pulled it closed with the other man's help, then held it while he relocked it.

"You can't go out," Stan yelled at Bethany. "It's too dangerous."

"It seemed fine a few minutes ago when I phoned you. What's going on?"

"We're not sure. The hail is getting bigger and stuff all over town is being smashed, including car windows. I know you're hardheaded but no one's head is hard enough to withstand that kind of punishment."

"Okay, okay. But what are you doing here? I thought you had to stay at the fire station."

"I got permission to ride out with the police chief.

He's going to sound his siren as soon as we're sure there's a tornado on the ground."

"Do you think that will happen?" she asked breathlessly. Before Stan could answer, they heard the high-pitched wailing of sirens begin.

Chapter Twenty

There was no place Bethany wanted to be except in Stan's arms. This dire situation left no room for bashfulness or hesitancy. If this was to be her last moment on earth, she wanted him to know exactly how much he meant to her.

Stepping into his waiting embrace, she slipped her arms around his waist and laid her cheek on his chest. "I'm glad you're here."

He pulled her closer. "So am I. It was tearing me up worrying about you."

She noticed that he was scanning the bank's lobby instead of giving her his full attention. "What's wrong?"

"This area is too exposed. Too much glass. If these front windows go they'll tear into us like shrapnel." With one arm around her shoulders, he hurriedly guided her toward the rear of the building.

"Where are we going?"

"Into the vault," Stan said. He nodded to the manager. "Everybody come with us. If your vault can keep thieves out, it can keep out a tornado, too. Just fix it so we don't accidentally get locked in."

"What if the whole building collapses?" Bethany asked him. She knew it was foolish to borrow trouble but her mind kept thinking of the worst.

"The vault will stand against even that," Stan assured her. He pushed her into the enormous safe ahead of the others, then followed last and swung the heavy door nearly closed with the manager's help.

Bethany reached out to him and laid her head on his shoulder. "Since this may be my last chance to tell you," she began, "I want you to know I love you. I have for years."

To her delight and relief, he not only didn't reject her, he smiled and replied, "I love you, too, Bethany. Not your sister or anyone else. *You.* I'm just sorry it took me so long to figure it out."

"It hasn't been that long," she said soothingly. "We only got reacquainted a couple of weeks ago."

"No." Stan was shaking his head as he cupped her cheeks, raised her face and gazed lovingly into her eyes. "It was a lot longer than that. I think I loved you all along. If Amy hadn't been in the picture I'd have come to my senses sooner. It was your character, your sweetness, that had always appealed to me. I just got my feelings confused when you acted so reserved and she was so forward."

"She threw herself at you, you mean." Bethany couldn't help grinning in spite of the terrible crashing noises outside and the whistling of the wind through the narrow crack the manager had left between the safe's door and frame.

"I didn't have to believe her," Stan countered. "I should have realized long ago that I was confusing you two." He paused to place a brief kiss on her trembling lips. "You looked so alike that I suppose I was combining your personalities, at least subconsciously. Now that Amy's out of the picture I can see that her contribution to my dreams of the perfect wife was the only part that didn't quite fit."

Bethany blushed. "Wife? Did you just say what I think you did?"

Laughing and pulling her closer, Stan confirmed her conclusion. "Yes. Wife. Will you marry me, Bethany?"

"Yes," she replied, clinging to him. "And you'd better see to it that we get out of this mess we're in because I intend to become your bride just as soon as possible. It seems like I've loved you forever."

"We'll survive," Stan vowed. "You're not getting rid of me for at least the next fifty years."

Rising on tiptoe, she kissed him soundly before she said, "That'll make a good start."

* * * * *

Originally published for Harlequin.com

INSPIRATIONAL

Wholesome romances that touch the heart and soul.

Love Inspired.

celebrating
15
YEARS

HISTORICAL

COMING NEXT MONTH
AVAILABLE MARCH 13, 2012

THE COWBOY COMES HOME
Three Brides for Three Cowboys
Linda Ford

THE BRIDAL SWAP
Smoky Mountain Matches
Karen Kirst

ENGAGING THE EARL
Mandy Goff

HIGHLAND HEARTS
Eva Maria Hamilton

REQUEST YOUR FREE BOOKS!

2 FREE INSPIRATIONAL NOVELS
PLUS 2
FREE
MYSTERY GIFTS

Love Inspired
HISTORICAL
INSPIRATIONAL HISTORICAL ROMANCE

YES! Please send me 2 FREE Love Inspired® Historical novels and my 2 FREE mystery gifts (gifts are worth about $10). After receiving them, if I don't wish to receive any more books, I can return the shipping statement marked "cancel". If I don't cancel, I will receive 4 brand-new novels every month and be billed just $4.49 per book in the U.S. or $4.99 per book in Canada. That's a saving of at least 22% off the cover price. It's quite a bargain! Shipping and handling is just 50¢ per book in the U.S. and 75¢ per book in Canada.* I understand that accepting the 2 free books and gifts places me under no obligation to buy anything. I can always return a shipment and cancel at any time. Even if I never buy another book, the two free books and gifts are mine to keep forever.

102/302 IDN FEHF

Name	(PLEASE PRINT)	

Address		Apt. #

City	State/Prov.	Zip/Postal Code

Signature (if under 18, a parent or guardian must sign)

Mail to the Reader Service:
IN U.S.A.: P.O. Box 1867, Buffalo, NY 14240-1867
IN CANADA: P.O. Box 609, Fort Erie, Ontario L2A 5X3

Not valid for current subscribers to Love Inspired Historical books.

Want to try two free books from another series?
Call 1-800-873-8635 or visit www.ReaderService.com.

* Terms and prices subject to change without notice. Prices do not include applicable taxes. Sales tax applicable in N.Y. Canadian residents will be charged applicable taxes. Offer not valid in Quebec. This offer is limited to one order per household. All orders subject to credit approval. Credit or debit balances in a customer's account(s) may be offset by any other outstanding balance owed by or to the customer. Please allow 4 to 6 weeks for delivery. Offer available while quantities last.

Your Privacy—The Reader Service is committed to protecting your privacy. Our Privacy Policy is available online at www.ReaderService.com or upon request from the Reader Service.

We make a portion of our mailing list available to reputable third parties that offer products we believe may interest you. If you prefer that we not exchange your name with third parties, or if you wish to clarify or modify your communication preferences, please visit us at www.ReaderService.com/consumerschoice or write to us at Reader Service Preference Service, P.O. Box 9062, Buffalo, NY 14269. Include your complete name and address.

LIHI1B

Love Inspired HISTORICAL

celebrating 15 YEARS

The heiress Josh O'Malley has courted by mail is on her way to Gatlinburg, Tennessee, to become his wife. But it's her sister who arrives, to end the engagement. Kate Morgan can't help but like the beautiful mountain town... and her sister's would-be groom. If only Josh would realize that his dreams of family can still come true...

The Bridal Swap
by
KAREN KIRST

SMOKY MOUNTAIN MATCHES

Available March wherever books are sold.

www.LoveInspiredBooks.com

LIH82908

*When Cat Barker ran away from the juvenile home
she was raised in, she left her first love, Jake Stone.
Now Cat needs help, and she must turn to
her daughter's secret father.*

*Read on for a sneak peek of
LILAC WEDDING IN DRY CREEK
by Janet Tronstad.*

"Who's her father?" Jake's voice was low and impatient.

Cat took a quick breath. "I thought you knew. It's you."

"Me?" Jake turned to stare at her fully. She couldn't read his face. He'd gone pale. That much she could see.

She nodded and darted a look over at Lara. "I know she doesn't look like you, but I swear I wasn't with anyone else. Not after we—"

"Of course you weren't with anyone else," Jake said indignantly. "We were so tight there would have been no time to—" He lifted his hand to rub the back of his neck. "At least, I thought we were tight. Until you ran away.

"She's really mine?" he whispered, his voice husky once again.

Cat nodded. "She doesn't know. Although she doesn't take after you—her hair and everything—she's got your way of looking out at the world. I assumed someone on the staff at the youth home must have told you about her—"

His jaw tensed further at that.

"You think I wouldn't have moved heaven and earth to find you if I'd known you'd had my baby?" Jake's eyes flashed. "I tried to trace you. They said you didn't want to be found, so I finally accepted that. But if I'd known I had a daughter, I would have forced them to tell me where you were."

"But you've been sending me money. No letters. Just the money. Why would you do that? I thought it was like child support in your mind. That you wanted to be responsible even if you didn't want to be involved with us."

Jake shook his head. "I didn't know what to say. I thought the money spoke for itself. That you would write when you were ready. And I figured you could use food and things, so…"

"Charity?" she whispered, appalled. She'd never imagined that was what the envelopes of cash were about.

Jake lowered his eyes, but he didn't deny anything.

He had always been the first one to do what was right. But that didn't equal love. She knew that better than anyone, and she didn't want Lara to grow up feeling like she was a burden on someone.

Cat reminded herself that's why she had run away from Jake all those years ago. She'd known back then that he'd marry her for duty, but it wasn't enough.

Can Jake and Cat put the past behind them for the sake of their daughter?

Find out in LILAC WEDDING IN DRY CREEK by Janet Tronstad, available March 2012 from Love Inspired Books.